DEATH
FOR
SALE

DEATH
FOR
SALE

A SALLY WITHERSPOON MYSTERY

ERIK S. MEYERS

To my sister & my late mother and stepfather for their love and support.

Chapter One

Holiday smells wafted through the hall. Sally leaned back against the wall and closed her eyes. She loved the cheerful aromas of cinnamon, cranberries, roasted turkey, and so much more. Thanksgiving had been one of her favorite holidays ever since she was a child.

Her nostalgia brought a twinge of sadness. She would be 60 next year, and her parents were aging.

But enough of that, she told herself, there was a job to do.

Opening her eyes, she took in a roomful of smiling faces. Around 250 people from across the county had come to the annual Thanksgiving Day dinner in the expansive ballroom at the Grand Hotel in Berry Springs, the center of life in the area.

The entire hall was decked out in Thanksgiving swag. Cornucopia baskets sat on each table, their contents overflowing with the abundance of the harvest. Each chair had a covering of soft, dark green fabric. Crystal wine and water glasses, as well as real silver flatware, added to the luxury of it all.

The manager of the hotel, Rose Cohen, had an eagle eye for detail, and every event there had people gushing afterwards for days. Since this was the highlight of the year in Berry Springs, even more so than Christmas or New Year, she had really gone all out, as always.

Rose flitted about doing last-minute checks of each table. Sally also noticed her quietly reprimanding some of her staff. This was evident as the two waiters she talked to had anguished looks of fight or flight on their faces.

With the guests, though, she was sugar and spice. Rose knew pretty much everyone in town, and they knew her. She had been a fixture at the Grand Hotel for over 50 years, starting as a chambermaid at 16 and working her way up to general manager. Many people came to Berry Springs and never left, like Sally.

At that, Sally smiled. She really did love living in the small town.

Pushing that thought aside, Sally checked her phone for the time. The festivities were about to begin.

Annette, her part-time bartender and bar helper, was there along with Magda, her full-time staff member, to help make sure thirsts were quenched and no one had to wait too long for a drink. As every year, she had also hired a few temp bartenders to deal with the vast number of people present.

The overstuffed buffet had been provided by the lovely Joanna, who owned The Nutmeg Café on Oak Street, not far from the town square. Joanna usually offered café food, but for this, she had gone all out with a magnificent Thanksgiving feast. From roast turkey to stuffing, mashed potatoes, cranberry sauce, pumpkin pie, and much much more, Sally knew no one would go hungry. It was Thanksgiving after all.

Sally always wondered why Joanna catered for the event, rather than the hotel kitchen staff. Well, actually, she did know. Joanna's food was so much better. Mind you, the hotel restaurant wasn't that bad, but it was basic fare like steak and potatoes or flounder filet, far from the fancy concoctions Joanna came up with. Her café cuisine was a delicious and unique fusion of so many food origins.

Looking around, this was one of those special moments Sally knew she had made the right choice those many years ago to leave Atlanta and move to Berry Springs, tucked in the Arkansas Ozarks.

Life had been fairly quiet, well up until the past year or so. She couldn't believe how much had happened in such a short time.

Just over a year ago, her best friend and business partner, Bill Arnold, had been killed and left in the dumpster behind her bar. Other deaths followed, and Sally helped the police get to the bottom of it, though she almost got herself killed in the process.

This was the second Thanksgiving without Bill, and it still hurt.

Then, about six months ago, she had booked a luxury paddleboat river cruise down the Mississippi to get away. Sally laughed to herself. Yeah, she really got away. Partway into the cruise, one of the passengers died mysteriously at dinner. Other deaths followed, and the rest of the passengers and crew got away within an inch of their lives.

Death seemed to follow Sally around, which wasn't very healthy, she considered.

Someone tapped her on her shoulder, stirring her out of her reverie.

"Sally, are you with us? You seem lost in thought," Magda said.

Sally smiled. "No, I'm fine. Just reminiscing."

"Enough of that, we have work to do," Magda retorted playfully.

They hugged.

A tap on the microphone got everyone's attention. Sally did a scan of the bar they had set up in the corner. Once the mayor's (hopefully) short speech was done, the bar and buffet would be officially open. Sally, Annette, and Magda would serve people at the bar, while the temporary bartending staff would take drink orders at the tables.

This was the new mayor's first Thanksgiving.

The long-time former mayor, Jennifer Milkowski, had resigned at the beginning of the year, a few months after Bill was killed and left town. Her long-time partner, Margaret Jackson, was implicated in the deaths, and was now awaiting trial in Little Rock. The legal process was slow, and Sally wished it would speed up so Berry Springs could try to put those events behind it.

Sam Pulasky, the former chief of police, had been elected mayor earlier in the year. He had run on a safety platform, and Sally was sure that was why so many people voted for him. Sally had worked with him and his team to track down Bill's killer, and many people saw Pulasky as the town's savior.

"Dear Berry Springs residents, dear county guests, dear friends, I'd like to welcome you all to the Berry Springs' Annual Thanksgiving Extravaganza," Mayor Pulasky began.

"This is a special occasion for us all to come together and remember what we are thankful for. It's also a time for everyone to see old friends, meet new people, and enjoy a wonderful time together. I am ever thankful for your votes to elect me as mayor. I will do my best to do you proud and make Berry Springs a safe, healthy environment again for everyone," the mayor continued.

Sally gagged. He was laying it on a bit thick.

"Thank you to Joanna from The Nutmeg Café and Sally Witherspoon from Sally's Smasher for the food and drink. And a huge thanks to Rose Cohen and her team for this beautiful setting! I know we will all enjoy the evening. So, without further ado, I declare the feast open. Enjoy!"

Mayor Pulasky stepped down from the podium and went over to sit at the head table with the town dignitaries, as it were. Sally saw Detective John Finnegan and his underling Sergeant Mark Soder together with the new chief of police, Tim Sanford. Chief Sanford was the son of her retired neighbor, Robert Sanford, who had passed away earlier in the year. He was sitting next to his gorgeous husband, Andy. Sally always had a warm spot for the chief's father, particularly for how he embraced Andy as his son-in-law. She knew Robert would be so proud of his son, and it was sad that he had passed away only a few months before Tim had been appointed chief.

She wondered what Detective Finnegan thought of his new boss. Though she had to admit to herself that while Finnegan had a hard crust, deep down he had a soft soul. Well, that's what she told herself at any rate.

Finnegan and Pulasky weren't married, but Sally did wonder where Mark Soder's wife, Candy, was. Maybe she was sick. Sally would have to try to get a chance to ask Mark later.

"Hi, Sally, I'll have a cold beer," a voice said.

Sally looked over. It was Randall Wentworth, the main lawyer in town. "Hi Randall, so nice to see you here."

Randall smiled. "Yes, I always try to get here and show my face. I think people expect it," he offered.

"I bet," Sally replied, hoping she didn't sound too sarcastic.

She glanced over at Detective Finnegan, who had also just appeared at the bar. The look on his face told her he thought the same of Randall Wentworth. He moved a few steps away from the lawyer to order a drink from Magda.

He nodded at Sally as he did.

She handed Randall his beer and moved on to the next customer, Jeff Bartholomew, a high school teacher and the basketball coach at Clinton High School.

Jeff had been charged as an accessory in Bill's death, but as he had been acting under duress, he got off with a six-month suspended sentence. This was probably more due to the fact that he was a beloved teacher in the county than anything else. His popularity with students and parents alike had also saved his job at the school.

Magda, her bartender, was particularly pleased. They had dated a while back and gotten back together.

"Jeff, why don't you let Magda help you?" Sally offered.

"Oh, I see her all the time, Sally."

"I guess," Sally said, chuckling. "What will you have?"

"The same as Randall, a nice cold beer."

Sally handed him his beer and went on serving other people.

After only about 20 minutes, they had somehow managed to get through the first round. The extra bartending staff was a godsend. There was no other way they would have been able to handle the extensive crowd on their own.

"Time for some photos for our social media presence," Magda said, moving through the room snapping away, as if she were an influencer in New York.

Sally never got the pull of social media, but Magda was a whiz at it. She always told Sally it kept up the buzz about Sally's Smasher bar, as if there was buzz. Though Sally had heard a few comments from out-of-town visitors who had been intrigued by the name of the bar and their posts on social media. This had prompted them to try to expand their social media activity. Sally's Smasher bar was a bit out of town, but Sally still had quite a good business going with the locals. The out-of-towners added a nice twist to the mix.

Magda came back, tapping away.

"Thanks so much, Magda. I couldn't do that social media stuff," Sally said.

Magda laughed, "OK, Grandma."

That got a giggle out of Sally as well.

With everyone seated and eating, a hush had filled the room as people dove in.

Sally took a moment to sit on one of the stools behind the bar and rest her feet. The night had just begun.

Chapter Two

Exhausted, Sally fell into bed, hoping to be able to sleep in on the Friday morning. She hadn't gotten home until two. The Thanksgiving dinner tended to go all night, with a lot of guests staying at the Grand Hotel. Easy access to their rooms meant more time for partying.

As she fell asleep, she realized she wasn't the spring chicken she once was, but decided she could milk her aches, pains, and aging for sympathy points. This made her chuckle and relaxed her enough to fall into a deep sleep.

She was awakened by her phone ringing.

Darn, she had forgotten to turn it off or put it on mute.

Glancing quickly at the alarm clock next to her bed, she realized it was a way too early 5:35 a.m. Ugh, so little sleep.

She picked up the phone and saw it was Sergeant Mark Soder.

She smiled. Sally definitely had a soft spot for him. Tapping the phone, she answered the call. "Um, hello, Mark, it's a bit early to call me, isn't it?"

"Sally, sorry to wake you, but something's come up."

Sally groaned. Again?

"Several people from the Thanksgiving dinner were rushed to the emergency room with food poisoning. Well, that's what it looks like," Soder explained.

"Wait, what? That doesn't make sense. Joanna is a stickler for food hygiene, and she's never had a complaint."

"True, but the people are vomiting and have stomach pains," Mark explained. "We are looking into it now. But it also means we need to test some of your drinks. You served cocktails with fruit, and maybe some of the fruit was contaminated."

Sally's stomach dropped. Oh no, what would that do to her bar? It was her life.

"I'm sure we were so careful with everything, Mark. Is that really necessary?"

His silence was clear.

"OK, I get it. We packed up the leftovers and put them in the hotel's cold storage. I would guess it's all still there," Sally explained.

"Thanks, Sally. I'm sure you have nothing to worry about, but you know we have to be sure."

She nodded as if he could see her. Her friends were always trying to get her to use video calling, but that was just weird to her. And anyway, she was now phoning with Mark Soder while in her nightgown in bed.

"Has anyone died?" she asked finally, adding, "Who are the sick people?"

"No, fortunately, no one has died. There are around ten people who complained of symptoms of what looks like food poisoning, including Randall Wentworth, Finnegan, Dr. Wiggams, and Gilbert Rock. Two people are in critical condition, Momma Arnold and Belle from Betty Jo's Diner," Mark said.

Ugh, Momma Arnold. She was a tough cookie who had been through so much when her son Bill and, later, her daughter Gillian, had been murdered a year ago. Sally hoped she would pull through.

And ancient Belle. She was tough, too, but very frail.

She really felt bad for Gilbert Rock. The town librarian was so beloved, always trying to help people. She hoped he would be OK.

It seemed obvious that the oldest people would be most affected, Sally considered. Even Randall Wentworth, who seemed to be nearing retirement for the last ten years. He would be incensed he was sick and probably had had to be dragged to the hospital.

"Oh, I can't believe it. I hope they make it."

"Me too. Um, can you meet me at the hotel at seven? I know it's early, but we need to get going on this," Mark said.

Sally took a deep breath. Of course, she was going to help. And did she really have a choice if it was potentially her fruit in the cocktails that got people sick?

Ugh, will the stress ever stop?

* * *

Sally had taken a quick shower and put her graying chestnut hair in her standard ponytail. Throwing on jeans and a Sally's Smasher bar sweatshirt, she pulled on a winter coat, scarf, and gloves. The temperature had dropped during the night, and it was just below freezing.

She stepped outside her aging Victorian and prayed Gladys would start. Her old blue Datsun 210 rarely failed her, but Gladys definitely did not like the cold.

The first challenge was getting the driver's door open. It took quite a bit of pounding and pulling, but Sally finally got inside the frozen car.

She turned the ignition, and nothing happened.

Oh, come on, not now. Sally took a deep breath and prayed to the car god.

Pumping the gas a couple of times, she turned the ignition again, and the car slowly turned over. She let it sit and tried again, finally the car started with a blue cloud bellowing out the back.

Sally said a silent prayer of thanksgiving, put the car in reverse, and headed across town to the Grand Hotel. It was on a hill overlooking Berry Springs, like a matriarch surveying her lands.

Luckily, the roads had been salted, considering the steep hill Gladys had to climb to get to the hotel.

Sally was relieved when she made it safely to the hotel parking lot without a slide or breakdown on the way. She pulled into a spot not too far from the door and already saw Mark Soder waiting for her at the entrance. He was as bundled up as she was.

Mark smiled as she walked over to him. "Thanks for coming in, Sally. What a Thanksgiving this has been."

Sally looked grim. "Always something going on in Berry Springs," Sally replied, trying to keep things light.

Her thoughts were with Belle and Momma Arnold, in particular, but she was overall worried about all the sick people. The town stuck together through thick and thin, and she hoped this would end well for all.

Sally led Mark inside to the hotel kitchen. The staff were ready for them. Mark must have called ahead, Sally thought.

She went over to the industrial fridge and showed Mark the fruit she had stored.

"What about your bottles of alcohol?" Mark asked.

"I thought it was food poisoning," Sally said.

"Well, we can't be too sure, and we need to get everything tested."

Sally pointed to several boxes in the corner. "That's the lot, some of the bottles are open."

Mark took the cart from next to the fridge and began loading up the boxes. The hotel staff helped him push everything outside to his police SUV. It took two trips to get it all. Meanwhile, Sally packed up the fruit and olives that had been chilling in the fridge.

She headed outside. Mark held the door open for her and helped her push the box in next to the alcohol. He slammed the door shut and hopped into the driver's seat. Before he could shut the driver's door, Sally tapped his arm.

"Oh, Mark," Sally said, "We missed Candy at the Thanksgiving dinner yesterday."

Mark nodded. "I know. She was really looking forward to it, but she wasn't feeling well yesterday, so she thought it would be better to give it a pass."

"That's too bad. Please give her my best, and I hope she's feeling better soon."

"Thanks, Sally. She's a bit better today. I'll pass on your good wishes." Mark smiled.

"When do you think you will have the test results back?" Sally asked, wringing her hands.

"Not too long. The lab is on alert. Should have them at the latest tomorrow," Mark explained.

"I hope everyone is OK," Sally said.

"Well, most everyone that was admitted to the hospital with symptoms should be released by tomorrow, except the critical cases."

"You mean Momma Arnold and Belle," Sally replied, just confirming what he had told her on the phone.

"Exactly. I hope both of them pull through, but it is good that the rest will hopefully be out soon," Mark said.

"I know. What a Thanksgiving they have had!" Sally replied, "Are you going to talk to them all?"

"Actually, yes. We just want to get their details of what happened and what they think they might have eaten," Mark explained.

"Do you need any help with that? I could talk to some of the people. Everyone knows I'm a busybody anyway," Sally offered.

Mark laughed at that. "No comment."

At that, Sally laughed as well.

"Well, actually, sure. I could use your help. Why don't you take Randall Wentworth and Bethany Wells? I'll handle the rest."

Oh joy, Sally thought: the arrogant lawyer and the town gossip. That was probably why Mark suggested she talk to them rather than him. Though maybe Bethany had heard something that might help. And both of them might be a bit more open than with the police, even if everyone in town knew Sally loved being an ace amateur detective.

Mark shut the driver's door, started the engine, and pulled out.

Sally wasn't ready to breathe a sigh of relief yet, but she was glad the results would be back soon.

What a way to start the holiday season!

Chapter Three

"How are you feeling, Momma Arnold?" Sally asked, tapping her arm.

"Oh, honey," she croaked, "I told you a while back to call me Carol."

Sally smiled. "Carol, how are you feeling?" Sally asked. She still couldn't get used to that.

"Terrible, but glad to be alive. How is Belle?"

"You heard about her?"

Sally wished the hospital staff had kept that from her. Momma Arnold put on a brave, tough-old-bird face, but Sally was always worried she was frailer than she let on. Any shock could be the end of her. Though maybe Sally was just being paranoid.

"Oh, not from the nurse, but Mark Soder was here asking questions, and I dragged it out of him."

"Already? Shouldn't he give you time to recover?" Sally asked, acting as if she were Momma Arnold's long-lost daughter.

"Oh, come on. Of course he's going to be here asking me questions. I'm awake, I'm fine, and I might have seen something. He should get it out of me as soon as possible, don't you think, Ms. Detective?"

Carol Arnold, the matriarch of the most prominent family in town, could get anyone to do anything she wanted. She was always using her sweet momma voice, but the dagger was in the background somewhere. And everyone knew it.

"Don't you want to know if I saw anything?"

Sally started to move toward her backpack to grab her notebook and pen to take notes, but decided that probably wasn't the most appropriate move at the moment. She was there to comfort Momma Arnold and listen.

Sally leaned forward. "Oh, yes ."

Momma Arnold laughed.

"You are such a dear. Well, I told Mark that there were so many people about, waiting staff bringing food to the buffet, removing plates and glasses, it really could have been anyone."

So much for that line of questioning.

"But enough about that. What about Belle?"

Sally hesitated, but then realized Carol would find out anyway. "Um, well, sadly, she passed away this morning," Sally explained slowly.

Momma Arnold gasped. "Oh no, that's terrible," she replied, her hand over her mouth.

"I know. She was such a lovely lady," Sally replied.

"Do they know what happened to us exactly?" Momma Arnold asked.

"Mark didn't mention anything?"

Momma Arnold shook her head.

"He treated me like his great-grandmother. I wish he had shared more, though I certainly tried to wriggle it out of him."

Sally laughed. "I bet you did."

"So, what's the latest, Sally?"

"Well, Mark told me they would have the test results latest by Saturday. They also took my fruit and alcohol for testing, too," Sally admitted.

Momma Arnold's brow creased. "But I thought it was food poisoning," she stated.

"Well, maybe the fruit was contaminated, or maybe it wasn't food poisoning," Sally blurted out.

"Why would someone do that?" Momma Arnold asked, tears filling her eyes.

Yes, it reminded both of them about the deaths a year ago.

"I'm hoping it was food poisoning, which is bad, but not as bad as the alternative."

Momma Arnold touched her hand. "Now, you keep me updated, you here?"

Sally nodded in obedience.

* * *

Momma Arnold had begun nodding off, so Sally headed to the bar. It was a bit early, but Black Friday was always busy with people still in the Thanksgiving spirit.

She pulled into the back lot and saw Magda and Annette's cars already there. She was so grateful for their help. One bartender helping her wasn't enough.

Jay used to work there, but Sally put that out of her mind. What a terrible time they had had a year ago. She looked forward, not back, as she headed inside to get ready for the evening.

"Hi Sally," Magda said in greeting as Sally walked to the front of the bar.

"How are Momma Arnold and Belle?" Annette asked.

"Oh yes, terrible," Magda added.

Sally hesitated a moment before replying. "Momma Arnold is awake and slowly recovering, which is great," Sally began. "Um, but, um, Belle passed away this morning."

"Oh no!" both women cried at once.

"It could be food poisoning. The food and drink from yesterday are being tested," Sally explained.

"Drink?" Annette asked, brows raised.

"Well, it could be anything. We had fruit for some of the cocktails," Sally replied.

"Ugh, what a terrible Thanksgiving," Magda said.

Sally nodded grimly. "OK, let's try to put that out of our minds and get ready for a busy evening," Sally said.

"Yes, ma'am," Annette replied, with Magda nodding.

* * *

The evening was thankfully busy, which meant it went by quickly.

Sally concentrated on serving guests, lending an ear when they had something to get off their chest, while a part of her was trying to process the events of the night before.

She also had her ears attuned to the conversation in the bar. She caught fragments of conversation from many of the guests. Not surprisingly, many were going over what they might have seen or heard at the Thanksgiving dinner.

She hoped to catch someone saying something she could consider suspicious, but alas, this was not to be the case.

She commiserated with several people about Belle, who had been a fixture at Betty Jo's Diner since the 1960s. No one could imagine the place without her. Though Sally had been trying to get her to retire for years. Her hands shook, and she didn't have much strength in her arms, so pouring coffee had been difficult for her. Sally had always been worried she would burn a customer or herself.

But Sally knew from her own passion about bartending that people who love to serve others also love the camaraderie and companionship that comes from having guests. Deep down, Sally had known Belle would never give that up. And in the end, she didn't have to. Advanced age and food poisoning had ended it for her.

"Sally, how are you holding up?" a voice asked.

She turned to find Pastor Johnson from St. Luke's Methodist Church standing next to her. He gently placed a hand on her shoulder.

"Oh, hello, Pastor. I'm well. OK, I'm not fine. Thanksgiving should be a time of thankfulness and being together with friends and family. This has really put a wrench in the works," she said, frowning.

"Yes, but we are a strong town that pulls together in difficult times. We will make it through," he replied sagely. "I wanted to let you know that Belle's funeral will be next Wednesday at 11:00 a.m. at St. Luke's."

Another funeral. She had been to enough of them over the last year, but this was not to be avoided. She and Belle had gotten quite close over the years, and it always cheered Sally up when she had breakfast at Betty Jo's.

"So soon? Doesn't there have to be an autopsy?"

"Well, yes, but the town wants to put this behind them as quickly as possible, so everything has been accelerated with help from the State Medical Examiner in Little Rock. The team has assured the police by Wednesday afternoon they will have examined everything."

Sally thought for a moment before responding as she pondered this strange development.

Was someone trying to hide something? She needed to talk to the town coroner, Dr. Wiggams, to get more information.

"I see the wheels in your mind turning, dear Sally."

Sally turned red and nodded.

"Conspiracy theories can be found everywhere if one is looking for them," the minister said and walked off.

Sally called after him. "Thank you for letting me know about the funeral. I will definitely be there."

"And at least half the town," he said, turning back to her and smiling.

Sally smiled back, her eyes glistening. Belle was popular, so it would be heartening to see her support in death.

Sally hoped that her death was the last in town for a while.

Chapter Four

Sally woke the next day at noon and lazily got out of bed. Stretching, she yawned and threw back the covers.

Saturday night at the bar was always busy, so she wanted to make the most of her afternoon to relax before the craziness started.

Then she remembered that Mark said they would have the food and drink test results by that day.

She was desperate to get them and clear her and her bar of suspicion. Though if she were completely honest with herself, she really wanted to get them to start investigating. If there was something to investigate.

She knew there was. She reached for her notebook and pen on her bedside table and was poised to write the solution down.

Slow down, Sally. It wasn't that easy. She scribbled in the notebook to help percolate her thoughts.

She still had to talk to Bethany Wells and Randall Wentworth. Bethany would probably be at Sally's bar that night, her usual Saturday evening haunt. And she could catch Randall at his office, Monday or Tuesday. She had plenty of time as the bar was closed both of those days.

She padded downstairs and started the coffee machine. Looking out on her patio, she saw frost everywhere.

Sally, you know you are not going to be sitting outside for breakfast in the mountains at the end of November. She sighed and headed over to the stove to scramble some eggs with cheese, one of her favorite breakfasts.

While she was working on the eggs, the coffee machine beeped, telling her it was finished. She turned around, pulled the pot out, and poured herself a cup, black, no sugar, into her favorite green ceramic mug.

The mug was her favorite, but brought back mixed feelings. She had bought it on her honeymoon in Ireland with her now ex-husband, Bart. She had loved Ireland so that was the good part, but it also reminded her of her failed marriage. Though looking back, she was glad she had decided to divorce him after they had taken a short trip to Berry Springs from Atlanta way back when, over 15 years ago. That had gotten her to where she was today, and she loved her life here.

She finished cooking the eggs and took the food and drink to the large wooden table in the kitchen. If she wasn't going to be able to sit outside, she would enjoy the frosty view.

* * *

Freshly showered and dressed, Sally finally felt like facing the world. Like the day before, she was in jeans and a Sally's Smasher sweatshirt.

In spite of the cold, she decided to walk to The Nutmeg Café. The weather app on her phone told her it was just 32 Fahrenheit, but she loved getting fresh air. The café was on the other side of the town square and only about a 15- to 20-minute walk, depending on her pace.

She donned her winter coat, scarf, hat, and gloves, grabbed her backpack, and headed out the door onto Maple. Shivering a bit, she locked the door securely. Even after all these years in Berry Springs, with everyone telling her not to worry about a break-in, too much time living in Atlanta had gotten her set in her ways. No way was she going to leave the deadbolt open or, horrors, not even lock the bottom.

She took the few steps on her short walkway and turned left on Maple Street, heading toward Oak Street. After a block, she took a right, toward the café.

She walked slowly and was looking down, contemplating and hoping Momma Arnold was still OK. She guessed as much, otherwise she would probably have been one of the first people to get a call.

As she approached Betty Jo's Diner, her stomach twinged. Poor Belle.

Betty Jo's wouldn't be the same without her. And if Sally were honest with herself, she wasn't sure when she would be OK to eat there again. Though they did have the best greasy Southern breakfast ever. It always reminded her of her mother's breakfasts growing up in Savannah.

She pulled out her phone and called Mark to see if there were any results from the tests. She crossed her fingers that there was nothing wrong with her cocktail ingredients.

Mark picked up after three rings. Mark answered in a voice that sounded like they hadn't talked in weeks.

"I was wondering if you had gotten the test results back yet," she asked, stopping as she spoke.

Mark laughed. "Already on the job?"

"Um, no, is there a job? I was just wondering because you were also having my stuff tested."

"Sorry, bad joke. I did just get the results in, as a matter of fact. Inconclusive," he replied.

Sally frowned. "What does that mean, inconclusive?" she asked, tapping her foot.

"Well, it means no poison or food poisoning bacteria were found in the food or drink. There were some curious results, however, but nothing that points one way or the other. As we both know, the people still somehow got sick. And Belle sadly passed away. It can't be an isolated incident of just Belle getting ill. Others were affected as well, but we aren't sure of what caused the breakout," Soder explained.

"That doesn't sound good," Sally said, stopping and tapping her foot on the sidewalk.

"Not really. It means Belle's death is now considered suspicious until we learn more," Mark replied.

Berry Springs was not the quiet place it used to be, Sally admitted to herself. She didn't think they would ever get back to normal, whatever normal was. Well, actually, she knew: when there weren't murders or suspicious deaths to deal with.

"This is a terrible way to start the holiday season," Sally said.

"Agreed," Mark replied matter-of-factly.

"Have you heard anything about Momma Arnold, Mark?" Sally asked.

"She's still in the hospital, but should be out soon."

"Oh, that's wonderful. I saw her yesterday, and she was certainly in good spirits."

"Or hiding it to show everyone she is still the town matriarch," Mark replied.

Sally laughed, "Yeah, that too."

"Take care, Sally. I'll try to keep you posted if I have any updates."

"Thanks, Mark, enjoy your Saturday."

Sally stuffed the phone into her pocket and continued onto The Nutmeg Café. She wasn't sure what she would, or should, tell Joanna about the results. On the one hand, both of them seemed to be cleared; well, their food and drink seemed to be. But Belle's passing was now considered a suspicious death, according to Mark. Whatever that really meant. She wondered if he had been keeping some piece of information from her. She doubted it, but then again, she had a hot-cold relationship with his boss, Detective Finnegan. He may have pressured Mark to only reveal certain things to Sally at this point.

Still, she hoped she would be able to get to the bottom of this soon, or maybe the police would beat her to it. Not that it was a competition.

After another 10 minutes, Sally arrived at The Nutmeg Café and walked in. It was early Saturday afternoon, so it was full of patrons.

Sally waved to several people she knew as she slid into the one available table in the corner near the counter. She saw Annette and Zeke Parker, Father Killian, Randall Wentworth, and the police chief and his husband. Magda and Jeff were just leaving.

Perfect. She could try to talk to Randall there, if she kept her voice down. He did not like being a part of anything suspicious or otherwise gossipy, though he himself certainly loved knowing about anything and everything that was going on in town.

Magda came over to Sally's table.

"See you in a bit, boss," she said, leaning down to give Sally a hug.

She watched Magda and Jeff walk out, the bell on the door chiming.

Leaning back, she inhaled the scent of cinnamon and reveled in the cozy atmosphere. Every chair had a bright cushion, the walls were painted a pale yellow, and the furniture was old-fashioned, harking back to a more genteel era.

As she was woolgathering, she felt a tap on her shoulder.

"Hey, hon," Joanna said in greeting, leaning down to give Sally a peck on the cheek.

"Hey, Joanna. How are you doing?" Sally asked, expecting the standard answer.

Joanna sat down at the empty seat across from Sally. She leaned in, whispering, "Oh, just terrible about what happened to Belle. I feel awful. I'm always so careful about my food. I hope I won't get shut down." Joanna was close to tears.

Sally had never seen her so upset. She was usually the tough cookie type, where nothing touched her.

Sally patted her hand. "Don't worry, Joanna. I don't think you are going to get shut down," Sally replied, whispering as well.

"I just don't know how Belle could have gotten sick," Joanna replied.

"Well, she was old," Sally admitted.

Joanna nodded. "True. Have you heard anything about the test results? I'm dying to find out if there was something wrong with my food."

Joanna frowned. "Sorry, bad choice of words."

"Actually, yes. I just talked to Mark Soder. The food and drink were clear of any poison or food poisoning bacteria. But since several people got sick and Belle died, they're now treating her death as suspicious," Sally explained as quietly as she could.

News, bad or otherwise, traveled like wildfire in a town of their size.

"Well, I'm relieved my food was OK."

"We seem to both be off the hook," Sally said, not quite believing it.

"Do you want a coffee or something to eat?" Joanna asked.

"Just a cappuccino to go. I had a big breakfast."

Joanna got up and returned quickly with the drink. Sally pulled her wallet out of her backpack, but Joanna shook her head. "On the house."

Joanna left Sally to get back to work, while Sally sat back with her coffee. Until Belle's death was explained, anyone could be a culprit. And the Thanksgiving dinner had been packed with people. Who would want to hurt Belle and Momma Arnold? Narrowing down the suspects would be a challenge, but Sally was definitely up for it.

As she was considering this, she saw Randall Wentworth getting up out of the corner of her eye.

She grabbed her backpack and the coffee and walked over to the door just as he got to it.

"Hi, Randall," Sally said. "Lots going on in town. How are you feeling?"

He turned and smiled. "Oh, hi, Sally. How are things?" Randall glanced around the café and quickly headed outside. Sally followed him.

"Randall?" Sally called.

He stopped. "Oh, sorry, Sally. I just didn't want to talk about this inside. You know how small towns can be."

Sally waited for him to begin speaking again. "So you asked how I'm feeling. Well, better. I don't know what I ate at Thanksgiving that would have made me, or the others, so sick. I usually have an iron stomach."

"Maybe just overeating?" Sally offered.

Randall smiled. "Maybe. You are probably right. I just hope we can put this behind us."

"Me too," she agreed.

He was about to leave when she put her arm on his. "Just one question, Randall," Sally said.

He turned and frowned. "Detective again, Sally?"

She winced. "Well, Mark, um, well, wanted me to chat with a couple people to see what they might have noticed Thursday night."

"Deputized again, I see," Randall said, peering down at her.

Sally ignored his tone.

"As you probably heard, Belle's death is being considered suspicious. So, did you see anything strange at the Thanksgiving dinner?"

Randall considered for a moment before finally responding. "No, not that

I recall. Everyone was enjoying themselves, chowing down."

"Sure, I guess celebrating was more on people's minds than watching for a poisoner or killer."

"Sally, it was probably just a bout of food poisoning that somehow didn't show up on the tests," Randall mansplained.

She decided to leave it at that. "I guess I'll see you at Belle's funeral."

He nodded.

"Her death is a real loss for the town. When I first got here so many years ago, she was a great person to talk to, and she helped me meet people. And get me my first clients."

As he was talking, Sally thought, wow, he is human. But the last sentence made her stop. Since he was a lawyer and new in town, he had needed to first build his client base oh so many years ago. Now he was a town fixture like Belle was, though she had heard he had been bigger than life ever since he arrived.

If she were honest with herself, Belle did the same thing for her when she first arrived in Berry Springs. A bar needs customers, and it also took a lot of work to first get the bar ready. Belle helped with many of those connections. Bill Arnold did the rest, and without his money back then as her business partner, Sally's Smasher would never have gotten off the ground.

Chapter Five

The Sunday after Thanksgiving was traditionally the day Sally and her crew decorated the bar for the holidays. This year, it was somehow extra special, taking a few hours to put the events of the past few days out of their minds and looking forward to the joy of Christmas.

Sally had arrived just before 1 p.m., with Annette and Magda coming in a bit later. Annette had told Sally she would bring her husband, Zeke, to help put up the tree and other trimmings. Annette had also agreed to get the big tree, and Zeke's pickup was great for that.

Sally's old Datsun 210 would barely hold one of the boxes in front of her.

Sally loved Christmas, but she tried not to go overboard with decorations. It was still a biker bar, she told herself. And she didn't want to stuff the place. Her guests still needed room to move around and enjoy themselves.

She had lugged the five boxes up from the cellar and was slowly pulling out the ornaments, garland, and the small ceramic Santas for the tables.

The tree would be stuffed in the corner near the door, present but out of the way. The red paneling in the bar was the perfect color for the holiday cheer. She and Bill hadn't chosen it for that, but it fit in nicely nonetheless.

She had debated removing Bill's vintage bike and its cage to make room for the holiday decorations, but she knew she couldn't. One reason was that it reminded her of Bill. It had belonged to him, and Sally had inherited it after his death. The other reason was that it was one of the main attractions Sally's Smasher had to offer. People loved admiring its polished metal frame and leather seat.

She turned to look at the machine, and a tear rolled down her cheek.

Drying it off with her sweater sleeve, she returned to the task at hand. She had just opened the last box when the chime told her the others had arrived.

She pushed herself up to see Annette, Zeke, and Magda.

"Where should we put this?" Zeke asked.

Sally pointed to the spot she had picked out near the door. Before they had arrived, she had moved the table that stood there to make room for the holiday accoutrements.

Zeke maneuvered the tree over to the corner. Sally had already set up the stand there and filled it with water. Pulling off the net covering, he set the tree in the stand and knelt down beneath the tree to tighten the screws.

"Oh, how beautiful," Magda cried, walking over to touch the tree and inhaling the earthy pine scent.

Magda's grandmother had been from Poland, and somehow a Christmas tree anywhere made her nostalgic, she had told Sally a few years back.

"Let's get decorating," Sally said, smiling while pointing to the ornaments she had laid out on the table next to the tree.

"Zeke, can you get the ladder from the back for the star on top?" Sally asked, pointing toward the back storeroom.

Zeke nodded and headed off.

As Sally, Magda, and Annette started decorating the tree with all the decorations and ornaments Sally had collected over the years, Sally decided it was the perfect opportunity to pick over the carcass of the Thanksgiving dinner, so to speak.

Magda selected a golden orb to place toward the front of the tree near the door. She looked at Sally as she hung the ornament. "I know that look, boss," she declared, laughing.

Annette added, "Yes. What do you want to know, Ms. Detective?"

Zeke came back with the ladder.

"Did I miss some of the fun already?" he asked, grinning.

"Well, Sally is just getting ready to interrogate us about the Thanksgiving dinner," Magda explained.

Sally threw up her hands. "You got me."

"So what do you want to know?" Zeke asked.

Sally considered for a moment, realizing the only information she had was that something had probably been added to the food to make the people sick. She realized she had just spontaneously come to that conclusion.

That did make sense.

Mark Soder had said the tests were inconclusive, but that no poison or food poisoning bacteria had been found in the samples tested.

And anyway, it was a buffet dinner. If something had been in one of the pans of food, the tests should have shown it. Though Mark Soder had been a bit coy about giving her details, that was probably more due to his boss, Detective Finnegan, not wanting to give Sally all the information rather than anything else. Sally knew Mark had the same soft spot for her as she did for him.

"I guess my first question is whether you saw anything suspicious?"

Magda laughed. "There were so many people about. What do you mean suspicious?"

Sally explained her thinking.

"Yeah, I guess that makes sense," Magda replied. "But it really could have been anyone. And you told us it's not clear what was in the food."

"Ugh, this is so frustrating," Sally replied, stamping her foot.

"We know you'll solve it." Magda gave her a hug. "Just keep asking us and everyone else questions."

"Like what?" Sally replied.

"Like if anyone had a grudge against any of the sick, or worse against Belle."

"Good point. Any thoughts on that, people?" she asked, her eyes sweeping the small group.

Magda, Annette, and Zeke were quiet for a moment.

"Well, everyone loved Belle, though she was getting on in years. Her coffee-pouring skills and order remembering were sometimes challenged, but that seems like a ridiculous reason to want to kill her?" Magda asked

Sally considered that for a moment. "I doubt any of this is random. And maybe getting a few people sick was a way to cover up a potential crime."

"But how would the killer know who would die?" Zeke asked.

"Hopefully no one else dies," Magda replied. "Why don't we get back to decorating? I doubt there's anything else we can help you with, Sally."

"OK, well, please think back to the Thanksgiving dinner, and if you do remember something, please let me know."

Annette saluted, and they all chuckled.

The group spent the next hour putting on all the decorations and ornaments and running the golden garland around the tree.

At the end, Zeke climbed the ladder and topped the tree with the silver star Sally's mother had gifted to her years ago. It had been in the family for at least 100 years, according to family legend.

Once the tree was done, the four finished putting the Christmas Santas on the tables and the rest of the decorations around the bar.

When they were finished, Magda went around taking photos. "For our social media accounts," she explained, as if no one in the room knew why she was doing it. Sally's bar was hyper-local, so they didn't get a lot of guests through social media, but it did help with the random tourist who often left a nice comment after their visit. *Best place I visited in Berry Springs*, someone had written the past summer.

Sally checked the clock on the wall and saw it was going on four, so they still had a little time to relax before the crowd arrived.

Everyone in town knew this was the day the decorations at Sally's Smasher went up, so they usually got an extra horde of guests to come and ooh and aah, or at least that's what Sally told herself. And that would be perfect for trying to catch a random tidbit or clue about the Thanksgiving dinner.

She went behind the bar and pulled out four chilled beers, opened them, and placed them on the bar. She knew she didn't have to ask. The four jumped on the barstools and toasted a job well done. Sally didn't usually drink before or during work, but this was a special occasion.

"Thanks, everyone. There is no way I would have been able to do this myself," Sally said.

"Glad to help, my dear," Annette replied, patting her husband's leg.

"Yeah, glad to help," Zeke added. He wasn't always a man of many words, but a great help, nonetheless.

Magda began posting the photos to their social media accounts in between glugs of beer.

Sally sat back and just enjoyed the moment.

As always, though, the moment didn't last that long. Before they knew it, it was time to open the door, and as expected, there were already a few guests waiting outside.

Chapter Six

Luckily, the past couple of days had been uneventful. After the Sunday rush coming to see the decorations, she was glad the bar was closed Monday and Tuesday, so she'd had plenty of time to rest and recuperate. She really needed to steel herself for Belle's funeral. A close friend had died, and the police still weren't closer to finding out what happened.

She had spoken to Bethany Wells at the bar on Sunday night. Sally had been surprised Bethany hadn't been there Saturday, but she told Sally she was still recovering from her bout of illness after the Thanksgiving dinner.

Unfortunately, Bethany couldn't tell her much more than Randall Wentworth had. Though Sally realized if she had gotten food poisoning after a big meal, she wouldn't have been able to pinpoint the source either. Or the source of whatever had happened to them all. Sally was still waffling between it being some kind of undetectable poison to something being added to certain plates of food.

Mark had called her the day before to give her an update, though there wasn't much of an update to give.

He explained that Detective Finnegan was now more closely involved, since Mayor Pulasky and Chief Sanford were putting pressure on him to solve Belle's suspicious death as soon as possible and rule it a natural death due to old age or such.

Sally knew this wasn't Finnegan's call. That was up to Dr. Wiggams, the town coroner. Everyone knew he should have retired years ago, now that he was over 70, but he wasn't going to give up. Sometimes Sally wondered if he wasn't getting a bit senile.

She decided to see if she could get any information out of him at the funeral, not that it was the best place for a conversation of that sort. But Sally was determined, as always, to solve puzzles and crimes, and he was going to be there anyway. She might as well make the most of the opportunity, she told herself.

The funeral was at St. Luke's Methodist Church across town. It didn't start until 11 a.m., which meant she had enough time to get ready. She was mainly focused on her mental readiness that morning as she sat in the living room on the couch, leaning back with her eyes closed, a cup of coffee on the table in front of her.

There were tears streaming down her face, but she was too shaken to get a tissue.

Looking back to the events of the past year or so, Sally wondered why she was so affected by Belle's death. Yes, she and Belle had gotten close over the years, and she loved to visit Betty Jo's Diner for the food and the conversation. For some reason, her death hit Sally almost as hard as Bill Arnold's death had a year earlier. She and Bill had gone to college together and had been friends for years. That had made sense why she would be so upset.

But Belle?

Then it hit her. Her parents.

George and Dorothy Witherspoon were retired and living in Bolton, Oklahoma, just across the state line from Arkansas. That meant they were only about a two-hour drive away, which was a perfect distance, Sally admitted. If they were in the next town, she would feel obliged to visit them regularly, and that didn't quite fit with running a bar or being independent, for that matter.

Dorothy Witherspoon was about the same age Belle was.

Ugh, she knew her parents were getting older, but prayed they would last forever. Though that wasn't realistic or honest.

She had talked to her parents on Sunday as she usually did and had filled them in on what was going on.

The Witherspoons had raised her to be honest and open, so she had felt obliged to keep them updated on all the terrible events, both a year ago and during her attempt at relaxation on the riverboat cruise down the Mississippi six months before.

Now she had had to tell them about the Thanksgiving dinner.

Her parents usually spent Thanksgiving in Bolton with close friends they had met just after they moved there years ago, not too long after Sally had moved to Berry Springs. She had wondered why her parents had left beautiful Savannah, Georgia, to move to Oklahoma. She considered that it was probably because their only child had moved away. And maybe her parents also liked the freedom of the distance, rather than being on top of their daughter in Northwest Arkansas. For years, their special tradition had been Christmas. Sally drove to Oklahoma to pick them up and bring them to Berry Springs to spend the holiday with her.

She glanced at the ceiling and was thankful she had finally upgraded the guestroom upstairs. Since the room originally only had had a single bed, Sally slept there when her parents visited and gave her parents her room. She had recently bought a queen-size bed for the guestroom so they could sleep in there now. She had then decided to move the guestroom down the hall to one of the bigger rooms, which she had completed just before Thanksgiving. It meant the two rooms were at opposite ends of the second floor, giving all the Witherspoons more privacy.

Sally's phone chimed as she was thinking about her parents and the house. She glanced at the clock on the wall. It was time to get ready for the funeral. Sally took a deep breath before pushing herself up from the couch to head upstairs to shower and change.

Oh, Belle, she thought as she climbed the stairs.

* * *

In spite of the frigid temperatures, Sally decided to get some fresh air by walking to St. Luke's, just like she had done on Saturday afternoon to check in with Joanna at The Nutmeg Café.

She wanted to be as clear-headed and focused as possible to give Belle the sendoff she deserved.

Admittedly, she also wanted to be sharp to question Dr. Wiggams about Belle's death and Momma Arnold's serious illness. If he would talk to her. She thought he would, as he was always going out of his way to help people, even waiving fees for medical services if someone couldn't afford it or visiting patients even in the dead of winter in heavy snow. And he was known as the deputy town gossip to Bethany Wells. He loved to chat about anything and everything, even if that meant divulging cause-of-death or other medical information. This more often than not got him in trouble with some families or the Berry Springs police. Usually, everyone just looked the other way, though, as he was an aging, gentle old codger whom everyone seemed to love.

As Sally strolled into town, she wondered who would be at the funeral. If she knew Berry Springs as well as she did, it would be a very packed funeral. Betty Jo's Diner was one of the few places to eat out in town, and it served a mean breakfast. Belle had worked there for what seemed like forever, and she was synonymous with Betty Jo's in many people's minds.

Her husband had passed away at a fairly young age in the mid-1980s, and she had no kids. Maybe that was why she had stayed working so long; serving coffee and food at the diner was her life.

The owner of Betty Jo's Diner, Roy Barnes, kept a very low profile in town. Though he was a bear of a man, he was rarely seen at the diner and was more of a hands-off manager. He was gruff, but everyone loved him almost as much as they loved Belle, but they rarely saw him. Sally wondered whether he would venture out for the funeral of his longest-term employee.

She arrived at St. Luke's just before 11, and the parking lot was packed. There was even a line to get inside.

Sally had expected a lot of people, but this was like the entire county turned out. OK, maybe the entire town, well or half the town. The county had maybe 50,000 people, so that might be a slight exaggeration. Berry Springs only had about 2,000 inhabitants.

Sally waited at the end of the line, and it slowly moved forward. Once inside, she saw there was absolutely no seat left, so she stood to one side to get as good a view as she could.

She felt a bit guilty she hadn't gotten there earlier for a better seat, as she had considered Belle a special friend, though so did most of the town, Sally realized.

Looking around, Sally realized how many people she didn't know or maybe had seen only once or twice in town. She had been in Berry Springs for over 15 years, and, with running a bar, she always assumed she was well acquainted with most of the town and a good part of the county.

Sally wondered if Momma Arnold was there. With all the people filling the church, she couldn't tell. Knowing the town matriarch, she was there for Belle, regardless of what the doctors were telling her or ordering. Carol Arnold did what she wanted, and no one was going to stop her.

As she glanced around, she was glad to discover Dr. Wiggams toward the back. Perfect, she could tackle him later, well, figuratively.

And she smiled when she recognized Roy Barnes sitting next to Dr. Wiggams. Belle would have been so pleased she got the hermit out in death. He was about Dr. Wiggam's age, Sally thought, though she couldn't be sure. He still had a full head of hair, most of which was still dark brown. Sally always wondered if he colored it. He wore a suit that looked like he had bought it in the 1960s.

As the organ began playing, Sally turned to the front of the church, and her eyes filled with tears.

* * *

The service had been beautiful. Since the church had its own cemetery, the attendees had followed the coffin around the back of the church, filling the rest of the parking lot and the grass between the church and cemetery.

They were now under a huge, enclosed tent on the other side of the church parking lot. There were heat lamps everywhere, and Sally was pleasantly surprised how warm it was.

Small tables were set up where people could stand for the refreshments.

Belle had always said that when she died, she wanted people to enjoy themselves and not be too sad. There was a huge buffet in the center, groaning with all kinds of appetizers and desserts.

Belle had enjoyed a glass of wine or two at times (well, maybe that was an understatement), so there was a full bar in the corner serving whatever people wanted. The drinks had been provided by Betty Jo's Diner, and a couple of Belle's colleagues were serving. If the church had asked Sally to provide the bar service at the funeral, she would have turned them down. Belle was too dear a friend, and she wanted to focus on remembering her and not be worrying about whether people had a drink in their hand.

She had just grabbed a soda when she saw Roy Barnes slide over to the bar, trying to keep to himself. That wasn't going to be possible here. Many people came over to offer him their condolences. And Sally overheard several of them trying to see how he was doing. Everyone was so sweet.

Walking over to the bar just as he had picked up his drink, she decided to rescue him. The only person left talking to him was Gilbert Rock, but he was just the person to try and cheer Roy up.

Roy smiled when he saw her. "Hi Sally, so nice of you to be here," he said, giving her a hug.

That was a surprise. "Oh course, I wouldn't miss this. Belle was a dear friend."

"To me as well. She will be sorely missed at the diner," he added, a tear running down his cheek.

"I know, she really was the life of the diner and such a wonderful person," she added.

"Yes, we all loved Belle," Gilbert added, touching Roy's arm.

He burst into tears.

Sally leaned in to give him a hug.

"It's all right, Roy. We're there to help you," Gilbert offered.

Sally pulled away. She wasn't sure what she could add to Gilbert's words, so she just nodded solemnly.

Roy seemed very upset about Belle's death. He finally stopped crying and wiped his eyes with his jacket arm. "I'm sorry, Sally, Gilbert. It's just I had some shocking news yesterday," he explained.

Now what is going on, Sally thought. Another death?

"Oh no, what happened?" Gilbert explained, his eyes wide with shock.

He sipped his coffee and finally spoke. "Randall Wentworth informed me yesterday that Belle left all her worldly possessions to me."

Sally and Gilbert gasped. Sally knew that Belle had no relatives or kids, but Belle had always seemed the type to leave her money to an animal shelter or the like.

"Yes, it seems she had a soft spot for me," he said, tears running down his face.

"That is… I just don't know what to say," Sally admitted. She decided to just give him another hug, which he seemed to need.

As they pulled away, he said, "Thank you, Sally. Thank you, Gilbert. You are both always so kind."

A part of Sally's brain was wondering what he got, but this was neither the time nor the place for that question.

Well, unless it involved a murder, which Belle's death could have been.

Roy coughed. "Wondering whether to ask me what I got, Sally?" Roy said, chuckling.

Gilbert joined in the merriment, giving Sally a wink.

"Oh, um, I no, I was just thinking about Belle," she stammered.

"Don't worry, Sally, I was going to tell you anyway. Belle was such a good friend to you. I thought you would want to know the extent of her generosity and what I'm planning to do with it."

Sally thought this was a bit disingenuous and bragging, but he did know her well enough that she was a very curious soul.

She kept her mouth shut for the moment, waiting for him to speak again.

Gilbert stayed quiet as Roy had seemed to have forgotten he was there as well.

"Well, she didn't have much. She rented her small apartment, didn't own a car, and I'm sorry to say I don't pay millions for waiting staff." He grimaced. "I've decided to use what money she left me to fix up the diner in her honor. In addition, one of the booths will be dedicated to her with a special plaque."

Sally gave him a spontaneous hug. "Oh, what a tribute to her," Sally said. There was a lot of hugging going around.

"Yes, so whenever people come to the diner and see the booth, they will remember her and her kindness."

Sally smiled. "I will definitely be sitting in that booth as often as possible," she told him.

As she said this, Roy looked at his watch. "Oh, I must get home to feed Tabitha."

Sally knew that was code for, "I've had enough of people for the moment." They hugged again, and Roy made his way out of the tent toward the parking lot.

As he left, Sally considered whether he might be a suspect. He had inherited something from Belle, albeit not that much. Had he known about this before? She didn't know Roy enough to be able to tell if he had really been surprised by the news or whether he had been acting.

Sally knew she would have to keep an eye on him for the time being. There wasn't much information to go on about Belle's death at that point.

As she was contemplating this, she noticed Dr. Wiggams head over to the bar. Just the person she was hoping to have a word with, in spite of the setting. She waited for him to be served his drink and walk away before she followed him.

As she did, Gilbert waved to her and headed off into the crowd.

"Dr. Wiggams, do you have a minute?" she asked.

Everyone called him Dr. Wiggams. It was as if he didn't have a first name, which Sally had heard years ago and promptly forgotten.

She watched as he stopped and looked like he was considering who she was. His hand holding the drink was shaking a bit. She hoped it didn't spill.

His eyes brightened. "Oh, Sally, nice to see you. Even though these are sad times again. I didn't recognize you at first. My old eyes, you know."

Sally wasn't sure it was his eyes that were the problem, but she was not going to go there.

"Nice to see you too. It seems you have been kept busy again, Dr. Wiggams."

He took a sip of his drink, and a bit spilled on the floor. Sally had just enough time to slide to the left to avoid the liquid.

"Yes, terrible about Belle. She was such a kind lady."

Sally nodded sagely. He looked up at her and leaned in. "I assume you are interested to learn what I found during Belle's autopsy?" he whispered.

Sally was taken aback. Maybe his doddering was just an act. She didn't think she would ever know. "How did you guess?"

He chuckled softly. "You are easy to read, my dear. And after the last year or so, you seem to be turning into an ace detective," he replied.

She wasn't sure if he was being sarcastic. "And what can you tell me, doctor?"

"Why don't you come by my office tomorrow morning at ten, and I can give you more information," he said, glancing off to the right.

Sally looked over and saw Detective Finnegan, Sergeant Soder, and the police chief. She knew exactly what he meant. "See you tomorrow," she replied, walking away quickly, though she assumed the police had seen them talking.

She steered away from the law enforcement and managed to find Momma Arnold. As Sally had expected, she was there as well. Her son, Jack, was pushing her in a wheelchair. Sally was surprised to see the matriarch in a wheelchair. Carol Arnold was not one to show weakness, so she must really still be feeling poorly to be seen in the chair.

She smiled when she noticed Sally coming toward them. "Oh, Sally, hello. Sorry, I can't get up."

Sally leaned down, and they hugged tightly. "What are you doing here, Carol?" Sally asked.

"Now don't you start with me, too. My kids and half the people here are concerned about my health. I couldn't stay away."

"Hi, Jack," Sally said in greeting.

"Hey Sally. Yeah, Momma insisted on coming."

"Yes, I did. Though I hate that it has to be in this weakling wheelchair," Momma Arnold said, banging her fists on the armrests.

"Now, Momma, don't get yourself worked up," Jack scolded.

Sally thought she was going to yell at him, but with half the town there watching, Momma Arnold just gave him a look, but said nothing.

"Yes, I didn't think you would stay away, but you need to get better," Sally replied, touching her arm.

"I am feeling better, though still weak. I should be home, though, by the weekend."

"That's great to hear," Sally said.

"OK, Momma. Time to leave," Jack said sharply.

That was the only way to deal with Momma Arnold. She sighed. "Oh, all right," she replied.

As Jack began to push the wheelchair, Momma Arnold turned. "Now you're coming to my annual Christmas get-together on the 16th, right?"

"Of course. That's a tradition I never want to miss," Sally replied, smiling broadly. One of the few days in the year when she wasn't at the bar when it was open. She loved Momma Arnold's party.

"That's a good girl," Momma Arnold called as Jack wheeled her out of the tent.

Sally shook her head and looked around. She saw Gilbert Rock had planted himself at a table surrounded by many of his fan club. He was wearing his traditional sweater vest and polka dot bowtie. His fairly substantial belly was straining the vest, though Sally couldn't quite see it fully, there were so many people around him. They looked like they were all admiring his outfit. He always dressed like a fashion maven. Or maybe they were talking about the Thanksgiving dinner.

She decided to join the crowd and also find out how he was doing after his bout of food poisoning, or whatever it was. She hadn't had a chance to ask him about that while they had both been comforting Roy.

Chapter Seven

The next morning, Sally was up bright and early.

Though bright might be an exaggeration. It was still pitch black outside. The sun didn't rise until around seven at the beginning of December in Berry Springs, and it wasn't even six yet.

She switched on her bedside lamp and was momentarily blinded.

Pushing herself up, she slid into her slippers and padded downstairs.

Though she usually got up later, considering she worked late almost every night at the bar, knowing she would see Dr. Wiggams and hopefully get some information about what had happened to Belle had jump-started her day.

Quickly making some toast and coffee, she brought everything over to her kitchen table.

She glanced around the room and smiled. She really did love living in the house and the town.

The holiday season was always particularly special. Partly because she saw her parents, who she admitted she should visit more often, but also because it really made Berry Springs shine with happiness, joy, and community.

Her backpack was on the table, and she reached in to pull out her trusty notebook and pen. Placing both in front of her, she didn't know what she was going to write down.

Unlike the last two crime adventures she had been on, there didn't seem to be a crime involved. Well, as far as she knew. That's what the visit to Dr. Wiggams later that morning would tell her.

But Belle was dead, and, according to Mark Soder, the police were treating it as suspicious.

Sally was relieved Momma Arnold was recovering. The town would certainly not be the same without her, and who would hold her annual Christmas do?

When Bill had been killed, she had considered who was around in the bar late that night.

Thinking back to the Thanksgiving dinner, there were around 250 people there, and many stayed late as they had booked rooms at the Grand Hotel. That was way too many people to consider. She put down her pen and sipped her coffee.

Glancing over at her notebook, she smiled. After seeing Dr. Wiggams, there would be much more to write down, getting her closer to the truth about Belle's death.

***

Walking out her front door, Sally stopped and shivered. In spite of her winter getup, it was frigid. And the fresh air was a bit too fresh for her liking that morning.

Sally turned right around and went back in to get her car keys.

Gladys started up right away for once, in spite of the cold, and she breezed down Oak Street to the police station, aka morgue, library, and mayor's office.

She had to drive around the town square a couple of times to get a spot. There were several boutique shops nearby, and people came from all over to shop and enjoy the Christmas cheer in Berry Springs. Another reason she loved living there.

Sally finally found a spot a block away and trudged over to the morgue. The air smelled like it was about to snow. Looking up, she saw ominous clouds above her. She hoped it would hold off. Gladys had her winter tires on, but she was definitely not as snow-worthy as a 4×4. Her friends had been telling her for years to get a better vehicle for the Ozarks. Winter could be rough, and there were a lot of hills to maneuver.

Sally wasn't going to give up Gladys until she died completely. She just hoped the car wouldn't skid off the road as she headed to her bar someday. Sally's Smasher was south of town, and the roads could definitely be treacherous.

Dr. Wiggams was waiting for her in the entranceway, and he led her downstairs to the morgue. "Coffee?" he asked as they entered his office.

She nodded vigorously. The temperature in his office wasn't much more than she had just come from.

He put a pad in the machine next to his desk, and soon she had a steaming cup of black brew to help her warm up. Dr. Wiggams sat down at his desk and motioned for Sally to take the seat across from him.

He pulled out a folder from the bottom of a pile of paper perched precariously on the edge of his not-so-large desk.

Sally leaned forward in anticipation.

Dr. Wiggams grinned. "You are enthusiastic, my dear." He opened the folder. "So we found a slightly elevated level of aspirin in her blood," Dr. Wiggams began.

"What does that mean?"

"I'm not sure yet. I know from Belle's doctor that she took a daily dose as a preventive measure after her heart attack ten years ago," he explained.

"But elevated?" she queried.

"Well, maybe she took a double dose, thinking it would be doubly good," he said, chuckling at his own joke.

Sally remained silent. She didn't find that funny at all. "So she died from aspirin poisoning?" Sally asked, rocking in her chair impatiently.

"Well, maybe. The symptoms of aspirin overdose mimic food poisoning: cramps, stomach pain, nausea," he replied.

"Is there a way to tell the difference?"

He shook his head. "Not easily. There was an elevated amount of aspirin in her blood, but as far as I can tell, it wouldn't have been fatal. Though she was quite old."

Sally was considering this when the door opened and Detective Finnegan walked in. He frowned when he saw her.

"At it again, Sally?" he said, laughing.

She got up. "Well, you know…" she replied, wondering if she was going to be thrown out.

He turned to Dr. Wiggams. "Can I speak to you a moment, Doctor?" the detective insisted.

Was she in trouble? Or worse, Dr. Wiggams.

They returned after only a minute or two. "Sally, I'm sorry. I can't give you any more information," Dr. Wiggams explained, looking at the ground.

She got up, looking over at Finnegan, who seemed to be glowering. "No worries. Thanks for having me." She grabbed her backpack and quickly left. It was not even 11 a.m., so she decided to head over to The Nutmeg Café for another coffee. It was going to be a caffeine-fueled day.

She walked the block to the café and was glad to step inside out of the cold. It still wasn't snowing, for which Sally was grateful.

Joanna wasn't there for once. Sally was glad she had taken some time off. Or maybe she was just out shopping for stuff for the café.

As a bar owner, Sally rarely took any time off. If she were honest with herself, this was more because she wanted everything to be just right. She loved her staff, but a part of her felt if she weren't there, something would happen. Thinking about it now, deep down she knew she fully trusted Magda, but somehow Sally still felt like she had to be at the bar whenever it was open.

It had certainly taken quite a lot of convincing on Magda's part to get her to finally book the Mississippi River cruise she had been on earlier in the year. She had been glad to get away, even if death had followed her there.

There were a few precious moments of joy, and she had met some great people. Brin Clarkson was one of them, a Canadian who ran a boutique hotel in Valencia, Spain.

That reminded her: she had to send Brin a text and wish her happy holidays. Brin had urged her to come to Spain for Christmas, but there was no way she could leave her parents.

Maybe next year, Sally thought.

As she made her way to the counter, the bell at the door jingled. She turned around to see Rose Cohen, the manager of the Grand Hotel.

"Hey Sally," she said as she joined her at the counter.

Joanna's son, Kent, was behind the counter. "What can I get you, Sally?" he asked.

"I'll have a double cappuccino and a blueberry muffin," Sally ordered, considering the treats on display in front of her. "Where's your mom?" Sally asked.

Kent walked over to the large professional machine to start her drink. "Can you believe she took the day off?" he said, shaking his head.

Sally laughed. "No, I cannot believe that."

"I had to confirm with her a hundred times that she was heading out this morning to do her thing," he explained.

He started frothing milk loudly, so Sally waited for him to finish before answering. "What did she say she was doing?"

"She wanted to head over to Jefferson for their town flea market and then maybe get some lunch there," he replied.

Jefferson, Sally thought. That was even smaller than Berry Springs, with one restaurant and a mini downtown, if you could call it that. Another puzzle to solve, Sally thought as she brought her coffee and muffin to a table in the corner.

Rose soon joined her and plopped herself in the chair. "Can we talk?" Rose asked. It came out like "tawk." Rose was Brooklyn-born and bred. And even though she had been in Berry Springs for decades, the New Yorker in her was hard to miss.

"What's on your mind?" Sally asked, munching on her blueberry muffin. Though she could surmise what Rose wanted to talk about.

"Well, it's Thanksgiving," Rose began. Surprise! "I just can't believe people were sick, and one person died on my watch." She looked like she was about to cry.

"Rose, it wasn't your fault."

"How can you say that?" Rose asked.

Their voices were quiet, both not wanting to draw attention to the conversation. Kent kept glancing over, perhaps overhearing Rose's stage whisper. Luckily for them, several customers came in at that point, and he was distracted serving them.

"Well, I was with Dr. Wiggams this morning, and he told me that it may have been an aspirin overdose. And anyway, you had nothing to do with the food or drink. If anyone, the police should be looking at Joanna and me. Though I don't usually put aspirin in people's drinks."

The words came tumbling out like a confessional.

Oh, that's a weird comparison, Sally.

Rose's mouth dropped open. "Who would do that?"

"That is the big question at the moment. I just can't believe anyone there would do that. But someone did something. Many people were sick, and now Belle…" Sally replied, giving Rose a quick hug.

"That hotel is my life, and if something happens there, I'm responsible," Rose explained matter-of-factly, pulling away.

Sally put her hand on Rose's. "I get it, but until the police know exactly what happened and who did it, if it is aspirin poisoning, you shouldn't be beating yourself up."

Rose looked at her coffee. "Maybe I should have ordered something stronger."

Chapter Eight

The morning of Momma Arnold's party, Sally was in the middle of a cleaning fit.

It had been a surprisingly quiet week and a half since Belle's funeral. Luckily, there had been no more deaths.

Sally had managed to talk to a number of people who had been at the Thanksgiving dinner, but no one had seen anything. She had kept the aspirin part quiet since she reminded herself she needed to stay on the good side of Dr. Wiggams and, more importantly, the police. She had done some online research on dosage and toxicity levels, but nothing conclusive. She also kept having to remind herself that she wasn't a medical professional, so a bit of online searching did not constitute expertise.

Since the crowd at Momma Arnold's party would have some overlap with the Thanksgiving dinner, she hoped this would be the place for a breakthrough.

As she whisked a duster around the living room and ran the vacuum, she considered other angles she could take to get to the truth.

The guest Sally Witherspoon was definitely looking forward to the party, but the detective in her needed to finally make some progress on her investigation.

She was putting pressure on herself to solve the crime quickly, which had caused her to toss and turn for a couple of nights over the last week. And she kept thinking back to her aging parents and what might have happened to them if they had been at the Thanksgiving dinner.

Perish the thought, Sally.

Finishing up the living room, she glanced at the clock on the wall and saw it was almost time to get ready. She hadn't realized she had been cleaning or thinking that long.

Momma Arnold's party that afternoon would be a blast. The Arnold mansion and compound were huge and could accommodate a lot of guests.

Sally wondered who was invited that year. She was always glad to make the guest list, but others weren't so lucky. There were a few regulars, like Sally, but most were added or subtracted each year, depending on Momma Arnold's mood and good graces. She was a picky hostess who wanted the mix of people to be just right.

Many people in town jockeyed for an invite, but those were the people that rarely, if ever, got an invitation. Momma Arnold hated people competing to take part. It was a party, not a rodeo.

Sally's stomach grumbled, reminding her she hadn't eaten anything yet. She had had a cup of coffee when she got up, but she decided it was time for more, and a snack to tide her over until the party.

Saturdays, she often made herself a treat of pancakes and warm maple syrup.

Considering the do in front of her, though, she decided to stick to some buttered toast.

The coffee felt glorious going down, and she enjoyed several cups before realizing she better hurry up or she'd be late. With the coffee, she had been reading her latest non-fiction book. This was a tradition started by her late uncle. He always read non-fiction at the first meal of the day.

"Always important to learn something new," he told Sally many a time.

Naturally, he would say that, having been a math professor at an Ohio university.

Her current read was about the continental drift and how the continents came to be as they are today. She was loving it and learning so much.

Maybe she could use some of the information at the party.

Sally laughed to herself. That would get her a de-invite faster than she could say "Momma."

Washing up, she headed upstairs to get ready. She needed to be at Momma

Arnold's around 2:30 to help finish setting up. Momma Arnold made her boys help, but Sally always offered to do any last-minute things to make the party just right.

Saturdays were for long, hot showers, which Sally relished.

She scrubbed, used a generous amount of coconut bath gel, and washed her hair with her coloring shampoo. Her chestnut ponytail wasn't as chestnut as it used to be. At first, she had loved the mix of gray and chestnut, but the reality of turning 60 the next year had hit her like a brick. Though she wasn't that vain about her appearance, she nonetheless decided to try and dim the gray.

She had found an all-natural, organic shampoo that claimed to help bring back natural hair color. Yes, she admitted to herself, she was a sucker for marketing tactics. She had been using the shampoo for about a month and didn't really notice a difference, though she pretended she did.

Drying off, she headed into her bedroom to choose an outfit. The Arnolds were wealthy, but there was no fancy expected or wanted for that matter.

Sally didn't want to go too casual, though, so she paired a pair of dark jeans with a cream blouse. Her grandmother's pearl necklace and dark blue flats completed the outfit. She thought for a moment before putting on a bit of her dusty rose lipstick. She rarely wore makeup.

As she looked at herself in the mirror, she remembered this was almost the exact outfit she had worn one night on *The River Queen*, on her fateful trip down the Mississippi.

Oh, Sally, how do you get yourself into these messes?

Though a part of her was glad she had had a crime to solve during the trip. That made her shudder. Maybe she was getting too used to death and dying.

Putting that out of her mind, she walked downstairs, put on her winter coat, scarf, and gloves, and headed out to Gladys and the party.

* * *

The party was in full swing with the *Who's Who* of Berry Springs in attendance.

Detective Finnegan was chatting with Mark Soder, his wife Candy, Chief Sanford, and his husband, Andy.

Sally had been pleased to see Mark Soder at the Arnolds' front door, greeting guests, or maybe better yet, looking over guests to bounce people at a moment's notice. The exclusivity of the event rose every year, and Sally was always grateful to be a part of it.

Momma Arnold was eternally grateful for Sally's help in solving the murders of her son and daughter the year before.

The shock waves of all that death were still touching everyone in town.

Next to them, she saw Magda with her partner, Jeff Bartholomew, talking to Joanna from The Nutmeg Café and Mayor Pulasky.

Sally had decided to close the bar that day, something she rarely ever did. It meant Magda and Annette got the night off for a change. Both had been quite surprised when Sally had told them, as they had planned on working, giving Sally a break.

Maybe it was because she was extra careful with both of them after what had happened to Bill a year before. Magda had been devastated by his death. Annette, Sally had learned, had been dating Bill secretly, or not so secretly. Everyone in town had known, except Sally. That was why Bill had left his share of the bar to Annette, rather than to Sally, as they had discussed years before. Annette had told Sally that her husband, Zeke, knew all about it. Sally seemed to be the last one in town to have been told.

Sally had been hurt by that, but she and Annette had made up. And Annette had sold her half to Sally, so it was now really Sally's Smasher 100%.

Continuing her inventory of the guests in attendance, she saw the religious crowd was there as well, with Bishop Billingsley, Father Killian, and Pastor Johnson sitting at a table eating together.

Annette and Zeke were in the corner with Gilbert Rock, the librarian.

She laughed when she saw Bethany Wells corner Randall Wentworth. He did not look happy. Bethany worked at the high school and was also known as the town gossip. He would remain as tight-lipped as possible, Sally was sure.

Two faces were not present, which Sally guessed meant they weren't on the guest list that year. Though she was surprised that Dr. Wiggams seemed to be one of them. Rose Cohen was the other.

Sally wondered if this was because Momma Arnold had gotten sick after the Thanksgiving dinner at the Grand Hotel or because Belle had as well and died.

Sally debated asking Momma Arnold about the two missing guests who she had expected, but decided it was probably better to keep her mouth shut. One always wanted to stay on Momma Arnold's good side.

Sally took in the party decorations. Momma Arnold always went all out.

Several round tables to stand at were distributed around the room, replete with cheery flowers, salt and pepper shakers, and a stack of napkins. There were also a few picnic tables set up near the buffet for those who weren't too steady on their feet or wanted to be close to the chow.

Unlike the catered Thanksgiving dinner, Momma Arnold had made most of the food herself, with her sons supplying all the drinks. Sally had been surprised Momma Arnold had been able to cook all the food, what with her hospital stay after the Thanksgiving dinner, but she seemed to have made a complete and speedy recovery, even if, behind the facade, she may still be suffering a bit. That was something Carol Arnold would never show outwardly.

Sally filled her plate with as much food as she could manage. There were mashed potatoes, green beans, fried chicken, salad, and two crusty rolls on the plate. She had slathered them with salted butter and was now maneuvering through the room, deciding where to sit or stand.

Momma Arnold was in the center of the room, decked out in gold and sequins everywhere. She had made a grand entrance on the arms of her two sons, Jack and Steve.

Sally knew why Momma Arnold wanted everyone to be fairly casual—so she herself could shine. This was the one day of the year when the Arnold wealth was on full display; most of it in the designer gown and jewels Momma Arnold was showing off.

Sally wondered why she did that.

Perhaps it was to remind everyone in town that the Arnolds were wealthy and powerful, but maybe that was too cynical.

Or Momma Arnold really did love the holiday season and just wanted to be all decked out for it.

Speaking of the devil, that's who came over to Sally next. "Enjoying yourself, Sally?" Momma Arnold asked.

Sally nodded in between bites and swallowed. "Yes, Momma Arnold…" she replied, which got her a look. "I mean, Carol," she added quickly.

"That's better," Momma Arnold responded, patting her shoulder. "You enjoy, dear," she said as she floated off to chat with the other guests.

Sally had offered to stay over and help clean up the next day.

It was a chance for Sally to get away, as it were, and stay in one of the hotel-quality suites, and also to help out Momma Arnold. She was getting on in years, though she would never admit it. Plus, Sally wasn't sure Carol Arnold really had fully recovered from the Thanksgiving ordeal.

Looking over at her talking to the mayor, she seemed OK, but Sally wasn't too sure.

With Sally there and her sons to help, the place should be cleaned up and put back together quickly the next day.

And staying over also meant Sally could enjoy a bit of wine for once and not have to worry about driving home. The Arnold compound was quite a way out of town, and the narrow, hilly roads were not a good idea after having something to drink, especially in winter, driving Gladys on potentially icy backroads.

As she was finishing her plate and debating whether to go for seconds, Mark Soder came over with his wife.

"Hey, Sally," they said. She gave Candy a hug. "What a party," Candy said, holding Mark's hand.

Sally nodded. "It's always a wonderful day and such a great way to celebrate the season."

"Oh, I am so glad she does this. It means one less day of cooking and washing up," Candy added.

"I know what you mean," Sally replied, "I closed the bar today to give us all a day off, and that means no serving or washing up."

"Wow, that's a first!" Mark exclaimed.

Sally nodded. "To be honest, I don't know why I never thought of it before. Over the past few years, it's meant Magda had to work that night and couldn't get to the party."

Sally only mentioned Magda, not her other long-time bartender, Jay. That was a person she wanted to forget, if she could.

"Yes, it's so nice to see Jeff and Magda back together," Candy said, nodding toward the couple.

"I seem to be the only one who didn't know they dated before," Sally admitted.

Candy laughed. "Well, he was her teacher just before, and she was just 19, so maybe she was just a little embarrassed."

"She admitted to me that they had dated and had wanted to keep it quiet because of the age difference, but I thought she would have told me at the time," Sally said, sounding a bit frustrated.

"Don't be too harsh on Magda. She hadn't been working for you that long back then. I'm sure if something like that were to happen today, she would be much more forthcoming," Candy offered.

Sally smiled. "I would hope at her current age she wouldn't keep who she is dating from her friends," Sally replied, not sure how they had gotten so deep into Magda and Jeff's relationship now or back then.

Luckily, Gilbert Rock, the town librarian, came over to talk to them at that moment, and they all got caught up in the latest books they were reading. Gilbert also wowed them with his latest vacation plans, two weeks exploring South America.

Chapter Nine

Sally opened her eyes and momentarily forgot where she was. That always happened to her when she was at a hotel or staying with friends. It was relaxing, but also disorienting at the same time.

She checked her phone and saw it was already 9 a.m. Had she really slept that long?

Momma Arnold's Christmas party usually didn't go that late these days. The matriarch got tired easily and didn't want to leave the party early, so she usually ended things earlier every year.

Sally laughed to herself whenever she thought of Carol Arnold and her vanity. She knew, though, that that was how she would be when she reached that age.

The house was quiet. She assumed Momma Arnold was in the kitchen at the other end of the house, cooking breakfast and wondering where Sally was.

Sally hoped she hadn't started to clean up the mess from the party without her. Steve and Jack were supposed to assist as well, but she didn't think they were early risers like their momma. She got up and put on the bathrobe that was always provided for her. Slipping into the fluffy house shoes at the foot of her bed, she headed down the hall to the stairs.

She made sure to be extra quiet as she went downstairs. Turning right, she headed down the long hallway toward the back of the house, stopping in the kitchen about halfway down.

Sally had noticed the hall light wasn't on, which she thought was strange. Pushing the kitchen door open, she stopped.

The room was dark, the oven wasn't running, and there was definitely no smell of fresh coffee or muffins.

What was going on?

Maybe Momma Arnold was really getting on in age, and the party had worn her out.

She headed out of the kitchen, down the hall, and up the back stairs to the Arnold family bedrooms. Walking to the end of the hall, she stopped at Momma Arnold's room. Sally debated whether she should knock and disturb her or just let her sleep.

It was very late for Carol Arnold to not be up, so she knocked lightly, not wanting to wake up the Arnold sons.

There was no answer, so she knocked louder.

Sally waited a few seconds and heard a door open down the hall. Footsteps got closer, and then a voice spoke.

"What's up, Sally?" Jack asked.

Sally turned to him.

"Well, your momma isn't up yet, which I thought was odd, but maybe the party wore her out," she replied.

He smiled. "Yes, she would never admit that to anyone, let alone herself. Though she usually gets up by 7 a.m., no matter what happened the day or night before," he said.

He knocked loudly. They waited for a response.

Nothing.

"I'm going in," Jack said, opening the door. Sally followed behind.

As they turned the corner toward the bed, she screamed.

Momma Arnold was lying on the floor on her side, a pool of vomit in front of her mouth.

Jack quickly went over and felt for a pulse.

He looked at Sally and shook his head.

* * *

The ambulance and police arrived quickly, with Detective Finnegan leading the pack. He quickly maneuvered his bulky frame into the house and up the stairs.

Sally could feel the ambition drooling off him, though with a new mayor and new police chief, he wouldn't be getting that sought-after promotion for a while.

Finnegan, Sally, & Jack and Steve Arnold stood outside Momma Arnold's bedroom.

"So, what happened?" Finnegan asked.

All three started talking at once.

Finnegan put up his hand. "One at a time," he said, pointing to Sally to start.

She took a deep breath to collect her thoughts. She needed to relay what happened as calmly as possible, but inside, she was churning. Belle and now Momma Arnold. Who was doing this to their quiet small town?

"I stayed over to help Momma Arnold clean up after her party yesterday. I slept so well and didn't get up until nine. I kind of felt something was wrong when I came downstairs and found the kitchen quiet and nothing baking. Momma Arnold always gets up, um, got up early," she explained, frowning.

Finnegan nodded. "Go on," he said.

"Well, she was getting on in age, so I thought she was just exhausted from the party. But I decided to knock on her door anyway. There was no response," she continued.

"I heard the knocking and came to see what was going on," Jack added.

"Right. And then we went in and… and found her," Sally said, finally breaking down.

Jack hugged her, and they both cried.

Finnegan shifted on his feet, clearly uncomfortable with the emotional outburst.

Steve was standing the whole time off to the side, looking at the ground, his mouth tight and his face red.

Sally pulled away and glanced at him. He looked like he might shoot someone at a moment's notice. He had pulled a shotgun a year ago as his mother had revealed her troubled past to Sally, which he had unfortunately overheard. She had never told her children before, and he had gone berserk. The gun had gone off and blown through the kitchen window.

As Sally was contemplating this, the paramedics came out with Momma Arnold's body on a stretcher.

"There was nothing we could do. She's been dead for hours," they said to Finnegan.

Sally thought he looked like he was going to ask the paramedics how she died, but they wouldn't have been able to tell him anything definitive at that point.

She had clearly been ill, but was it food poisoning like Thanksgiving or something worse?

Finnegan grunted and moved aside to allow them to head down the stairs and outside to the ambulance.

Sally, Finnegan, and the Arnold boys went downstairs to the living room. Finnegan didn't ask them to, but Sally could figure he would try to get more out of them.

Sally's immediate thought was aspirin, and she wondered if Momma Arnold took it like Belle did. She also began to consider suspects, though a part of her shuddered at the thought of another murder. The other part of her couldn't wait to get started with the investigation.

Sally and Finnegan took the sofa while the Arnold boys took two of the easy chairs across from them to sit. Neither of them dared sit in the middle easy chair, slightly elevated as it was. This was Momma Arnold's throne-like seat to survey all she owned.

Now Steve and Jack got everything, Sally assumed, including the Arnold business. Great-grandpa Jesse Arnold had built a logging empire in northwestern Arkansas and, over the years, the family had expanded it into housebuilding and furniture-making. Sally wondered what would happen to it all now that Momma Arnold, the glue that kept everything and everyone together, was dead.

Finnegan glared at the Arnold boys, who glared back.

"What?" Steve barked.

"Just wondering what happened here last night," Finnegan began.

"Well, you were here too. Maybe you did it," Steve yelled, getting up, his face getting even redder.

"That's enough!" Finnegan bellowed.

Steve sat down and murmured, "Sorry."

Finnegan turned to Sally. "Can you tell me anything?"

Sally shook her head. "There were so many people here. And we don't know what killed her," Sally began.

"True. I guess I was jumping to conclusions after Belle's death," he admitted.

That was magnanimous, Sally thought. Her other thought was that maybe he hadn't been promoted because he jumped to conclusions, seemingly more eager for power than actual proper police procedure.

"She did have a heart condition," Jack said.

Sally's grandmother had had a massive heart attack and had been vomiting hours before her death. Her mother had been a nurse before she retired, and she had told Sally this can be a symptom of a heart attack about to happen.

Finnegan didn't say anything for a few seconds. "Well, I want you all to stay in town. I'll be in touch after we get the results of the autopsy," he explained finally.

"Autopsy?" Steve asked.

"It was maybe natural, but after Belle's still unexplained death, I want to be sure about what happened to your momma. Don't you think she deserves that?" Finnegan asked, really laying it on.

Every time she had contact with the detective, she wondered if she would ever understand him or his methods, if he had methods or wasn't just winging it.

"I guess," Steve admitted.

Finnegan got up and motioned for Sally to follow.

"One moment, Detective," she said, first going over to hug the Arnold boys.

They reluctantly stood up for the hugs.

"If you need anything, you let me know, OK?" she said, looking both in the eyes.

Steve and Jack nodded.

Looking at the detective, she said, "I just need to get my overnight bag from my room."

Finnegan shrugged.

She ran upstairs, grabbed the bag, and then headed back downstairs to follow the detective outside and let the boys grieve quietly.

Outside, she went over to her car. "Wait a minute, Sally," Finnegan said, coming over.

"Yes, Detective?" she asked.

"This is just so strange. What a holiday season," he began.

Sally nodded.

"If you do think of something strange that happened, let me know, OK?" he continued.

Sally started up Gladys and headed out, driving by Finnegan, seemingly lost in thought in his police car.

As she headed east toward home, she contemplated what Finnegan had asked.

Thinking back to the party the night before, she couldn't think of anything suspicious off the top of her head. It had been a fun party, as usual, with lots of food and booze. Everyone just seemed to be having a good time. Nothing that would point to another death about to happen. With all the people milling about, grabbing drinks from the bar or food from the expansive buffet, anyone could have slipped aspirin powder onto someone's plate or into someone's drink without anyone noticing.

Sally wanted Momma Arnold's death to be natural, though that in and of itself was so sad.

But somehow she knew it wasn't going to be. That's why her first thought had gone to aspirin. There must be a pattern here, she told herself.

Sally pulled into her driveway and parked Gladys. She took off her seatbelt and leaned her head on the steering wheel.

Sally knew what she had to do. It wasn't going to be easy.

Chapter Ten

Sally sat in her living room, a glass of bourbon on the rocks in her hand.

Usually, she didn't drink a drop on days she worked, but she thought the bourbon might steady her nerves. She had to figure out what to do. Her first thought was to close the bar that day, for mourning or something. On the other hand, the people of Berry Springs would want a place to gather to go over the events of the last few weeks.

But she knew she had to do something else, though she was dreading it. She and her parents were open and honest with each other, sometimes to a fault. But this would be one of the most difficult things she would have to do.

More difficult for them or you, Sally?

She took a deep breath, gulped some more bourbon, and put the glass on a coaster in front of her.

Looking over at her phone lying next to her on the couch, she felt she was ready. She picked it up, selected the number she wanted, and tapped dial.

For the sake of convenience, she tapped speakerphone and placed the phone on her thigh.

It rang a few times before someone answered.

Her parents didn't have a cell phone, and they hated caller ID. She kept trying to get her parents to at least add that to their phone plan so they would know who was calling. With all the spam callers these days, she wondered how her parents put up with it. Though her mom had once admitted to her that, since they were retired, it was kind of entertaining to lead the spam callers on, or worse, play tricks on them like banging a spoon on a saucepan as they answered.

"Hi, Mom," Sally began.

"What's wrong?" her mother asked.

Both Sally and her mother had a "something is wrong voice."

If her mom called her with that voice or, worse, asked her if she was sitting down, Sally always immediately insisted on knowing who had died.

"How do you know something is wrong?" Sally replied.

"Oh, Sally, come on," her mother said sharply.

This wasn't going to be easy. "Mom, there have been some strange things going on in town. Two people have died. I don't think you should come here for Christmas," Sally blurted out.

There was dead silence on the phone.

"Is it murder?" her mother asked just as directly.

Her parents had been very upset and worried about Sally's own safety when she had called them the year before to tell them about Bill Arnold's murder, but they weren't surprised she was getting right in the middle of the investigation. And they had also been not surprised when she called them after her river cruise to tell them about the deaths and investigation.

So it wasn't surprising that her mother quickly jumped to conclusions. She decided to be honest with her mom. "It's not clear. The first was Belle, as I think I told you," Sally began.

"But you said that was food poisoning," her mother replied.

"Well, it was, at first. Now it seems it may be something else," Sally explained. "There was an elevated amount of aspirin in Belle's blood…"

"Which could account for the food-poisoning-like symptoms," her nurse mother replied.

For some reason, Sally sometimes forgot her mother knew much more about medicine and health than she did.

"And who is the other person?" her mother asked.

"Well, I was at Momma Arnold's annual Christmas bash yesterday and stayed overnight to help her clean up this morning…" Sally began, using a pause to sip some bourbon.

"Don't tell me, Momma Arnold," her mother said, sniffling.

Sally took another sip before having the courage to reply. "Yes, sadly so," she said, breaking down into tears. She began shaking and was just able to put the glass back on the coaster before collapsing on the couch, the phone tumbling onto the shag rug.

"Sally, Sally?"

It took Sally a few moments to compose herself before reaching for the phone that had found its way under the coffee table. "Yes, Mom, I'm here," she said into the speakerphone.

"Oh, Sally, I'm so sorry to hear about Momma Arnold. What happened to her?"

Sally shook her head as if her mother could see her. "It just happened this morning. We don't know exactly," she replied, leaving out all the details of what they had found that morning.

"Well, you should come here today and stay with us over Christmas," her mother urged.

Sally looked at the clock on the wall. If she left soon, she'd definitely be there before dinner. She wanted to see her parents, but she knew she needed to stay in town. There would be another funeral to attend, and then there was the investigation to conduct.

Sally knew that both deaths were still unexplained, but she was sure they were murder.

Thinking about this took a minute or so. Her mother didn't say anything, but Sally could tell she was thinking too.

"You want to investigate," her mother said finally.

"Well, yes," she replied, "And I need to help the Arnold family. It's just Steve and Jack left."

"You are such a strong woman," her father said. "You do what you need to do, and please visit us soon."

"I love you both!" Sally replied, wanting to cut the conversation short before she would start tearing up, knowing she wasn't going to see her parents for Christmas.

Putting down her phone, she hoped it was murder because otherwise she would be missing a wonderful Christmas with her parents.

Telling herself it must be murder, she sat back to plan her next move.

Chapter Eleven

"Hi Sally, I'm so sorry to hear about Mother Arnold. How terrible," Magda cried.

It never ceased to amaze Sally how fast secrets traveled in Berry Springs, let alone happenings and goings on. The news of Momma Arnold's death seemed to have made it at lightning speed through the town.

"I know. What a blow to the town and her family. And after Bill's death and Gillian's as well," Sally said, sniffling.

"I bet you can't wait to investigate," Magda replied, which got a laugh out of Sally.

"How did you know?" Sally asked, half-joking.

"Boss, I've known you a long time and, after last year's events, I know what you love to do, besides running the bar."

Sally did love both, though juggling them at the same time was not always easy. Sally hoped the murderers would time their killings far enough apart to not interfere too much with her life. Yeah, that's going to happen.

"So any clues so far?" Magda asked.

There really wasn't much to go on this time, except the elevated aspirin levels in Belle's blood. Sally wondered what Momma Arnold's autopsy would show.

She'd have to call in on Dr. Wiggams on her way to work, and hope Detective Finnegan wasn't there to interfere in her questioning this time, even if it was Sally who was really the one interfering.

She put that thought out of her mind.

"The reason I'm calling, Magda, is to ask you a question," Sally began, though she had really decided for herself just before she called her parents to tell them the bad news.

"Question?" Magda asked.

Sally paused before answering. "Well, in light of the events over the past two weeks, I was considering closing the bar today."

After Bill's death, Sally had decided to change the opening days and times. The bar used to be closed Sunday only, but that was now Monday and Tuesday to give everyone a breather. Early in the week had never been that busy, anyway, though people had been asking her about opening Sunday nights for years.

"Don't you think people will want to get together to chew over the murders?" Magda asked.

"Who said they were murders?" Sally countered.

Magda laughed. "Oh come on, Sally, it's obvious."

Sally knew that was obvious, though she didn't want to say that out loud until she had concrete evidence to back that up.

Speaking of concrete evidence, she saw it was almost two o'clock. She'd have to hurry up and get ready if she was going over to see Dr. Wiggams. She assumed he would be in his office working on Momma Arnold. She decided not to call ahead for a number of reasons.

"OK, we'll stay open," Sally finally replied. "I've got to go and get ready. See you at five."

"Bye, Sally, see you later," Magda replied, ending the call.

Sally put the phone on the coffee table and sat back for a moment of thought. She wondered whether it might be better to see Dr. Wiggams the next day, since it was Monday. That way, she might have some information or questions based on what she heard at the bar that evening. And that would give him more time to collect the results for her.

As if he was doing the autopsy just for her.

Sally laughed and went upstairs to get ready for the evening shift.

* * *

It was 9 p.m. on a Sunday, and the place was as busy as ever. This was not a surprise since Sundays tended to be the busiest night next to Saturday and, with the two deaths in town, people were desperate to gossip. Sally was sure of that. And they would all be thinking she would be involved and probably at the bar to get information out of her.

Though that is what she was trying to do herself, drag any inkling of what happened out of her customers. Well, in a nice and, hopefully, subtle way.

She had hoped Mark Soder would be there that night, but he wasn't. Sally guessed this might have to do with Momma Arnold's death.

Sally was glad Joanna from The Nutmeg Café and Rose Cohen from the Grand Hotel had stopped by. Somehow, those two knew when Sally needed support. Or maybe they were just there to gossip like the others.

Sally had just handed Gilbert Rock, the town librarian, his second very dry martini when the two came over to the bar. Gilbert took his drink over to sit with Bethany Wells, the high school assistant.

Sally was surprised Gilbert was in jeans and a sweater. He usually spiffed up, though he probably guessed the appropriate gear for a biker bar was exactly what he was wearing. Gilbert rarely came to the bar, preferring to sip wine at one of the few restaurants in town.

"So how are you doing, hon?" Joanna asked, reaching across the bar to give Sally a hug. Rose did the same. They hopped onto stools and pointed to the whisky bottle behind Sally.

She served a lot of beer, as befitting a biker bar, but she always kept some wine and other booze on hand for people. She wanted everything to be just right, and the last thing she wanted was to not have something someone ordered. It was still a biker bar, though, so things never got too exotic.

This made her think of her favorite cocktail bar in Atlanta, The Blue Whale. She and her ex-husband often went there Friday nights after work to unwind. It wasn't too far from their downtown apartment, and their frequent visits meant they were treated like VIPs. Her favorite drink was a Margarita Imperial, while Bart usually went for a very dry martini, just like Gilbert.

After two each, they headed home—though occasionally they stumbled home when the two became four. Ever since they had gotten divorced and she had moved to Berry Springs, Sally had put off hard alcohol, though she did serve a selection at her bar.

Over the years, some regular guests had asked her to start serving a wider selection of cocktails, but she always had to remind them that this was a biker bar, with beer the main beverage on tap, literally. She had expanded the selection of beers she served, adding some exotic labels from places like China, New Zealand, and Chile. She particularly liked the latter from Chile, corn beer. It was delicious, ice-cold.

Thinking about beer was getting her thirsty, so she poured herself a glass of water.

"Hon, are you there?" Joanna asked.

"Sorry, woolgathering," Sally replied.

"Glad Magda is here to serve the couple of guests that were just in line," Rose said, laughing.

Sally realized she was talking about them. "Sorry," she said, turning around to get two glasses and the whisky bottle they had pointed at.

She knew they both liked it on the rocks, so before she poured the whisky in, she used tongs to add a few ice cubes to each glass. She handed them their drinks and sipped her water.

"Cheers," they said, toasting.

"So how are you, hon?" Joanna repeated. "We were both so sorry to hear about Momma Arnold."

Rose looked grim. Sally was thinking she was probably glad it hadn't happened in the Grand Hotel, like the Thanksgiving food poisoning incident, or whatever that was. It was really still too early to tell.

Sally frowned. "I just can't believe it. She was so full of life yesterday at her Christmas do. And then… this morning…" Sally couldn't continue. Partly because she was still in shock, but partly because she didn't want to be gossiping herself about what might have happened to the matriarch.

Rose patted her hand. "I know. Belle, and now Momma Arnold. Any clues?"

Sally shook her head. She leaned down to a whisper, though this was difficult with all the ambient noise from the many guests. "I'm going to talk to Dr. Wiggams tomorrow. I wanted to stop in and see him today, but somehow I was running behind," Sally whispered. "I'll keep you both posted." She winked.

"Got it," Joanna said, taking another sip of whisky.

Chapter Twelve

The next morning, Sally padded around the house, tidying things that didn't need tidying.

She kept glancing at the clock, but decided it wasn't quite time to head over and interrogate, um, talk to, Dr. Wiggams. Sally didn't want to jump in right at the start of his week, as it were.

Her main goal that day was to talk to Dr. Wiggams and find out what happened to Momma Arnold. Thinking about the investigation, she decided she should also talk to Mark Soder. He would probably be more forthcoming than his boss.

When the clock said it was 11 a.m., she decided it was time to make her move. She packed her backpack, poured the rest of the coffee into a travel mug, and headed out.

As she walked into town, she decided to call her parents again. She had been thinking about it quite a bit since their last call.

She pulled her phone out of her pocket and tapped her parents' number.

"Hi, Mom. I'm calling to apologize," Sally began.

"Oh, honey, for what?" her mom asked, though Sally could feel the emotion through the phone, indicating her mother knew exactly what she was apologizing about.

"I'm sorry, I said that I had to stay here to investigate. I don't know what I was thinking, or maybe I wasn't. You and Dad are more important. I'll drive to Oklahoma to see you for lunch Christmas Day," Sally explained, relieved she was getting it all out.

"Sally, that is wonderful," both her parents replied.

"Will you stay overnight?" her dad asked.

Sally thought for a second, but knew she couldn't say no. "Sure, but just one night. I really do want to figure out what happened to Belle and Momma Arnold."

"It will be wonderful, Sally. You know we love you so much," her mom said, her voice cracking.

"I love you too. See you Monday!" Sally replied.

"Bye, dear," her mother said, signing off.

Phew, that was done.

* * *

After finishing the call with her parents, she decided to first make a stop at Betty Jo's Diner before talking to Dr. Wiggams. She hadn't been there since before Belle had passed, but she felt she owed it to herself to move on. And she wanted to comfort the owner of the diner, Roy Barnes, who had always been so supportive.

Walking toward the door of the diner, she was glad she had come.

The only guilt she felt was that she always went to Betty Jo's Diner rather than the other diner next to her bar.

One part of her wanted to help her business neighbor, but her stomach always told her the breakfast was better, more Southern, and greasier at Betty Jo's.

Looking through the window, she saw Roy Barnes pouring coffee for Gilbert Rock.

Sally was glad to see he had shed the jeans of the night before and was now back in his dapper apparel. Gilbert was sitting next to Rose Cohen.

Sally was never surprised to see anyone with anyone in Berry Springs. In a small town, everyone knew everyone else, so there were connections left and right, many years or decades old.

She pushed open the door and headed inside.

It was a very cold day, and she was glad she had on her heavy winter getup. Besides the winter coat, she had also smartly put on a heavy turtleneck cable sweater over her jeans.

As Sally breezed into the diner, Roy Barnes gave her a huge smile and came over to give her an even bigger hug. He was a bulk of a man, and Sally could barely breathe, but she appreciated the gesture.

"Sally, so happy you are back," he said, making her feel guilty for not showing up sooner.

"I'm sorry it's taken so long. Belle…" she began, choking up.

"Come on over and have a seat," Roy said.

"Yes, Sally, come over and sit with us," Gilbert said, patting the stool next to him.

She stopped to give Rose and Gilbert quick hugs before jumping on the stool.

Roy had already poured her a mug of coffee. Sally realized she still had coffee in her travel mug, but there was something about diner coffee that just hit the spot. Or maybe it was the company and atmosphere that made it so.

She admired the mug that said "NY Diner."

Rose had told her years ago that she loved coming to Betty Jo's because Roy had mugs and dishes from a New York wholesaler. By coincidence, it was the same chinaware that Rose's hometown diner in Brooklyn used.

She had never been to New York, so this was the closest she would probably ever get. She and Rose had talked for years about going to Brooklyn to visit Rose's sister, but both admitted they really wouldn't want to get away for a long time. The bar and the hotel really did take precedence.

By this point, anyway, Rose's sister was in a home in the early stages of Alzheimer's.

Sally knew that if this were one of her parents, she would be there regularly, in spite of her obligations to the bar, but it was Rose's life, not hers. Gilbert spoke, pulling her out of her thoughts. "So sorry to hear about Momma Arnold," he said.

There was a lot of that sentiment going around. Both Belle and Momma Arnold were beloved citizens, and their loss would leave a huge void in town. Sally wondered spontaneously who would take over as town matriarch, now that Momma Arnold was gone.

"It's just been terrible," Sally admitted.

"And during the holiday season," Rose added.

At that point, Roy brought Sally's regular breakfast, though, glancing at the time, it was more like brunch. She tucked into her all-day breakfast special with extra bacon and extra sausage. The diner knew her; she never changed her order, so it always came even faster than normal.

Rose laughed as she watched Sally eat. "My grandmother is probably turning over in her grave having that much pork in my vicinity."

Sally laughed, "Yes, this is probably the opposite of kosher."

"I'm glad I never kept kosher, though she always admonished me when I was in college. I love eating anything and everything and hate to be restricted," Rose explained.

That sounded just like Rose, always doing her own thing.

"Do you know when Momma Arnold's funeral will be?" Gilbert asked.

Sally shook her head.

"Everyone in town will be there. Literally," Rose said.

"Probably. I wonder where they will hold the funeral. Smith Funeral Home is definitely not big enough. What about the hotel?" Sally asked.

"I guess in the grand ballroom, like Thanksgiving, but that room is giving off bad vibes at the moment," Rose replied.

Sally looked across the counter at Roy. "Any details on your rework here?"

"Not yet. I have to admit Belle's death has hit me harder than I thought it would, so I don't have much of a mind for it at the moment. I'm hoping to spend time thinking about it over the holidays and not just jump in. But let's see how I feel."

"Roy, if you need any help, let me know," Rose offered. She had done a lot of the decorating at the Grand Hotel over the years.

Gilbert got up. "Well, I have to get back to the library. End of year tasks and such. Nice seeing you all."

Gilbert headed out after hugs all around.

Sally turned to watch him go.

"He's so dedicated to his work," she said, turning back.

Roy nodded: "The library, and town, wouldn't be the same without him."

Rose slid over to the stool next to Sally.

"We all live vicariously through him and his travels," Rose declared.

Sally laughed.

"That we do," she replied, picking up her mug to take a sip of coffee.

Another mug of this and she would be shaking all over.

"What are you up to today, Sally, or do I even need to ask?" Rose said, hands on her hips.

Sally smiled. "You got me there. I'm hoping to talk to Dr. Wiggams about Momma Arnold. I'm hoping her death was something natural, like a heart attack or stroke. Maybe the excitement of the party was too much for her."

"What does your gut say?"

Sally wasn't sure she should say what she was thinking out loud. "I'm not sure at the moment. I need more information."

"Fair enough," Rose replied, winking. Rose hopped off her stool. "I'm off for the afternoon shift," Rose said, hugging Sally before leaving.

Sally scooped up the last bit of pancake, drowned it in maple syrup, and chewed it down quickly. It was time to get on with the investigation.

Chapter Thirteen

Since Betty Jo's Diner was just diagonally across the square from the main town building, she made it there quickly without getting too chilled. Even so, she wished she had taken her car into town instead of walking,

As she approached the town hall building where all town offices were situated, she glanced around for signs of Detective Finnegan. Not seeing him, she swept up to the door, wrenched it open, and slipped inside.

She hurried down the corridor to the stairwell, which led to the basement where the coroner had his office. Just as she came down the stairs, she heard the door open at the bottom. She was glad to see Mark Soder coming up them. "Oh, Sally, what are you doing here?" he asked, laughing.

"I'm glad you're not your boss," she said in greeting.

"Yeah, he is in a bad mood today. With two prominent deaths, the chief and the mayor are getting very impatient, as if we will solve the crimes in three seconds."

"Any word on what happened to Momma Arnold?" Sally asked.

"Yeah, I was just talking to Dr. Wiggams about it," Mark replied, "But have a chat with him yourself."

Sally wondered why Mark was being so mysterious, but maybe he was just in a hurry.

"Nice seeing you, Sally. Chat soon," Mark said as he headed upstairs.

"You too," Sally called as she opened the door to the basement.

Just as she turned to head down the hall to Dr. Wiggams' office, a burly guy pushed past her in a hurry, almost knocking her over. "What the..." she called.

As she steadied herself, she saw that he was headed into Dr. Wiggams' office. Sally had never seen him before. She hoped he wasn't trouble for the good doctor.

She opened the door to Dr. Wiggam's office and found him standing at his desk, the unknown visitor standing over him.

She coughed.

"Oh, hi, Sally. What a surprise to see you," he said loudly. "So sorry, I don't have time for our coffee now. This gentleman from the Little Rock medical examiner's office is here to consult on what's been going on in town."

Sally got the hint. There was no way she was going to get any information out of him with someone from Little Rock here.

"Oh, that's too bad. I was looking forward to it. Well, why don't you stop by this afternoon, and we can catch up? I can't wait to hear about your trip," Sally improvised.

"Sure, will do. Say four o'clock?"

Sally nodded. "Sure, see you then."

Sally slipped out, not before getting a glare from the visitor.

As she headed upstairs, she wondered if he suspected she had an ulterior motive for visiting Dr. Wiggams. Though in the end it didn't matter, as they hadn't talked about Belle or Momma Arnold.

She'd just have to wait until the afternoon to find out what killed Momma Arnold.

* * *

Just before four, Sally had a small spread ready on her kitchen table. There were blueberry muffins, a couple of chocolate croissants, and a plate of sugar cookies she had just baked. She never really cooked or baked, but somehow she had felt like making it comfy and cozy for Dr. Wiggams' visit.

The coffee was almost done, and there was milk and sugar on the table. She had even pulled out her grandmother's gold-plated dishes for the occasion. She poured the coffee into a blue china pot her uncle had brought back from a trip to London and set it on a trivet in the middle of the table.

Then she sat down to wait for her visitor.

She should make notes, but there wasn't much at the moment to make notes on. She grabbed her notebook and pen from her backpack, ready to write down whatever the doctor told her.

Maybe it was a good thing she hadn't talked to him earlier. By now, there might be more information he had gotten from the Little Rock representative.

She glanced at the kitchen clock above the door to the terrace and saw it was already ten past four. No sign of Dr. Wiggams, which was odd as he was always on time.

She hoped he would show up soon, or the coffee would get cold in the pot.

She went out to the front porch to see if there was any sign of him. Her street was as quiet as it usually was. She loved living close to the center, but on a side street. It was just far enough away from town to give her peace and quiet. Shivering, she went back inside and wondered what had happened to the good doctor.

She poured herself a cup of coffee and considered calling his office. Maybe he was still in discussion with the state medical examiner. She decided to wait until 4:30 and then call.

* * *

"Hi Sheryl, is Dr. Wiggams there?" Sally asked.

"Oh, Sally, I was just about to call you," Sheryl replied, audibly sobbing.

Oh no, Dr. Wiggams?

"Dr. Wiggams was walking out to his car to head home before meeting you. He slipped on some ice in the parking lot and had a bad fall, and hit his head. Oh, Sally, he's in a coma," she cried.

Chapter Fourteen

The call with Sheryl the day before had really thrown her. She couldn't believe Dr. Wiggams was in a coma. She planned to visit him in the hospital that afternoon. She had offered to go to the hospital right after Sheryl called her, but she had told Sally that they were working on Dr. Wiggams and a visit wouldn't be possible until the next day at the earliest.

People were sick or dying left and right in Berry Springs. What was going on? Was the town cursed? Sally wasn't superstitious, but something weird was going on. The karma was definitely bad. This would definitely be a holiday season that people would never forget.

She was sitting in the kitchen thinking about this, sipping her third cup of coffee, when her phone rang. She looked down and saw it was Detective Finnegan. Ah, maybe she would get some answers.

"Hey, Detective, what's up?" she asked casually as if she wasn't desperate to get more information.

"Good morning, Sally. How are things?"

"OK is about it. Momma Arnold and Belle gone, and now Dr. Wiggams is in a coma. What a way to start the holiday season," she replied.

The detective sighed. "I know. I thought this would be a quiet month. Well, it's about Momma Arnold that I'm calling. I know you two were close, so I wanted to give you a heads up."

Ah, the good side of the detective was showing, or Momma Arnold's influence was continuing beyond the grave. "Oh, have they found out something?" Sally asked.

"Well, Dr. Wiggams' last report shows elevated aspirin levels, just like Belle," he explained.

"But what does that mean?" she asked.

"Good question. The Little Rock medical examiner, Dr. Meadows, is still working on his report, he told me early this morning. I hope he can get some answers soon."

"We need to put this behind us for everyone's sake," Sally said.

A part of her was very sad about Momma Arnold and Belle, but the detective within her couldn't wait to get out. And she was sure it was murder.

There was silence on the phone. Finnegan coughed. "Is there something else, Detective?" Sally asked. She could feel him thinking. Was he keeping something from her?

"Well, I do have some additional information about Belle and Momma Arnold. I know you were a help last year, but I kept it from you, thinking I'd solve this thing myself."

Finnegan human? Perish the thought.

"Um, yes, what is it? I really do want to help, and the two women meant so much to me."

"Well, I updated you on the aspirin results. But I should have told you that aspirin was found in some of the Thanksgiving food and the food at the Arnolds. Since there were so many people there, I don't really have a suspect at the moment."

Did he think she put the aspirin in the food?

Reading her mind, he added, "Don't worry, Sally. I don't think you did it. If you have any ideas about it, though, let me know."

That was a relief.

She began squirming in the chair as she considered the excitement of another investigation. Then she frowned. Two of her best friends had died, and poor Dr. Wiggams was in a coma.

Finnegan brought her out of her reverie. "Well, I'll let you get back to your day," Finnegan said.

"Thanks for the call, Detective, and trusting me with this new information. I'm off soon to see Dr. Wiggams in the hospital."

He ended the call without another word. Sally shook her head. He was weird. But what a call that had been. Aspirin in the food? Why would someone do that?

Well, at least they now knew why there were elevated levels of the substance found in both Belle and Momma Arnold. And that would explain the food-poisoning-like symptoms the others suffered.

Sally was glad she had steered clear of the tainted food at the Thanksgiving event. She had been working, so she hadn't eaten too much. At Momma Arnold's do, on the other hand, she had eaten her fill. But she had felt fine afterwards.

* * *

Sally looked outside and saw snowflakes. Just what I needed, she thought. Gladys did not like the snow, and she barely worked in the winter.

Sally glanced back at Dr. Wiggams, who was still in a coma, tubes and lines all over the place.

She prayed he would make it. The town definitely didn't need another death, particularly the death of another one of the town's beloved citizens.

Dr. Wiggams was in a single room at the back of the hospital. It was set against a hill, so the view outside was breathtaking. Sally sighed. Dr. Wiggams would have loved the view, but he hadn't woken from his coma.

The doctor had been in a few minutes ago to check on him.

Sally had asked him about a prognosis, but the doctor wouldn't offer any hope. They all just had to wait.

She did learn that the good doctor was actually over 80. He really should have retired years ago. His hands shook a bit, and he was often forgetful. Sally couldn't understand why the town hadn't pushed him out. Knowing small-town politics, he probably knew someone in high places in the county or maybe even the state.

Hopefully, when he woke up from his coma, he would realize he was too old to continue.

He had never married, had no kids or pets, and seemed literally married to his job. Maybe that was the reason he had held out so long.

She had had an uncle, a math professor who had retired after many decades of teaching and had sadly passed away only a few months later.

She walked over to the bed and sat back down, placing a hand on his.

She felt a finger move, but maybe that was just a reflex. She really hoped he would wake up.

Chapter Fifteen

The klaxon was as loud as a rock concert. She jumped up and screamed as doctors and nurses poured in.

They quickly pushed her aside, and she headed out of the room to wait in the corridor. She was already shivering when she sat down on a chair nearby.

"Sally, what's up?" Mark Soder called as he walked toward her quickly.

Sally raised her eyebrows. "How did you get here so fast?"

"What do you mean?" he replied, sitting down next to her.

"Dr. Wiggams, something happened," she started, but her voice caught in her throat.

The klaxon had stopped, but the medical team hadn't come out of his room. She wasn't sure if that was a good sign or a bad sign.

Sally pointed to the door across the hall. "Is he…?" Mark asked.

Sally shrugged her shoulders. "What is going on in Berry Springs, Mark? I'm scared," she said, finally saying out loud what she had been thinking about all afternoon watching Dr. Wiggams.

Mark took her hand in his. "We're going to get to the bottom of this. Of that, I am sure." His voice wobbled as he spoke, contradicting what he was saying.

Sally ignored that and just squeezed his hand. "I know you will," she said.

But not without a bit of help from Sally Witherspoon.

At that moment, the doctor came out of Dr. Wiggam's room and walked across the hall. Sally looked at him, and he shook his head. "I'm sorry. We couldn't save him," he said in a monotone.

Sally burst into tears, and Mark pulled her in for a hug. The doctor shifted on his feet and headed away, clearly uncomfortable. The hug lasted a long time until Sally pulled away, feeling uncomfortable herself.

She glanced up and down the corridor for Mark's wife, Candy.

"I want to see him one last time," Sally said.

Mark pulled her back down. "I don't think that's a good idea." As he said it, the orderly wheeled out a bed covered in a sheet.

Sally's hand went to her mouth, stifling a scream, and Mark pulled her in for another hug. That hug was going to get her in trouble, she thought, even as she was weeping inside for Dr. Wiggams.

Mark got up. "Let me take you home."

Sally remained seated and shook her head. "No, I have my car here. I just want to sit a bit by myself."

Mark turned to go and stopped. "Are you sure you're OK to drive?"

Men. "Um, thank you, kind sir, but I think the lady will make it safely home herself."

"Sorry. Didn't mean for it to come out that way," he said. "Just let me know if you need anything."

"Thanks, Mark. I will. I'm going to sit here and think and head home for a relaxing dinner and movie on the couch."

Mark smiled and walked down the corridor toward the stairwell.

Sally sat back and closed her eyes.

* * *

Back home, Sally got started on one of her favorite dishes: roasted potatoes and peaches.

Tonight, she needed to get her mind off what was going on.

She fiddled with chopping some garlic and shallots, and then cut up some potatoes and peaches. The latter had been canned by her mother. Opening the jar, she had gotten a whiff of summer.

She dumped way too much olive oil on the mix, added some salt and pepper, and stuck it in the oven. She had an old cast-iron pan from her grandmother, who lived in Savannah. Every time she used it, she thought of her beloved Nana. It was over 100 years old and still going strong.

She poured herself a small glass of red wine as a starter. The next day was Wednesday, which meant the bar was open, but she thought she would treat herself to a bit of wine. She rarely had any alcohol when she was working the next day, but after the events of that day, she decided it was ok to make an exception.

She took her glass of wine into the living room to wait for the food to finish. It was an easy dish where the oven did all the work.

Dr. Wiggams. Poor man. Slipping on the ice and hitting his head. He didn't last long at all.

Three deaths now.

At least Dr. Wiggams went naturally, Sally thought. Not like Belle and Momma Arnold.

Though a part of her kept telling her that there was no proof of murder, yet. There was possible food poisoning and elevated aspirin levels in their blood, but no conclusive evidence.

This was not like the other two times she was called upon to solve murders. Or rather, the two times she insinuated herself into an investigation.

When Bill and the others had died a year or so ago, that had clearly been murder. And the deaths on board *The River Queen* the last summer had not been natural either.

She felt like she should do something. She fiddled with the notebook she had brought in from the kitchen, but there wasn't much to jot down.

Putting her glass down, she went out into the hall to rummage in her backpack for the latest mystery she had picked up from the library. She had stopped there on her way home from the hospital, desperate for some distraction from the goings on in town. It was located in the same building as the police, centrally on the square.

Gilbert Rock, the librarian, had been shocked when she told him about Dr. Wiggams.

"What a nice man he was. We often had coffee together in the morning," Gilbert had told her, brushing some lint off his colorful sweater.

Ah, Dr. Wiggams.

She opened the thriller, *Spy in Spring*, and lost herself in a thriller with fast-paced action across Europe.

Chapter Sixteen

At noon the next day, Sally was puttering around the house, cleaning. It was partly to think about the events of the past few weeks and partly to distract her from all the deaths. The weird combination wasn't helping either way.

She was vacuuming the living room when she heard the phone ring. She stopped the vacuum and listened for another ring to try to figure out where she had left her phone.

She finally discovered it deep in her backpack. How had it gotten there? It was her friend and part-time bartender, Annette Parker.

"Sally, have you heard?" Annette asked.

Sally sat up. Now what was going on? "Heard what, Annette?"

"About Dr. Wiggams. Terrible."

Sally had called Magda the night before to tell her, but had neglected to call Annette. She was well-connected in town, so she could have heard it from any number of people.

"Three deaths," Annette said, her voice breaking. "I hope the police find out who did it."

"Well, Dr. Wiggams slipped, so that was just an accident," Sally replied.

"Do you really believe that? It must be murder."

Sally wasn't sure what to think without any evidence, but she let that question hang in the air.

"I've been hearing that people in town are starting to panic."

"Panic?" Sally replied, not really believing what she was hearing.

"Three people are dead, Sally. Who knows who could be next?" Annette shrieked.

"Annette, Annette, we don't know what's going on, yet," Sally said, trying to calm her without telling her to calm down, which just does the opposite. "Let's talk later at the bar. Everything will be OK," Sally said. As the words left her mouth, she knew they weren't true.

Like Annette, she hoped no one else would die, but she wasn't about to verbalize it to her.

Apparently, her words worked. "OK. I'm sorry for freaking out, but you need to find out what's going on and make it stop," Annette pleaded.

Sally definitely couldn't wait to do that. "See you later, Annette," she said a bit abruptly.

Sally sat thinking about Annette's call. She hoped the town wasn't freaking out. What would that do if everyone locked themselves in their homes, not wanting to go out for fear of death?

Sally had learned strength and resilience from her parents. Just keep going no matter what and make the most of life. That had given her the strength to finally leave her husband, Bart, and move to Berry Springs to start a new life.

And that had kept her going through the investigations she had been privy to. And now it would help her get to the bottom of what was going on in Berry Springs. She was sure.

For once, though, she wasn't sure how to continue. So she decided to put it out of her mind and take a brisk walk. Well, she would try to put it out of her mind to get the creative juices flowing. Maybe she would run into somebody with an idea.

Or better yet, maybe Mark Soder would call her with the final details on Momma Arnold and Belle's deaths.

Oh, who was she kidding? Why shouldn't she just call him on the pretext of thanking him for being there for her in the hospital? Though that had been a coincidence.

That made her think of his help to get her home from New Orleans after her last adventure, which had started as a vacation to get away. Yeah, that had worked.

Sally realized that Mark had been on her mind way too often the past few weeks and months. He was married to his high school sweetheart, Candy. Sally thought they were an amazing couple and that they should stay that way.

Sally checked the temperature on her phone, shuddered when she saw it was below freezing, grabbed her coat, scarf, gloves, hat, and walking stick, and headed down Maple Street to Queen Street. Taking a right away from the center of town, she walked briskly.

She loved hiking, and she usually carried her walking stick more for the fun of it than actually needing a cane.

While she walked, she swung it around a bit.

She thought this would help her warm up faster, but she was still shivering after 15 minutes.

At the edge of town, she debated where to head next. The roads out of town could be treacherous. On her left was a path up the hill into the woods. She looked down, realizing she didn't have the proper foot gear on, but she took the path up anyway. At the top, there was a bench to sit on with a glorious view of the town nestled in the hills.

Sitting down, she pulled her coat tighter, wrapping her scarf securely around her neck. The air was cold, but at least there wasn't a sharp wind. She scrolled through her contacts. When she got to S, she made a decision. Even if he might not help her, she needed answers.

After three rings, he answered. "Good morning, Sally," Chief Sanford said.

"Hi Tim, sorry to bother you."

"Don't worry, I'm just cleaning out my office. Andy is always complaining about it when he comes to see me at work."

Sally laughed to herself. She doubted he was going to change his ways.

Sally had known Andy and Tim for years. They often had had dinner with his father, who had lived next door to Sally.

She thought they were a wonderful couple, and she was so happy when they got married. But she also knew this was a case of opposites attract. Tim Sanford was messy. The few times she had seen his office, she couldn't believe the piles of paper and stuff everywhere. It wasn't dirty, but he loved to collect. But when she went to their home, it was always spotless thanks to Andy. The only room that was a mess was Tim's home office, purposely tucked away at the back of the house for no one to see but Tim.

"So how can I help you?" Tim asked, "Or, let me guess, you want to know what the Little Rock medical examiner has discovered and thought you would come to me to bypass my team," he said matter-of-factly.

Oops, gotcha.

"Um, well. OK, yes. It's been a few weeks, and I'm starting to hear about worried people in town. Now that Dr. Wiggams is dead too, people are wondering what is going on, Tim."

The chief coughed. "Dr. Wiggams' death was an accident, Sally."

"Do you really think that?" she blurted out.

He laughed. "You are ready to find murder everywhere these days, aren't you?" he replied.

"No, but it just seems strange, doesn't it?"

"Coincidence. Nothing more."

Sally was wondering when he was going to get to the two ladies. He seemed to be evading them. "So what about Belle and Momma Arnold?" she asked, perhaps pushing her luck. "I know that there were elevated levels of aspirin in their blood and that aspirin was found in the food at both events."

"Who told you that?"

"A little bird," she replied, being evasive herself.

"You are well-connected, I have to give you that. Though that isn't news to me," he said, laughing.

There was silence on the phone for a bit. Sally didn't want to push him, so she waited patiently. Well, as patiently as she could. She tapped her fingers on her thigh.

Finally, he spoke. "OK, the medical examiner from Little Rock believes both women were poisoned with aspirin."

"How is that possible?" Sally asked.

"I'm not a doctor, but he told me high doses of aspirin mimic the symptoms of food poisoning and would quickly be lethal, particularly for older people."

"Wouldn't they taste that?" Sally asked, not knowing if that was true.

"Spicy or bitter food or drink would probably mask that, though I'm not sure myself. But that's what he has concluded."

"So they were both murdered," Sally said.

"Looks like it." Sally heard a knock in the background. "One sec," Sanford said. She heard shuffling sounds and a door opening. "Thanks," she heard him say. "Well, you are in luck, Sally. I just got some information from one of the security cameras outside town hall," he explained.

Sally held her breath. What was coming?

"I can't believe it."

"What is going on?" she asked, leaning forward on the bench as if they were sitting across from each other and she could look at what he was seeing at the moment.

"We have a photo of a hand pushing Dr. Wiggams. He didn't just slip on his own."

Sally sat back, stunned.

"Man or woman?" she asked, activating detective mode stat.

"Looks like a man's hand, but could be a woman. We don't have the best cameras, and the image is grainy."

"Wouldn't the camera get the whole person behind Dr. Wiggams?"

"Well, yes, but if you know where the cameras are and how they turn, you could probably time it so you weren't seen, or in this case, only your hand."

"There's a killer loose in Berry Springs."

"Again," Sally added.

Chapter Seventeen

In spite of what she had learned from Chief Sanford, Sally knew she had to put on her "brave boss" face to open the bar that night. A part of her was glad Christmas was just around the corner. She would need a break from the goings on, and the drive to Oklahoma across the state line to see her parents would be just what she needed to recharge her batteries and try to make sense of the killings.

Three deaths in as many weeks. When would it end?

This time, she felt like there was no rhyme or reason to the killings, and someone was just enjoying killing off the old folk.

Who would be next?

She was just about to get her coat on and head over to the bar to get ready for the evening's happenings when her home phone rang.

"Oh, hello, Sally, it's Randall Wentworth."

"Oh, Randall, you just caught me at home. I'm just about to head out," Sally said, one foot moving toward the door.

"Sorry to bother you, but I thought I'd catch you at home before you go to work."

He was well-connected and had been in Berry Springs for years, but she still wondered how Randall seemed to know everything that was going on in town and where anyone was at any given time.

"Smart man," Sally blurted out.

Randall chuckled. " How do you think I got to where I am? My family has always been the smartest wherever we live."

Sally's stomach lurched. What a mansplainer.

"So what's going on?" she asked, trying to get him to stop talking about how amazing he was and get him to tell her why he was calling.

"Well, I have some news," he began.

Sally walked over to her backpack and pulled out her notebook and pen. This might be important to jot down.

"Momma Arnold's will specifies no funeral, only family. So that would be just Jack and Steve. She had no other relatives she was in contact with. Well, except her long-lost daughter, Diane, as we know, who is on death row."

Sally froze, both from the information Randall had just given her and the memories of Diane and what had happened in town a little over a year ago.

"No funeral? But the town loved her," Sally replied.

"Well, yes, I know, but that's that."

Sally thought for a moment. "Maybe we could have some kind of memorial service for her?"

"In a church?" he asked.

"Well, you know, just a get-together."

He shuffled some papers, and Sally guessed he was perusing the will. "Well, as long as it is not in a public place, you will be OK," he responded.

"Oh, that's good to know. But why didn't she want a public service?"

"That is a question we will never know the answer to, my dear," he responded in his hoity-toity way.

Sally knew he knew more about that, but she wasn't going to push him. She and everyone else always wanted to stay on his good side.

"But that wasn't the main reason I called. I wanted to let you know as soon as possible that Momma Arnold left you $50,000." The last part came out like he was a robot.

$50,000!

Was she now a suspect?

"Are you kidding me?" Sally shrieked. She didn't mean to be so loud.

"I'm not," he replied in a meditative voice.

Sally moved into the living room and sat on the couch. She was stunned, her hands shaking.

"Momma Arnold loved you and was so happy about your friendship over the years and your detecting stardom last year," he explained.

Now he was laying it on a bit thick. But she hadn't wanted money for that. She had never thought an Arnold would leave money to a non-family member.

Reading her thoughts, he continued, "She didn't trust either of her sons, so she has left a good sum to you, an enormous amount to charity, and the sons get just enough for upkeep on the manse."

Neither had kids nor wives, so who knew what would happen to the family compound when they were gone? But that wasn't really Sally's problem, was it?

"It's a lot to process, but you needed to know. Why don't you come by after Christmas to sign the papers? Once the will is processed, I can get you your money. You might want to start thinking about what you are going to do with it."

Sally sat back and breathed deeply. Finally she replied, "Sure, thanks."

He ended the call.

$50,000. That was a hell of a lot of money.

Sally was already running ideas through her head about what she would use it for. One idea hit her immediately, and she wouldn't even have to use it all to do it.

She got up, walked to the hallway, put on her coat, and headed out to work. Checking her watch, she saw she would still be right on time.

She locked the door and stopped on the porch to look over at Gladys. The snow was still falling lightly, and she hoped she would make it to work in one piece. The winters were the worst, even with snow tires.

She sighed.

Yes, Gladys, she said to herself, tearing up. It was time for you to go.

Chapter Eighteen

"Have you noticed?" Magda asked Sally.

Sally put down the beer stein she was drying and looked over at Magda.

"What do you mean?" Sally asked.

"Look at all the people here tonight," Magda said, pointing.

Sally looked out at the crowd, if you could call it that. The deaths in town certainly seemed to have put a damper on the festivities. There were maybe ten people at Sally's Smasher that night, when a Wednesday night, particularly before Christmas, had at least double that.

Sally furrowed her brow. "OK, I see, um, people?"

Magda huffed. "Look at the people. Look closely," Magda said, pointing again, her voice a tad louder.

Sally looked from person to person, trying not to stare and hoping no one was listening in on their conversation.

Though it wasn't that crowded, the conversations were loud. The tall ceilings helped make it a loud place to be. For Sally, that was what had drawn her to the old bakery building in the first place. She wanted a loud, lively place to serve beers and provide cheer to the town's residents.

Sally looked back at Magda. "Look closely."

Sally looked back. Then it hit her. There were no older people there tonight. She knew most of the regulars and their ages. She guessed someone from out of town might have slipped in, but then she told herself she recognized every face. All young people.

"What does that mean?" Sally asked, already knowing the answer to her own question.

"Isn't it obvious?" Magda replied. "The old people are worried."

Sally sort of agreed, but she wanted to defend her place. "But we didn't kill them," Sally pleaded.

"Well, no," Magda replied, "But someone's been doing something, and it could happen here, couldn't it?"

Sally nodded, thinking back to Bill's murder a year ago. She always thought she had locked that sad memory into a memory cage, never to be opened again, but it kept opening when she least expected it.

"You need to solve this fast," Magda said.

"And how am I going to do that?" Sally asked, putting her hands on her hips.

"You've been successful up to now, haven't you?"

Sally thought back again to the events of a year ago and then her attempt at vacation on the Mississippi, which turned into a disaster.

Maybe she was just lucky. And it wasn't like she solved the cases completely on her own; she had to admit to herself.

She needed to go back over the events of the Thanksgiving dinner, Momma Arnold's party, and maybe even when Dr. Wiggams was pushed. Who was there the whole time? And even if she figured that out, who would have a motive to kill them all? Then there was the aspirin bit. Who would know that an aspirin overdose could kill? Sally had never heard of that, and her mother had been a nurse. Not that she spent much time researching poisons or drug overdoses. And while both she and her mother love reading murder mysteries, they hadn't spent a lot of time discussing ways to kill people.

She would have to interrogate her mother about it, though, when she was in Oklahoma in a few days over Christmas. That would hopefully give her much more to go on.

"Earth to Sally," Magda said, tapping her shoulder.

Sally got back to the job at hand. She scanned the room, but didn't see Mark Soder, or Detective Finnegan, for that matter. Too bad, because she would love to have had a conversation with them.

Then she remembered, oops, she had gotten her latest information from their boss. She hoped they wouldn't be too mad about it.

At that moment, the door jingled, and in walked Detective Finnegan.

She was both overjoyed and nervous.

He came right over to her. "Sally, hi, can we talk?" he asked, or rather demanded.

Uh-oh. "Sure, uh, Detective. Why don't we go in the back to my office?"

"I can handle it out here," Magda said.

Sally led the detective to her small office in the back. He sat his bulk on the cracked leather sofa in the corner, while Sally sat behind her desk.

"Would you like a drink, Detective?" Sally asked, realizing she should have checked with him before they had settled down in her office.

"No, thanks, this won't take long," he grunted.

Sally sat bolt upright on her chair, waiting for the lashing.

"Listen, Sally. I know you have been a help to us in the past, and I know you mean well, but you can't go over my head like that," Finnegan bellowed.

He got louder and louder and, by the end, the level almost hurt her ears. She wondered if Magda had heard and would come running. Though Magda knew how Finnegan could get, Sally surmised.

Sally's stomach lurched as she debated what she should say in reply. She took a deep breath and shouted back. "Fuck you! Don't you come into my bar yelling at me!"

Where did that come from?

Finnegan was obviously taken aback. His mouth opened, but he shut it just as quickly.

Sally took a few deep breaths to calm down. It was at least three minutes before either spoke.

Sally started. "Look, Detective. I know you are upset, but I really was just trying to find out what happened to our beloved friends. Just as I was talking to Tim, he got the photo of Dr. Wiggams being pushed and just told me. Isn't that his choice? And you know we are friends." The words came out in rapid fire.

Sally avoided admitting the fact that she had gone over Finnegan's head by calling Chief Sanford directly in the first place.

"Sally…" he began, waiting a few seconds.

She thought that was his way of apologizing, without bursting a seam again.

"Why don't we agree that I'll provide you with information that I am allowed to share, and you come to me with any questions first, OK?"

Sally nodded.

Though the devil in her knew that she could still call the police chief, her friend. She hated any semblance of legal gray areas, but her duty to herself and the town was to solve these murders. Period.

That made her think of her friend Nancy in Little Rock, who worked at the registry. Sally wondered if she could help get any more information.

"Sally?" Finnegan asked.

"Um, yes, Detective."

" I have your agreement?" he asked. "Please say it."

Sally gave him a look that could kill and squeaked out. "Fine."

"Good. Have a nice evening," Finnegan said, getting up and walking out.

Sally remained seated, her fists clenched.

Chapter Nineteen

Sally beamed across the table at her parents.

The three had just sat down to a lovely Christmas afternoon repast. The table was groaning with food, though they were only three. That was their Christmas tradition the last few years. They had stopped exchanging gifts when Sally was still a teenager.

Each was dressed casually in jeans, wearing their traditional Christmas sweaters. Sally's sported a mini version of her bar. Her mother had knitted the sweaters years ago, a few months after Sally had gotten divorced and moved to Berry Springs to set up the bar.

At that time, her parents had still lived in Savannah, though they had told her they were already planning a move to be closer to her. In the end, they had moved to Oklahoma only a couple years after that.

"Merry Christmas," her father said, raising his glass of wine. They clinked glasses and dug in.

Sally was glad she had made the decision to visit her parents for Christmas, after all. They were definitely getting on in age, and she realized seeing them was more important than solving the latest Berry Springs murders. Though they were on her mind constantly since they happened.

"Everything OK, Sally?" her mother asked, putting down her fork and knife to take some more rice.

"Oh, I'm sorry, Mom. It's just the deaths in town are keeping me occupied."

"Of course they are, dear," her father said, chuckling.

"I just would love to solve them soon. And I hope no one else dies."

Sally dipped her bread roll in the creamy sauce her mother had made for the roast chicken and downed that before responding. A soft moan escaped her lips. Foodgasm, the best.

"Mom, this is delicious," Sally said, reaching across the table to take her mother's hand.

"Why, thank you, Sally. You know I love cooking."

"Oh yes. I wish I spent more time doing it, though I'm definitely not as good at it as you are."

Her father patted his stomach. "Yes, she's very good at it," he said.

They all laughed.

Sally took another bite of chicken. She was debating what to tell them. Though there wasn't much more information than she had already told them over the phone the weekend before.

"Well, someone has been adding aspirin to food and poisoning people. I don't know why I wasn't affected," she explained.

"Any suspects?" her mother asked, taking a sip of wine.

Sally shook her head. "Both events where they were apparently poisoned had tons of people. It's hard to tell who could have done that. It would have been very easy to slip something into someone's food without being noticed."

"So, the aspirin was added to someone's plate and not doused on the buffet?" her father asked.

Good question. "Actually, that's hard to tell, though there were several people ill after the Thanksgiving dinner."

Sally thought the previous murders she had to solve were difficult, but these seemed almost impossible.

Her mother must have read her mind. "You'll figure it out, dear. You're a very smart woman."

"Thanks for your confidence. I'm not so sure. There's nothing linking the three deaths," Sally admitted.

"Well, beyond the fact that they were all elderly like we are," her father declared.

Sally's stomach lurched. That topic was something she didn't want to think about.

"Yes, we are elderly, Sally," her mother said, smiling, "But we are going strong."

Sally smiled. "Yes, you are."

She thought for a moment before continuing. "Well, yes, they were all elderly, which seems the only common thread. Though maybe there is something else I'm missing. They all might be related, but maybe they are just random."

"Sally, you live in a small town. Are you saying three different people have done the killing? But two were aspirin, so those must be related," her mother concluded.

"Maybe you two should come back with me to Berry Springs. We can be the Witherspoon crime-solving family," Sally said, chuckling.

"Oh yes, dear," her father replied, smirking.

"More wine?" her mother asked.

Sally nodded, and her mother filled her glass.

"My first thought is that someone is targeting old people, but why?"

"Cleansing the town of the old?" her father asked, always the kidder.

Sally shuddered. "That would be awful."

"Well, you said three people were murdered. That sounds pretty awful to me," her mother asserted.

"True, it just makes me sick to think we have a killer in our midst. Again."

Sally took up her fork and knife, eating in silence, trying to piece together all the clues and information she had heard over the past few weeks.

Putting down her cutlery, she looked across at her mother. "Mom, how long would aspirin stay in someone's blood?"

"Ah, that's my detective," her mother replied. She took a sip of water before responding. "Well, it can actually stay in your body up to ten days, but that depends on someone's metabolism. And the higher the dose, the longer it will take to flush out."

"OK, so there would be plenty of time after death to detect it?"

Her mother nodded, "Oh yes."

"And how would a coroner know there was an elevated amount?"

"Well, that might be a bit difficult, but I guess they would use the standard aspirin dose and calculate the time since those dinners. And I think you mentioned Belle or Momma Arnold may have been taking a daily aspirin for heart problems," her mother explained.

Sally nodded.

"Though that isn't necessarily a good idea. Aspirin can cause bleeding and isn't recommended any more, I was just reading," her mother added.

"Oh, I didn't know that," Sally replied.

"I hope you aren't taking one," her mother said.

"Well, I don't have any heart problems, knock on wood, and I would definitely consult you first before starting or stopping any medication, Mom."

"That's my girl. Just like I know you will solve what's going on. This seems like a clever murderer using aspirin and not a standard poison."

Maybe the killer is a doctor, Sally thought. Though these days, the internet had answers to everything. She made a mental note to do some aspirin research when she got home. Or maybe she should just ask her own doctor.

She was glad when her parents changed the subject, well, slightly.

"How wonderful that Momma Arnold left you all that money, Sally," her mother said, breaking the quiet at the table.

Sally nodded. "I still can't believe it."

"Lucky lady," her father added.

"What are you going to do with it?" her mother asked.

Sally thought back to her drive there that morning. She had neglected to tell her parents she had almost gotten into a bad accident on the way to their house. Gladys had hit a patch of black ice and had started to slide off the road toward a steep drop-off. The guardrail was a flimsy wire thing which would definitely have not stopped her from tumbling into the ravine.

She was able to gain control of the car with a quick mix of brake, gas, and steering.

"Well, I've been thinking about replacing Gladys," she admitted.

Her mother gasped, "You've had that car forever."

"Mom, I think that's the problem. This winter has been really bad, trying to get her started in the freezing temperatures. My friends have been telling me to replace her for god knows how long. They are pushing me to upgrade to a 4×4, while guilting me with the whole pollution thing. Gladys is definitely not fuel-efficient. Maybe I would actually save money running a new car. And with the money from Momma Arnold, I can definitely afford one."

"What about the bar or your house?" her father asked.

"I'm going to do over another room upstairs and maybe try to get the back yard freshened up. There will be plenty left over after I've gotten a car. After Christmas, I'm going to go to the local used car dealer and see what they have."

"Maybe someone you know in town is selling a car?" her mother suggested.

"I know I'll find one," Sally replied. She took a sip of wine and sat back.

"Who's ready for dessert?" her mother asked.

Chapter Twenty

"Thanks for coming in, Sally," Randall said, sweeping into the conference room and taking one of the high-backed leather chairs across from her.

It was Wednesday morning, two days after Christmas, and she had gotten there at nine on the dot as the lawyer had requested. She wanted to get this over as quickly as possible. She never felt comfortable in the lawyer's office. It reminded her too much of her old office back in Atlanta. And Randall Wentworth reminded her of her old toxic boss. Every time he had walked through the open-plan floor, every employee had frozen, hoping he wasn't going to talk to them. If someone was called into his office, it felt like being called to the principal's office, or worse.

She was surprised he didn't sit at the head of the table as he usually did.

The cherry-wood table was huge, and she felt like she was sitting across town from him.

Wentworth of Wentworth, Shilling, and Barnesworth acted like a big-city lawyer.

Every time she was there, she was impressed that he had so many clients, and he came from money, or at least that's what he let everyone believe. Sally would never really know the truth, she admitted.

He had brought his standard leather binder. He looked across at her and smiled. "I hope you had a nice time with your parents," he began, the human in him peeking out.

She hadn't remembered telling him she was going to Oklahoma. How did he get all his information? She would have to be a bit more careful about what she told people.

"Yes, it was nice. I, well, I went to Oklahoma this year instead of having them come here," she replied.

"Yes, I can see why you would do that," he said.

She nodded.

"The town, well, at least the older folk, do seem to be in a bit of a panic," he admitted, wringing his hands.

She explained what she and Magda had talked about at her bar. "It's a weird situation. They weren't poisoned," she began.

"Yes, I've been getting updates from the mayor." Of course he was.

"But who would do this?" she asked.

"Someone with extensive medical knowledge, I would guess. Aspirin."

Sally nodded. "Exactly. That's what my mother said. She was a nurse. I think I must have mentioned that over the years."

"Yes. Did you get anything helpful from her?" he asked, leaning forward.

"She explained a bit about aspirin, the symptoms, and the like, but she would have no idea who did this."

Randall narrowed his eyes. "I guess not. Do the police suspect you or Joanna?" he more or less blurted out.

Sally had been pushing that thought to the back of her mind. "No," she replied emphatically.

"Sorry, just wondering. You both did cater Thanksgiving, and you at least helped Momma Arnold."

Sally wondered, though, what information he had gotten from the police or mayor. Or what Randall was thinking about who might have done this. He seemed to be goading her, or maybe he was just trying to milk her for information, or worse, try to get her to confess to something she hadn't done. Randall could make anyone do anything, she realized. She really would have to watch her back.

Sally took a couple of deep breaths before responding. "They don't seem to have any suspects at the moment. There were so many people at both events, so who knows who did it? And no one has come forward, as far as I know, to say they saw something suspicious. Though I'm not sure what someone could have seen. The murderer probably didn't take out a bottle of aspirin and crumble it onto a plate of food."

"No, I wouldn't think that was the method used," Randall agreed.

"Who do you think did it?" she asked bluntly. He knew everything that was going on in town and knew most of the residents intimately.

He put down the pen he had been fiddling with. "To be honest, I have no idea. I do hope the police find out. I'm still upset at this person for making me and others sick, and killing two of our own."

Sally considered whether he was telling the truth or telling her what he thought she wanted to hear.

That got Sally thinking about the killer's motive. She would have to sit down when she got home to make notes. "Are you feeling any side effects?" she asked, though it had been a month since Thanksgiving.

"No, luckily, I seem to have gotten a small amount, and I was much better after a day or two."

Sally smiled, "That's great to hear."

Randall gave her a wan smile. As she looked at him, she saw a lovely print behind him that looked new. "Oh, Randall, lovely new print," she said, pointing to the painting behind him.

"Oh yes, it is. Such wonderful artists, those Impressionists." It sounded like he wished he had the original. He coughed. "Shall we get back to the matter at hand?" Discussion over, it seemed.

He picked up the paper in front of him and read it out loud. "To my dear friend, Sally Witherspoon, who did so much over the years and recently helped solve the case of my poor children's murders, I leave $50,000."

So Momma Arnold had changed her will fairly recently. Sally wondered if she had been in the last version of the will.

"I assume you are wondering if you would have gotten anything if there hadn't been the terrible tragedy last year."

He was a mind reader as always, though wouldn't anyone want to know that? Sally smiled.

"Yes, you were in the last version of the will, though I will tell you, the amount was less."

Sally began to speak.

"I'm sorry, I can't reveal that," answering the question that hung in the air. "Please read, sign and date the papers laid out in front of you, well sign them once my staff members appear," he said, getting up to push a button on the fancy teleconference system in the middle of the table.

Sally began reading the few pages of legalese, basically saying she signed and would have no recourse to try to get more money, as if she would want to.

The door of the conference room opened, and two staff members came in to witness her signature along with Wentworth. Sally wasn't sure of the law, but she thought three witnesses was excessive.

She picked up the pen that was next to the papers, signed and dated as marked on several pages.

Then one of the staff members took the papers and pen from her, signing and dating the papers before handing them to the next colleague. Once all had signed, the first one picked up the papers and walked out. Wentworth opened his binder and pulled out what looked like a check.

He handed the paper to Sally, and she noticed it was a cashier's check in the amount of her inheritance.

Sally felt like she should have a bodyguard at that point.

"Congratulations," he said, as if she had just won the lottery, which from a certain point of view she had.

"Thanks, Randall, for the chat and the check. Let's keep in touch, and maybe you have some more ideas about what's going on."

"Have a great day, Sally," he said as he escorted her out.

Sally bolted out of the building and straight to the bank.

Chapter Twenty-One

Thursday morning, Sally was quite out of character, baking up a storm in her kitchen. There were bread and muffins already cooling on the counter, and she had just put in a batch of cinnamon buns. She looked over and smiled at the bread, her mother's recipe. Sally still couldn't believe it had come out more or less perfectly.

In some ways, she felt like she was channeling Momma Arnold. And maybe she was.

Just after leaving Randall Wentworth's office and depositing the check at the bank, she had spontaneously decided to invite friends over for a Thursday afternoon memorial do in memory of Momma Arnold. If there wasn't to be a funeral for the town, there should at least be some kind of remembrance get-together for the town matriarch, which Randall had told her was allowed as long as it wasn't in a public space.

The get-together would also be a tribute to beloved Belle of Betty Jo's Diner and Dr. Wiggams, the lonely old man tied to his job to the death.

In another bout of spontaneity, she had decided to close the bar that night in Momma Arnold's honor. Thursday was never busy at night compared to the weekend, anyway.

Sally wiped her hands on a towel before heading over to the kitchen table to check her guest list. Everyone she had invited had agreed to come, even though it was very last-minute. Sally was sure this was more due to Momma Arnold's popularity than her own.

Steve and Jack Arnold

She had debated just inviting Jack, since Steve was the one with a temper.

She still couldn't believe the shotgun incident a year ago in the Arnold kitchen. But her politeness got the better of her, so she invited them both. It was a memorial get-together for their mother, after all. She was surprised when both had said yes.

Magda and Jeff

She smiled. They were turning into quite the cute couple.

Rose Cohen

Sally admitted to herself that this was a bit more than a memorial get-together. She wanted to get people's take on the deaths over the last month. She was sure Rose must have seen something at the Thanksgiving dinner.

Gilbert Rock

The town librarian was the life of every party with the many tales he regaled the party guests with, mainly about his travel adventures and other luxurious happenings.

Joanna and Kent

The owner of The Nutmeg Café and her son were essential at any get-together. She and Joanna had become close friends over the years. And they had helped each other build their businesses. Food and drink were a great combination, and Sally and Joanna were masters of their craft. Sally had learned so much from Joanna over the years.

Zeke and Annette Parker

Annette was now her bar helper and, after Bill's death, they had become closer friends. Sally admitted to herself it was still difficult knowing Annette and Bill had had an affair, but she let bygones be bygones, or at least tried to.

Roy Barnes

Roy was another guest she was surprised had said yes. She definitely wanted him there, since he was the owner of Betty Jo's Diner, where Belle had worked. But he was something of a recluse who rarely showed his face. Sally guessed, though, that he was maybe starting to come out of his shell now that he had to spend more time at the diner helping out since Belle had passed. Sally wondered whether he would hire a new waitress to replace her. Not that Belle could ever really be replaced.

Bethany Wells

Bethany was a dear, but she was also the town gossip. While she might be able to contribute something to the discussion, being the eyes and ears of the town, she would also be the one to try everyone in the court of public opinion. Anything and everything she heard at Sally's house might be used against someone or at least leaked to whoever would listen. In the end, though, Sally thought, this might bring the killer to the surface sooner than later.

As Sally reviewed the list, she realized there were 13 people, including herself. Hopefully this wasn't going to bring bad luck. She had considered adding Mark Soder and his wife, Candy, or even Chief Sanford and his husband, Andy. And she had also thought about inviting Pastor Johnson and Father Killian. In the end, she decided the police and spiritual presence would probably hamper the discussion. And she hadn't even thought of inviting Randall Wentworth. He knew way too much about everyone in town and his aristocratic air of superiority would have put a damper on the whole affair.

The alarm on her phone beeped, telling her the cinnamon buns were done. As she pulled them out of the oven, she inhaled the glorious aroma.

This was going to be a fun and hopefully insightful party.

Opening her tablet, she checked the latest news. Her eyes widened as she saw the latest headline on the Berry Springs *Gazette*'s website.

"WHO WILL THE SENIOR SLAYER KILL NEXT?" it screamed.

Chapter Twenty-Two

After discovering the headline, Sally wondered whether anyone would show up. Though she knew her neighbors to be tough old birds, no pun intended.

To Sally's relief, the 12 guests showed up between 1:00 and 1:15 p.m. Each had brought a small gift for Sally, and all were dressed in black as befits a memorial get-together. It was not a happy time, but Sally hoped the camaraderie would help people cope.

The *Gazette*'s "Senior Slayer" moniker was on everyone's lips.

They were all seated or standing in Sally's living room. She had laid out all the food in the dining room so that the living space wasn't too crowded.

She was delighted when Rose and Joanna had brought some warm dishes to go with the breads, rolls, and cheeses she had laid out.

Sally scanned the room to make sure everyone had a drink. The sideboard in the dining room was full of beer, wine, water, and juices. She had told everyone to help themselves. She hated parties where the host spent most of the time filling people's glasses. She loved to chat, and playing bartender would take away from talking and investigating time.

She clinked her glass with a spoon and the room went silent. Smiling, she began the short speech she had prepared the night before.

"Thank you, everyone, for coming. I am really glad you all made it. I'm sure Momma Arnold, Belle, and Dr. Wiggams would have been so pleased you all made the effort. This has not been an easy time, but if I've learned anything in my many years in Berry Springs, it's that everyone in town sticks together to help each other and comfort each other. I wish us all a wonderful party in honor of three of our own. Please eat and drink and be merry. Cheers!"

She lifted her glass of wine, and the rest joined in a chorus of cheers and salute!

The chatter started back up, and Sally took the opportunity to slide over to Rose Cohen, who was standing at the mantelpiece, seemingly in thought.

"Hello, Rose. Thanks again for the food. I don't know what I was thinking when I sent out the invite. I had baking on the brain but little else. And that headline really threw me for a loop. I didn't think anyone would show up."

"Oh, pooh. Don't worry about the food. You know I'm glad to help. And of course everyone was going to show up. If there is one thing Berry Springs loves, it's gossip. And while many people are a bit nervous, thinking they might be next, we all want to know what our little town detective has found out."

Sally was glad Rose had lowered her voice. She didn't need everyone leaping over for some murder insights.

Sally shook her head. "This is just so confusing and complex. The police don't seem to be getting anywhere, there aren't any suspects—"

"Or maybe there are too many?" Rose interjected.

Sally cocked her head. "What do you mean?"

Rose stared at her and grinned. "Well, Momma Arnold's kids for one," she said, her eyes glancing over at Jack and Steve who were chatting with Zeke and Annette.

"OK, maybe, but they did love their momma," Sally replied.

Rose tsked. "Maybe they like money even more," she suggested.

Sally shrugged. "What about Belle? Everyone loved her."

"Roy Barnes did get a bit of money, didn't he?" Rose said.

"True, but he owns the diner, so shouldn't he have a lot more money than Belle?"

"Maybe. I've heard he has a gambling problem, like you know who did," Rose whispered, looking over at Jeff Bartholomew, who was standing next to his girlfriend, Magda, talking to Gilbert Rock and Roy Barnes.

"I guess I should ask Bethany that," Sally said, laughing out loud. Luckily, the volume in the room was high enough not to stop everyone talking, though, unfortunately for her, Bethany was exactly the person to look over at her at that moment.

She waved to Bethany, who waved back. Phew, crisis averted.

At that moment, Joanna came over to join them. Sally saw Kent head into the dining room to top up his plate or drink. Joanna gave Sally a side hug. "Thanks so much for the invite. What a nice idea."

"I'm glad everyone came, including Steve and Jack," Sally replied.

"Yes, that is a pleasant surprise," Rose agreed.

"I just hope they behave themselves," Joanna added, as Kent came over with a soda for himself and a refilled glass of white wine for his mother.

"Great spread, Sally," Kent said, grinning.

"Thank you, sir," Sally replied, clinking glasses with him, "And thank you, Joanna. You and Rose were such dears to bring the warm dishes."

"Oh, you do know I love to cater," Joanna replied.

"And everything is so delicious," Sally added. Joanna's face lit up at that.

"Well, I'm going to leave you bunch to chat. It's time for me to work the room, as it were," Sally said, leaving the group to chat, catching a wink from Rose.

Yes, Rose knew exactly what she was doing.

The bartender in her was antsy to see how her other guests were doing, and she also wanted to do some listening in. Maybe a clue would jump out at her about who was doing the aspirin poisoning and why. Or maybe someone had seen the person who pushed Dr. Wiggams. It had happened in broad daylight in the center of town. Somebody must have seen something. Unless they were covering for the culprit.

That was the main reason she had invited everybody, she reminded herself. She took a stroll around the room to try to have a chat with each of her guests. As expected, they were all wondering whether she had an idea of who the Senior Slayer was or who she thought might be next.

Sally shuddered at the thought. She would be glad if no one else had to die. Though if she were honest with herself, she really wasn't sure that would be the case.

In between the questions she was getting, she tried to work out if anyone knew anything. Everyone seemed as shocked as she was and had even less clues than she seemed to have.

And Dr. Wiggams' death threw a wrench in the works. He was apparently pushed, not poisoned with aspirin. How did that fit into all of it? Everyone wanted to know.

Sally tried to be helpful, but since she was still stewing over the facts herself, she didn't want to give too much away or reveal to the guests that she didn't have an answer yet. Not that she was a perfectionist, mind you.

After an hour or so of chat, she decided to tackle the most important person in the room, Bethany Wells, the town gossip.

She sauntered over to the high school assistant. Sally was desperate for information, and Bethany was the one to know, Sally admitted. "Hello, Bethany. I hope you are enjoying yourself."

"Oh yes, Sally. Thank you so much for inviting me. I was so excited when you called yesterday."

" The event wouldn't be the same without you," Sally offered.

Bethany chuckled. "You mean, without the town gossip," Bethany replied, winking.

Oops.

"Oh, Bethany, you are such fun to be around," Sally explained, not too convincingly, she felt. "Can I get you something else to drink?"

"I would love another glass of white wine. Oh, wait, I'll come with you."

Bethany followed Sally across the hall into the dining room, which was conveniently empty.

Sally was glad to see that the food and drink were going well. Scanning the table, she admitted to herself that there would still be a ton of leftovers. She wondered whether she should head back to the living room to get people to eat more, but she had Bethany exactly where she wanted her.

Sally poured Bethany a glass of white while she refilled her own glass with red. They took seats at the table. Bethany took a few grapes and a few slices of cheese, while Sally helped herself to a piece of Joanna's plum quiche, a weird, but yummy combination.

"Can you believe the *Gazette*?" Bethany started.

Sally shook her head. "No, I don't know why they are making it so panicky," Sally replied, wondering whether that was even a word.

"Exactly. I mean, Belle and Momma Arnold have been poisoned somehow… and poor Dr. Wiggams."

"Yes, sadly. As I was telling the others, apparently Belle and Momma Arnold were killed with some kind of aspirin overdose," Sally said.

"Oh really?" Bethany replied, not too convincingly, as if she hadn't already heard that, "But why would someone do that?"

This is what Sally had been considering over the past few weeks. "Well, it seems much harder to detect than say strychnine…" Sally said, choking up. That reminded her of the events of a year ago, which she kept telling herself were fully behind her.

She sipped her wine. Now she was tearing up. "Sally, are you OK?" Bethany asked, touching her arm.

"Yes, just a bit of wine gone down the wrong way." She coughed for effect.

"Maybe someone really is the Senior Slayer," Bethany said.

"But kill old people. Why?"

"Another good question. Maybe it was just a coincidence they died. Others were sick from the Thanksgiving dinner," Bethany replied.

"True. But Momma Arnold? No one else was sick after her party, as far as we know. And she was definitely the only person to die."

Bethany lowered her voice to a whisper, though there was still no one else with them in the dining room and the volume from the next room was loud enough to cover their conversation.

"I heard Dr. Wiggams was pushed," she declared as if she had just revealed a state secret.

Sally nodded vaguely. "He was such a kind man."

"But he really should have retired years ago, poor fellow."

Sally felt bad for him, too. He had literally worked to his death.

"Do you think the person that pushed him was the same person that killed Belle and Momma Arnold?" Bethany asked, finishing her glass. She was a much faster drinker than Sally, who still had about half a glass left.

"Well, if the *Gazette* is right, I would think so. He was definitely old. But why push him?"

Now Bethany tsked. "Aren't you our local celebrity detective? He was the coroner and maybe knew something about their deaths that might reveal the killer."

"Sorry, I'm a bit slow on the uptake, for some reason."

If Dr. Wiggams had known something that would help, he had taken it to his grave. Just as Sally was about to ask Bethany if she had any idea of who the killer was, there was a loud roar from the living room and a crash.

Both women jumped up and ran to the other room.

Chapter Twenty-Three

Sally and Bethany raced into the living room to find Zeke lying on the floor on top of the collapsed coffee table. He was groaning.

"What the hell is going on here?" Sally demanded, looking over at Steve and Jack Arnold, who were standing over Zeke.

Steve jabbed a finger at Sally. "You sh-tole our money," he yelled, slurring.

"Yeah," Jack added, both men now surrounding her.

Petite Rose Cohen came over and stood between the men. "You boys calm down, or I'm calling the police," she yelled.

Both Arnold men looked at each other, not sure how to proceed. Steve pushed Sally, and she fell.

At that, the other guests jumped on the two Arnolds and pinned them down.

"I'm going to sh-ue you," Steve yelled, struggling to break free.

Sally was hoping neither of them had brought a gun. That would put a damper on the party. Sally struggled to get up. Joanna came over and lent a helping hand.

"Are you OK?" Joanna asked.

Sally checked whether anything was sprained or broken. "Yes, I think so."

Gilbert Rock helped Zeke up.

Sally went over to him. "What happened?"

"They started on the 'Sally stole our money' bit, and I just jumped on Steve. We had a tussle, and then I fell on your coffee table."

The table was just thin wood, no glass table top. For that, Sally was glad. Otherwise, Zeke's back would have been in shreds. She gave him a hug.

"Thanks so much," she said.

"That's my man," Annette added from behind them.

Jeff and Kent were helping Steve and Jack to their feet. They looked calmer, though their faces were still beet red.

"Look, I didn't steal your money. You know your momma, and I were friends. Why wouldn't she leave some to me if she wanted to?" Sally said in a huff.

She neglected to reveal the fact that it was only the help she gave the Arnolds last year after Bill died that the amount was so much.

Jack shook his head. "I'm sorry, Sally. It's just we are upset we didn't get much. The Arnolds always pass on their money to the next of kin, not some stupid charities or friends," Jack explained.

"Why don't you two leave now?" Jeff suggested. Well, more demanded.

Both Arnold men headed toward the door, grabbing their coats from the coatrack and heading out. Jeff stood at the open front door to make sure they actually got in their truck and left.

Jeff returned to the living room, where everyone had found a seat. No one spoke, just a lot of shaking heads.

Sally broke the silence. "Thank you, everyone, for helping. I'm sorry I invited them. I just thought it would be a kind gesture in remembrance of their mother," Sally explained.

"You're such a kind soul," Gilbert Rock said, getting up to come over and give Sally a hug. The others nodded.

Sally neglected to mention that a part of her had been worried the Arnolds might pull something, in particular because of the $50,000 Sally had inherited from their mother, but her kindness got the best of her. In the end, she should have listened to her gut.

"I think it's time for us to leave," Zeke said, guiding Annette to the door.

That broke up the rest of the party as everyone said their goodbyes and headed out. Sally thought of asking them to stay, but she knew after the fight nobody was really in a mood to continue the get-together. After the last person had left, she went into the dining room to see what was left.

There was a lot of food still on the table. She made a mental note to call

Rose and Joanna to come and get their dishes the next day.

She began to pack up the food and put it in the refrigerator and freezer. There was enough to last her at least until after New Year. Or maybe she could have Magda and Jeff or Joanna and Kent come over to toast in the New Year.

That made her stop. The next year was the year she turned 60, a number she still wasn't quite ready to face. Just like she had no desire to go into the living room to survey the damage. She would leave that for the next day.

She looked at the clock on the wall in the dining room. It was already coming up on 5 p.m.

She decided she would have a bowl of Joanna's soup with bread and a glass of red wine in the kitchen. After that, she would clean up the dining room and put the rest of the food away. And then have an early night, curling up with a good book upstairs.

She finished the glass on the dining room table and filled it up from the sideboard. She took it into the kitchen to get a fresh bowl and spoon.

As she headed back to the dining room, her stomach lurched.

Sally dropped the bowl and spoon and rushed to the bathroom. Sally moaned in agony as she knelt over the toilet. It was the worst stomach pain she had ever felt.

Once she was done, she fell back to catch her breath, leaning against the wall to try to relieve the terrible cramps. As she wiped her mouth with a towel, she noticed blood.

Sally hated to admit it to herself, but she seemed to be the next victim. But why?

Someone must have put something in the food. She thought back to the get-together. Had it been one of the Arnold boys? There had been a lot of confusion after the fight, and she couldn't remember exactly who had been where all afternoon.

Even in agony, she jumped into detective mode. Pushing that to the back of her mind, she focused on herself. She needed immediate medical attention. She pushed herself up slowly, took several breaths, and crawled into the kitchen to get her phone.

Dialing 911, she told them she was seriously ill, and the voice on the line said they would send an ambulance quickly.

With that, she collapsed on the floor.

Chapter Twenty-Four

Sally woke disoriented. She felt sunlight on her face, and she turned her head to look out the window. This wasn't her bedroom window, she realized.

The events of the night before came rushing back, and her head fell back on the pillow.

She groaned. She felt like she had died and come back from the dead. Looking down, thin tubes and wires snaked across her. She pinched herself to make sure she really was alive. She winced.

"Feeling better?" a voice asked.

She slowly raised her head and found Mark Soder sitting on a chair next to the bed. How had she not noticed him? She really must be out of it.

Sally croaked a quiet, "Yes, I think."

"You gave us quite a scare," he admitted.

Sally smiled wanly. "I am so glad I didn't die," she said, whispering.

Mark got up and helped her take a sip of the water that was waiting for her on the tray next to her bed. "Thank you, Mark," Sally said, sounding more like herself.

Pushing herself up, she asked, "Aspirin?"

Mark nodded.

"But why me? I'm not old. Well, not that old."

Her stomach lurched again but she knew it was more her fear of getting older than another bout of poisoning.

"Good question. Maybe the killer is just going random?" Mark offered.

Sally shook her head. "No, he, or she, seems really smart," Sally replied, wondering where that thought was coming from or whether it even made sense.

Mark took her hand. "I think someone thinks you know something and thought they would try and get you out of the way."

Sally felt a tear as she realized what that meant. "Someone I know well is a killer," Sally admitted out loud.

"Looks like it," Mark replied. "We tested the food and glasses, and there was one that had aspirin in it. A full glass of red wine sitting on the dining room table."

"That's mine. I had just refilled it and gone to the kitchen to get a bowl for soup. Bethany Wells and I had had a drink together in the dining room and were chatting about the goings on in town."

"You think it's Bethany?"

Sally shook her head. "I was there the whole time with her, and I poured the drinks," Sally replied. "Though I guess I turned my back at one point to get the wine bottles off the sideboard. No, I don't think it's Bethany. What's her motive?"

Mark didn't hesitate. "To make her own gossip?"

Sally laughed, well as much as she could laugh in her state. "No, Bethany doesn't seem like a killer. But someone there was," Sally said, running through the guest list in her head. Her head hurt and she was a bit jumbled in her thoughts. She needed to get well, out of the hospital and really put her thinking cap on.

"No, you're not getting out of here quickly," Mark said, reading her mind. "Well, not for a day or two."

"I need to get out and question everyone," Sally said, as if the killer would just blurt out that they did it because she was coming around to interrogate them.

"We've already taken care of two of your suspects," Mark revealed.

"What are you talking about?" Sally asked, trying to lean toward him.

"We arrested Steve and Jack this morning. Zeke told us about the incident at your house yesterday. They will be charged with assault and now that Momma Arnold is gone, they won't be able to get out of charges this time."

"That's a bit callous, isn't it?" Sally asked, admitting to herself that it would be good for an Arnold to finally face justice for something they've done.

"Those two need to be taken down a notch," Mark said, turning red.

"Down, cowboy," Sally said.

They both laughed.

Getting serious, Sally asked, "But you think they had something to do with the deaths? If they did, that was pretty stupid considering Momma Arnold had changed her will."

"They aren't that smart, are they?" Mark replied.

"Well, um, maybe… but you don't think they did it, do you?"

Mark shook his head. "I'm not sure what to think. They certainly had a motive…"

"… to kill me," Sally finished his sentence.

"And their mother?" Mark added.

Sally shook her head, her ponytail flailing. "No way. They loved her. At least I thought they did."

"So where does that leave us?" Mark asked.

Sally thought for a moment before responding. "My first instinct is to say the three deaths are connected. Two aspirin overdoses and a push to Dr. Wiggams to stop him from revealing something."

"But what about your poisoning?" Mark queried, taking her hand.

Sally quickly pulled it away, worried Candy would appear at any moment.

"What I don't get about the attack on me is if the killer was there, wouldn't they also try to kill the oldest person in the room, which was Rose?" Sally asked.

"Maybe they had a plan of who to kill and they were done. They just wanted to get you out of the way so no one would solve the murder," Mark replied, realizing he had just criticized himself and the Berry Springs police force.

"Um, I mean…" Mark started.

"Don't worry. Your secret is safe with me," Sally replied, smiling.

Mark smiled back. "So did you see anyone or anything suspicious last night?" he asked, turning on police mode and taking out his notebook.

Sally shook her head without thinking. "No, I don't think so. I was talking to everyone and they were going in and out of the dining room and living room the entire evening. Anyone could have doctored my glass during the evening or doctored the wine. I didn't always have my wine glass in my hand. And if I recall, I was the only one drinking red wine, though I can't be 100% sure."

Mark scribbled in his notebook. Looking up, he replied, "Well as I mentioned before, aspirin residue was found in the glass, which seems to suggest it was added to your glass, not to the bottle of wine. We're testing the glass for fingerprints, so I'll need a list of your guests."

Mark handed her his notebook and pen, and she scribbled the names.

Handing it back, she said, "I doubt you will find any fingerprints besides mine. If the killer poured in aspirin powder, they wouldn't need to touch the glass, would they?"

"You never know. Maybe we will get lucky. And wearing gloves to hide fingerprints would have seemed out of place inside your house."

"True, but there were so many people going in and out of the downstairs rooms, anyone could have done it quickly, or say used a towel to hide fingerprints."

Sally was now thinking out loud. Someone there the afternoon before had poisoned her and tried to kill her.

She still couldn't believe someone she had known for years was a killer. But it had to have been.

That somehow got her tired, and she yawned.

"OK, I'm going to let you get some sleep," Mark said, getting up.

"Thanks, Mark, for coming. I know you needed to talk to me, but it was still nice seeing you," Sally said, blushing slightly.

Mark couldn't look at her, but just replied, "Get better soon, Sally. And yes, I'll keep you updated on any developments."

"Thanks," Sally said, her head hitting the pillow as she drifted off into never-never land.

Chapter Twenty-Five

A day later, Sally arrived back home with the help of Gilbert and Rose.

Rose carried in Sally's duffle bag while Gilbert helped her navigate the steps inside and into the living room. He gently let her down and she sank into the cushions with a sigh.

"Thanks, you two," Sally said.

"Naturally, we want to help you, dear," Rose replied.

"Whatever you need, Sally, you just let us know. Though I was surprised you got out of the hospital so soon," Gilbert added.

Sally grimaced. "The doctors wanted to keep me longer, but I was going stir crazy in there. They told me I was out of danger, so I more or less demanded they release me," Sally admitted.

Rose tsked. "I hope you know what you're doing," she said, leaning in for a hug.

"Can we get you anything before we head out?" Gilbert asked.

This kindness was another one of the main reasons she loved living in Berry Springs.

Her stomach felt better and she seemed to have had no serious consequences from the aspirin poisoning. But she didn't want to chance it. The doctors at the hospital had told her to call 911 if she had any pain, vomiting or the like.

She leaned back and closed her eyes. "I'd love a cup of herbal tea if that's not too much to ask," Sally replied.

"I'll make it," Rose offered, walking toward the kitchen.

"Actually, I do have to get back to the library," Gilbert said. He leaned down and gave Sally a hug. "Remember, you call if you need anything," he said as he walked out of the living room, his fine woody scent following him.

What a way to end the year, she thought, as she replayed the events of the past few weeks in her mind. She couldn't believe the next day was New Year's Eve and the town had lost three of their own between Thanksgiving and New Year's.

She hoped the New Year would be brighter, even if she did have a big birthday coming up at the end of June.

She gave herself until the end of January to solve the murders, if the police didn't get there first.

Rose brought the herbal tea in, placing it on a coaster on the side table. She had also thoughtfully brought a plate of plain crackers. "I thought you might want something light to nibble on," she explained.

They hugged. "I'm off. Like Gilbert said, please call if you need anything."

"I will. Thanks again. Oh, could you bring me my backpack from the hall before you leave?"

Rose went out to the hall and returned with the backpack, which she deposited on the couch next to Sally.

"See you soon," Sally said as Rose strode out of the house. Sally glanced out the window and saw her hop into her huge SUV. A gigantic car for a petite lady. Sally loved the contrast.

Reaching over, she opened the backpack and pulled out her notebook and pen. Time to review the suspects as it were. But first, she made a quick call to Magda to see how things had gone at the bar the last couple of days while she was in the hospital.

"Oh hi Sally, I was just about to head over to the bar for my shift. Annette will be there too."

"Do you need extra help? I can maybe come over," Sally offered, knowing that was definitely not going to be happening. She was better but not that much better.

Magda laughed. "Boss, I think you need to rest up and get your strength back. Jeff's helping out tonight."

It was the Saturday night before New Year's Eve. It was one of their busiest nights of the year. She loved the camaraderie, but she knew she wasn't going to be able to be there. "Sounds like you've got all the bases covered. You're a star," Sally replied.

"Thanks!" Magda replied.

"Let me know if you need anything and I hope I will be fit enough for the New Year's Eve party tomorrow," Sally said. That was the best part of her bartending job, ringing in the New Year with all her friends and customers. She really hoped she would be strong enough to make it.

Though knowing herself, she would get there come hell or high water.

Sally put her phone down and opened the notebook.

Now that she was feeling better, she needed to whittle down the list of suspects if she was ever going to solve the deaths.

But then she realized she needed to make one more call.

Putting the notebook back down, she picked up the phone and called her parents. She hadn't yet let them know that she had been hit with the aspirin overdose. She hadn't wanted them to worry, even if the family was straight-talking.

Her heart jumped in her throat as she realized what they would have felt if she had died from the poisoning and they hadn't been able to say goodbye. A tear rolled down her cheek as the phone rang.

Her dad answered. "Hi, Sally, a day early aren't you?" he asked guffawing. Ah, yes, her father, always the comedian.

"Hi, Dad," Sally replied.

"OK, what happened?" he asked, his tone darkening.

"I wanted to… um… let you know that I've been in the hospital the last two days," she began, breaking down in tears.

She heard her father calling her mother to the phone. "Hospital, Sally? Why didn't you call sooner? Was it serious?" her mother asked, nurse mode activated.

She debated what she should tell her parents, but she decided to tell them all. There were a lot of gasps and "oh my gods."

"I'm sorry I didn't call sooner. I didn't want to worry you," Sally explained, feeling defeated.

"You could have died!" her mother wailed.

There was what seemed like silence on the phone as her parents processed the information. Sally heard whispering at one point.

"We should come for a visit and help you until you are better," her mother declared.

Sally hesitated. She did want to see them, and they could help her, but she was worried they would get hit by the Senior Slayer, as the local press had dubbed the killer. And she had just seen them a few days ago for Christmas.

"I really don't think that is a good idea, Mom," Sally replied, croaking out the words, "There is a killer still loose and, well, the local paper has dubbed them the Senior Slayer. I don't know what I would do without you." Sally started blubbering again. This was not going to be easy.

"Don't cry, Sally. We love you, and we will see you soon," her father declared.

She could hear her mother admonishing him, but he tried to shush her up.

Finally, she gave in too. "Well, you get better soon, and please come visit us in the New Year, dear," her mother said matter-of-factly.

"I will. I love you both. Bye," Sally replied, tapping the phone to end the call.

To push that phone call out of her mind, she reached down for the notebook. Back to the investigation, she told herself. As she tapped her pen on the notebook, she thought back to Thursday evening.

Maybe the get-together at her house was exactly the catalyst she needed to find out who had killed Momma Arnold, Belle and Dr. Wiggams. She laughed to herself: someone might actually think she poisoned herself to bring the killer out of the woodwork, but that would have been too much of a gamble even for her. And it's not like she could ask her mother for the proper dose to poison herself but not enough to die.

Focus Sally.

She tapped her pen on the open page.

The first thing to do was list everyone that had been there for the memorial get-together. The pen scratched the paper as she listed them all:

CHAPTER TWENTY-FIVE

Steve and Jack Arnold
Magda and Jeff
Rose
Gilbert
Joanna and Kent
Zeke and Annette
Roy Barnes
Bethany Wells

She wanted to dismiss the Arnold boys. She knew they really loved their mother, and she couldn't imagine them coming up with the aspirin scheme. They were not so subtle. If they wanted to get someone, they'd probably just pull out a shotgun. But she admitted it could be anyone at the get-together who had poisoned her, so she needed to leave the whole list open. And anyways, with all the information available online, anyone could have done the aspirin poison research.

If she were honest with herself, though, she wished she could cross everyone else off the list. But she knew she couldn't. Someone at the memorial get-together had put aspirin powder into Sally's wine glass, with her ending up in the hospital, lucky to be alive.

Thinking back to what she and Mark had discussed, maybe this poisoning was more a warning to Sally than an attempt to kill her. Or maybe she really had just been lucky.

She wasn't getting any younger, but she tried to hike often and eat well. Hopefully, that had played an important part in her bout with aspirin. She didn't think she would ever be able to take one of those pills ever again, but luckily, there were many alternatives in the 21st century.

She ran her pen along every name, considering motives and opportunity. She finally decided to cross off Magda and Jeff. If Magda or Jeff had wanted to kill anyone or her, they would have probably done it during the events a year ago, Sally thought. And they seemed to still be reeling from those events. Sally just couldn't believe that one of them would be the killer.

Tapping her pen on the list, her eyes then jumped to Joanna and Kent. Though she had known them for years, they had catered the Thanksgiving dinner and were also at Momma Arnold's. Sally couldn't come up with a motive that Joanna, or her son, would have for killing the three older citizens, but one or both of them certainly had the opportunity.

Zeke and Annette, she considered for a few minutes before crossing them off, too. Annette had been so helpful with the bar, and Zeke had defended her against the Arnold accusations, collapsing her coffee table in the process. She also didn't see a motive for them.

That left Rose, Gilbert, Roy, Bethany, and the Arnold boys.

Roy Barnes definitely had a motive, though a bit of a weak one. He inherited Belle's money, though, as she had told herself before, he must be rich in spite of a potential gambling problem.

Bethany's motive could only be for attention, though, like the Arnolds, she didn't think Bethany was capable of the scheme.

Gilbert Rock was literally that, a rock. The town loved him, and he loved everyone in the town, a town fixture. What motive would he have for the killings? She just couldn't see it.

Finally, there was Rose. She was another fixture, like Gilbert, and why would either of them risk that with a potential jail sentence, or worse? Though Rose did like publicity, maybe she was looking to get herself in the news.

Rose definitely had an opportunity, at least at the Thanksgiving dinner. As general manager of the Grand Hotel, she supervised the entire evening. Sally recalled she was constantly walking the floor and could easily have slipped something into someone's food or drink.

The ones she was least sure of were the Arnold boys. They certainly seemed to be angry about Sally's inheritance of part of her mother's fortune, but were they that subtle to come up with the aspirin scheme?

Unless they had help, she thought, considering the possibilities of that.

She put the notebook and pen down and leaned back, and closed her eyes. She needed to talk to everyone that had been at the memorial get-together at her house to see if they had a clue about what went on or maybe had seen something.

The next night's New Year's Eve party at her bar would be the perfect place. Now she just needed to rest and get her strength back so she was in optimal detective shape for the last day of the year.

Chapter Twenty-Six

Sunday morning, Sally sat on the couch, sipping coffee, considering a mid-morning nap. She felt so much better than the day before, but she still wasn't sure she really was fit enough for the New Year's Eve party at Sally's Smasher bar that night. She looked at her mug and considered whether coffee had been such a good idea. Her stomach seemed ok so far, but maybe she should have just made herself a cup of herbal tea.

She looked across the room at the sun streaming in the windows overlooking the backyard. That probably meant it would be frosty outside. The frost made her think of Gladys, her old Datsun, which wasn't quite as trustworthy anymore. That was one of the first, and very difficult, things she would have to do in the New Year.

Randall Wentworth's son, James, worked part-time at the local dealership while he attended community college. He was the main connection she had to the car world, so she would give him a call the next week to see when he was working. She didn't think she would get much for Gladys, though she was considering keeping her as a memento of times gone by. Her property was big enough to house Gladys on the side.

Thinking her neighbors might complain about the eyesore, it probably would be better to sell her or give her away for a clean break with the past.

Pushing that thought from her mind, she picked up her phone off the temporary coffee table made of cardboard box and texted Magda to let her know she would be able to be there that evening, but probably wouldn't be able to do any bartending.

"No problem. Will be great to have you there, boss," Magda replied after a few seconds.

That would give Sally extra time and headspace to talk to the guests.

Sally was really hoping for a breakthrough that evening. This Senior Slayer nonsense had been going on for far too long. She hoped, though, that the breakthrough didn't involve another death.

* * *

Sally was pleased that Magda and the crew had gotten all the New Year's Eve decorations up, replacing the Christmas bits, though the tree was still in the corner, looking a bit ratty.

Sally, you aren't a micromanager, just a perfectionist, she told herself, chuckling silently.

She was glad that Magda and Annette were aware of her quirks, and they all got along so well. Sally was fully conscious of her need for perfection, but she tried to tone it down a notch. Well, now and again. She definitely didn't want to turn into that toxic boss she had back in Atlanta.

"Magda, everything looks great!" Sally declared.

Magda beamed. "Thanks. Annette, Zeke, and Jeff helped," she said, motioning to the rest of the crew behind the bar getting everything ready for the opening soon.

"How are you feeling, Sally?" Annette asked, holding her hand.

"I'm better. I'm glad I made it, though I guess it wasn't as bad as, you know, the others," she replied, not mentioning any names.

"Well, you are certainly not as old as they were," Annette said, knowing exactly what to say in a difficult situation.

"Can I do anything to help?" Sally inquired, knowing she had already admitted to Magda that she wasn't really up to it.

"No, you just sit yourself down on a bar stool and enjoy," Annette replied, showing her over to the counter.

Sally hopped on a stool while Zeke took her backpack and put it in the back.

"Would you like a glass of wine?" Jeff asked, reaching for a bottle.

"Are you sure you should be drinking so soon?" Magda asked, mother-henning.

Sally considered that for a moment. She'd had coffee and a good breakfast and felt much better.

"Just a sip to get in a festive mood," Sally replied. "As you know, I do enjoy a glass of wine now and then."

Magda gave her a look, but Sally pretended not to notice.

Jeff grinned and poured her usual glass of Italian red, but only a few drops. He placed it on a coaster in front of her and ran a cloth across the bar one last time.

"Now sip slowly," Annette said.

"Ugh, don't you start too," Sally replied. "I'm fine."

Annette walked away, and she and Magda made sure everything was ready before the first guests arrived.

It was coming up on 5 p.m., and the doors would open soon. Magda ran around straightening some of the chairs while Annette adjusted the table decorations. As it turned five, Magda unlocked the door.

Roy Barnes and Bethany Wells were the first to arrive. They looked like they had come together. This was probably more due to the fact that Bethany didn't have a car than any romantic entanglement. They settled themselves at a table in the corner near the Christmas tree.

Zeke went over to take their drink order while Magda and Annette welcomed other guests as they arrived.

By 6:30 p.m., the place was packed. Sally was glad to see everyone at her party had shown up. This included Steve and Jack Arnold, which surprised her a bit, though maybe they didn't want to be alone on New Year's Eve. Their desire for company apparently overrode any social hesitance about showing their faces in this crowd after what had happened at her house.

Sally made a point of going over to welcome them. "So nice to see you both."

Jack smiled, while Steve just nodded. "Um, Sally, we're sorry about what happened at your house on Thursday. That wasn't right, and we know Momma would have been pissed," Jack confessed.

"Don't worry about it. I know it's been a difficult time for you both," Sally replied, neatly neglecting to mention the will or her inheritance. She wasn't going to bring it up if they weren't.

"Enjoy yourselves," she added as she saw Joanna and Kent motioning to her.

The men headed to the bar.

"Oh, Sally, we heard what happened, and I'm just devastated," Joanna declared, giving Sally a big hug.

"How are you feeling?" Kent asked.

"Thanks, you two. I'm much better. Just glad I made it," she let slip.

"I can imagine. What a terrible time for you. And for the town," Joanna said.

Leaning over, Joanna whispered, "Any closer to finding out who's doing this?"

Sally shook her head.

"It has to be one of us at the party at your house, doesn't it?" Kent asked matter-of-factly.

Sally still had a hard time admitting that to herself. "Yes, it must be. I don't think someone slipped into the house while we were all there, though that is certainly a possibility. Did you two see anything?"

Mother and son exchanged glances. "No, we spent most of the time in the living room," Joanna said.

Sally wondered if someone had told them about the wine glass. They must have, or they had guessed.

Considering it had been some of Joanna's food on the table, she wouldn't want to talk about any overdose of anything from her food. Maybe Sally would have to take a closer look at the owner of The Nutmeg Café and find out what she knew about aspirin overdoses, if anything.

She would have to take a closer look at all the guests, she realized, even if most of them had become her close friends over the years.

The door jingled, and Sally looked over to see Gilbert and Rose walking in. What strange couplings this evening, Sally thought. And her four main suspects had come in pairs. That just added to the weirdness of it all.

"Have fun and let me know if you need anything," Sally said to Joanna and Kent.

"Thanks. And don't do any work tonight. You need to fully recover," Joanna replied, touching Sally's arm.

Sally smiled and walked over to greet Gilbert and Rose. "So nice to see you two here," Sally said, giving them each a hug.

Rose leaned over and whispered, "Are you feeling better?"

"I'm feeling much better, just not working tonight. I couldn't miss our New Year's Eve bash, though."

"Of course not," Gilbert added, taking Rose's coat and placing it on the one table that had just opened up in the back corner near the bar. Sally saw her two neighbors, Paul and Ezekiel, head over to the bar and take the two seats there.

As if they knew to make way for Gilbert and Rose. They were such dears, so they probably intuited it. The theme of friendship and caring was a recurring one in Berry Springs, even if someone wasn't quite the caring type at the moment, poisoning the elderly with aspirin.

Sally walked Rose over to the table and sat down with them.

Annette came over to take their order.

"I'll have a lemon spritzer," Rose said.

"A glass of dry white wine, please," Gilbert ordered.

"Anything else for you, Sally?" Annette asked.

"A sparkling water would be perfect," Sally replied.

Annette left to get the drinks.

"So sorry about what happened to you," Gilbert said, echoing the thoughts Sally had gotten from other people that evening.

"Yes, it was a scare. I'm glad I made it, unlike… " Sally said, leaving the names of the dead unspoken.

Rose and Gilbert nodded.

"I should be fully recovered in a day or two," Sally added.

"Do the police have any clues? It's been a month, and no one has been arrested yet," Gilbert declared.

At that, Sally scanned the bar for any police. She saw Mark Soder with his wife, Candy, but Detective Finnegan and Chief Sanford weren't about as far as she could see.

Tim Sanford and his husband, Andy, usually hosted their own bash at their house. Sally had been invited there a couple of times, along with her neighbor, Tim's father. She had only gone once, since she was usually hosting the bash at the bar.

"Not as far as I know," Sally said. "It seems time has flown by with almost an incident a week. But the aspirin overdosing is a challenge. Anyone could buy it. And anyone at the events could have slipped it in."

"Did either of you see anything?" Sally asked.

Gilbert and Rose exchanged glances. "Well, your poisoning must have been from someone who slipped into the house," Rose declared.

Sally went red as she realized her questioning was not quite as subtle as she had hoped. But since she had broken the ice, she decided to continue.

"Do they know how you were poisoned?" Gilbert asked.

At that point, Annette returned with the drinks, and the three stayed silent until she had left.

"Cheers," Sally said, with the others clinking glasses with her.

The noise level of the bar was such that any topics discussed would be less likely to be overheard, even if someone was standing nearby. In any case, they were seated in the back corner.

"Well, it looks like someone slipped the aspirin powder into my glass. It could have been in the living or the dining room," Sally admitted.

"Wow, that is terrible," Gilbert replied, frowning.

"I think I heard the front door open at one point," Gilbert said, "Though I can't be sure of it."

"Whoever did it must have been when your glass was out of your sight. Anyone could have slipped into the house," Rose added, echoing Gilbert's thought of a potential intruder.

Sally wished it was an intruder, but her gut told her it was someone at the memorial get-together at her house. And all of them had been at the Thanksgiving dinner, and Momma Arnold's Christmas do.

"Well, whoever did it must know about aspirin overdoses. Maybe someone with a medical background?" Sally considered.

"These days, the Internet can help turn up all sorts of information," Rose said.

Sally nodded. "True, but getting the dosage right for the people at the Thanksgiving dinner who were ill but not killed would probably require more information than some internet 'research.'" The last word got air quotes.

"Just a terrible time for Berry Springs. I really don't know what the world is coming to," Gilbert commiserated with a sigh.

Rose shook her head.

That was Sally's signal to not ask any more questions. "I'm going to mingle, you two enjoy," Sally said, getting up. Both smiled as Sally made her way to her next victims, um, friends.

As she walked over to talk to Roy and Bethany, she wondered whether she had gotten something of importance out of Gilbert and Rose.

"Sally, hi, how are you feeling?" Mark Soder asked, stopping her near the bar.

"Oh, Sally, I'm just so shocked at what happened to you," Candy said, frowning.

She gave them both a hug. "I'm much better, and so glad I was feeling up to coming here tonight. I wouldn't want to miss this for the world."

"You're not working tonight, are you?" Mark asked, his eyes narrowing.

"No, sir, just here for the fun," Sally replied.

"You let us know if you need anything," Candy said.

"Well, um," Sally began.

"You want to know if I have any news on our investigation," Mark said, finishing her thought.

Sally smiled. "Ugh, you know me better than I know myself."

"Well, stop in on Tuesday, and I can give you an update," Mark said.

Since it was a New Year's Eve party, she didn't want to push it. And anyway, she needed to talk to more people, and anything she found out or thought she could tell Mark in private at the station.

"Excellent, will do," Sally said, leaving them to head over to Roy and

CHAPTER TWENTY-SIX

Bethany.

For some reason, her main suspect at this point was Roy. He was the only one who she knew who directly benefited from one of the deaths. Well, besides Steve and Jack, though, if they had done it, they didn't quite get the windfall they would have hoped for. But they probably weren't smart or subtle enough to pull off this aspirin caper.

That made her think: she herself could be considered a suspect, what with the large inheritance she had gotten from Momma Arnold's will. She was glad no one had mentioned that up to now, and anyway, she hadn't known about the will until Randall Wentworth had called her about it. And she was certain he would vouch for her. She knew him to be an arrogant yet honest attorney.

Roy, on the other hand, could be a bit gruff, and Sally couldn't ever tell whom he liked or hated.

She found Bethany and Roy standing on the other side of the bar, leaning on it.

"Oh, Sally, so nice to see you," Bethany said, pulling her in for a hug.

Roy grunted and nodded. Always the charmer. "How are you feeling?" Roy asked the question of the evening.

When Sally was living and working in the big city of Atlanta, she felt there were so many fakes. When someone asked how she was feeling or how she was, she rarely believed they actually meant it. In Berry Springs, she felt the warmth from almost everyone.

"Oh, much better, thanks. I still can't believe I got it," Sally replied.

Bethany leaned over. "So it was aspirin poisoning," she whispered.

Sally nodded, wondering why the town gossip hadn't already gotten that information. Though maybe she had and didn't want to seem too nosy. Sally chuckled silently. Everyone in town knew that if you wanted to spread news, you just had to tell Bethany Wells about it.

"Terrible, terrible," Roy said, shaking his head.

"Someone got into your house and did this to you," Bethany declared.

Everyone was deflecting, it seemed. But maybe that was more due to the fact that no one could believe it was someone at her party, many of them close friends for years.

"Well, probably," Sally replied, frowning.

"You don't think one of us did it, do you?" Bethany asked, taking a step back, her mouth wide.

Sally considered a moment before answering. She didn't want to start an incident at her own party. "Well, it is a possibility, isn't it? But someone just as easily could have gotten into the house. The doors were unlocked, and we spent most of the evening in the living room."

"I can't believe one of your friends would do that to you," Roy said.

"Logically, the Senior Slayer is someone in town or in the area. The Thanksgiving dinner, Momma Arnold's bash, and my get-together all had locals there."

"… as far as we know," Bethany added.

"OK, maybe at the Thanksgiving dinner. But the other two events were more intimate," Sally said.

"I just don't understand why someone would do this," Bethany declared.

"Killing the old seems so cruel," Roy added.

That seemed to be the crux of the whole thing, Sally thought.

Was someone trying to rid the town of the old? Or was it more serious and personal? In her experience, not that she had that much experience with death, killings were usually personal, not random.

Though if someone did want to murder the old, that wasn't completely random since two elderly women had died.

Then again, others were sick at the Thanksgiving dinner and didn't die, even older folk like Randall Wentworth, Detective Finnegan, and Gilbert Rock. Though none of those men were as old as Momma Arnold or Belle.

"Sally, are you still there?" Bethany asked.

"Oh, sorry, woolgathering," she replied.

"You mean wondering who the killer is and why? The with what we already know," Roy said matter-of-factly.

"You got me," Sally replied, "Figuratively, of course."

The three laughed. Sally yawned and realized she needed a short break. She headed over to her office and ended up spending 15 minutes straightening up her desk before a sit-down on the couch.

She enjoyed hearing the sounds from the front, but was glad to get off her feet for a few minutes.

After another 15 minutes, she headed out for a quick check-in with Magda and Annette, who looked like they were running around like headless chickens.

Sally glanced around the room. Still packed, and it was only 9 p.m.

"How's it going? Looks like everyone is enjoying themselves," Sally said.

"Oh, it is so busy, boss," Magda replied, wiping sweat off her forehead. "I've been up and down the stairs to the basement several times, keeping everything stocked up here."

"Why didn't you have Jeff, Annette, or Zeke help you with that?" Sally asked, activating manager mode.

Magda shook her head. "We are so particular about inventory and the stockroom; I'm the only one who knows our system."

You mean my system, Sally the perfectionist thought, but definitely did not verbalize.

"That makes sense," Sally said. "I'm sorry I can't help you. I don't want to overdo it."

"Sally, don't worry. The four of us have it covered," Annette declared, putting her hands on her hips.

"I know you do," Sally replied, smiling. "I'll leave you to it."

Sally went around the rest of the evening talking to many of the customers, including the rest of the crowd at her memorial get-together. No one had seen or heard anything, and all of them were sure it must have been an intruder and not someone actually at the party.

There also didn't seem to be anyone there with detailed medical knowledge, though that was a difficult question to slip into a conversation. "Hi, do you know what the dosage is of aspirin to make someone sick or better kill them?" Um, no, that wasn't going to be asked directly tonight.

By then, it was already coming up on midnight anyway, and only about half the guests were left, including everyone that had been at her party. She caught a glimpse of Detective Finnegan and wondered if he might have time for a chat. Sally pushed that thought out of her mind. Mark Soder had invited her to come in on Tuesday for a chat, and maybe that chat would be with Finnegan and Soder. She did wonder how long Detective Finnegan had been there. She hadn't noticed him before.

Magda had turned on the big-screen TV hanging on the side wall in front of Bill's vintage motorcycle. As she looked at the bike, she thought of Bill. He had always been the life of the New Year's Eve bash, and it was now the second without him. Her best friend and business partner had been murdered over a year before, and she still had a twinge of sadness when she came into the bar and saw the bike.

10… 9… 8… 7… 6… 5… 4… 3… 2… 1!

"Happy New Year," everyone yelled, clinking glasses or bottles.

"Happy New Year, boss," Magda and Annette said in unison, both with glasses of water in hand.

"Happy New Year, Magda. Happy New Year, Annette," she said, toasting in the New Year with them.

Sally went around toasting with others. As she did, she realized how quickly every year flew by as she got older. And as she got to the back of the room, it hit her.

Older, ugh. This was now the year she would turn 60.

She needed to sit down for a moment, so she headed down the hallway to her office, and its old, but comfortable couch. She switched on the light and was just about to collapse on the sofa when she stopped and screamed.

There was a big bottle of aspirin in the middle of her perfectly clean desk.

Chapter Twenty-Seven

Mark Soder was the first person to race into Sally's office. For some reason, her immediate thought was wondering whether he cared about her more than he should or whether it was his policeman instinct. Probably the latter, she told herself.

"Sally, what's wrong?" he cried.

She couldn't speak, but just pointed to the aspirin bottle. His mouth dropped.

Others quickly filed into the hallway to find out if Sally was OK and what was going on. As people saw the bottle of aspirin, there were a lot of gasps.

Then a lumbering figure came into view. "OK, everyone, back into the bar. Soder, make sure no one leaves and call for backup. Oh, and call forensics to take care of this room," Detective Finnegan ordered, pushing people out of Sally's office, including Sally, and shutting the door.

Sally stood in the hallway while Finnegan did something inside her office.

After only a minute or two, he came out with two evidence bags in his blue-gloved hands. He had the aspirin bottle in one bag. Sally tried to see what was in the other bag; it just looked like paper. Did he always carry that gear with him? She surmised he probably did.

He went over to shut the door to the bar and leaned against the wall.

She really wished she could be sitting down at this point, but Finnegan was right to get everyone out of her office until it was checked and dusted.

"What's that in the other bag, Detective?" Sally asked.

He held it up for her to read. "DEATH TO THE OLD AND INFIRM," it read in what looked like cut-out letters from a newspaper or magazine. She now felt like a real amateur detective. Her first anonymous note made from cut-out letters. She had to stifle a laugh at that thought.

"I doubt we'll get fingerprints off this or the bottle, but one never knows. Maybe the killer is getting careless, or just annoyed we haven't caught him or her yet," Finnegan surmised.

It did seem a bit like showing off, Sally thought, and unbelievably bold for someone to slip into her office to plant the evidence with so many people in the bar for the New Year's Eve party.

While her office was tucked away at the end of the hallway in the back, it was diagonally across from the restrooms. Anyone needing the restroom could have seen the person going in or coming out of her office.

For years, Magda had suggested she keep her office locked, even with the safe secure. But Sally believed that didn't fit the openness and honesty of Berry Springs.

"Have you gotten anything from anyone here tonight?" he asked her, assuming that's what she had been doing all evening.

Sally shook her head. "Many people told me my poisoning was probably an intruder in my house and couldn't be one of my guests. No one could believe one of their own was a murderer. And sadly, everyone claimed they didn't notice anything strange. Though that could be more to protect an old friend than anything else," Sally summarized.

Finnegan nodded as he took a few notes. "Do you have another room to question your customers?" Finnegan asked.

"Sure, you can use our small storeroom across from my office," Sally said, moving down the hallway to open the door. It was small, just containing some cleaning supplies, but big enough to hold two people. Sally looked at Finnegan and hoped he would fit.

Finnegan came down the hall to look at the room. "Small," he said, "but it'll do. Thanks."

While he was in there talking to people, she would be outside seeing what she could discover about the aspirin on the desk. Someone must have definitely seen something this time, and maybe it was time to put a bit of pressure on her friends and neighbors.

Who knew, maybe Sally would solve the crime right on the first of the year. Wouldn't that be cathartic?

***

Finnegan had gotten through about half the customers at the bar when he came out of the back. He walked over to Sally and motioned for her to follow him to the storeroom.

As Sally followed him, she looked into her office. It looked like they were just finishing up. She wondered, as always, how quickly there would be results. She was not optimistic that the team would find any fingerprints besides those of her and her crew, but one never knew.

While Finnegan had been questioning customers in the back, Sally had tried to chat with as many people as possible in the bar proper. She had checked in with almost everyone and had a few nuggets to share with the detective. Though not surprisingly, most were still staying quiet about what they might or might not have seen, or did, for that matter.

She hoped he had something to share with her.

From all the information she had gathered up to now over the last several hours, she felt she was getting closer to finding out the identity of the killer. It was definitely someone at the bar at that moment, of that she was certain. But there were still a few clues and facts missing.

"Have a seat," Finnegan said, motioning for her to sit on the one chair in the storeroom. He leaned against the shelving. Sally saw it move slightly, but luckily, it held. "So, what have you gotten so far, Sally?"

"Well, several people saw Magda go in and out of my office tonight, but that's to be expected. She would be putting away the cash into the safe."

"And pretty safe to say, wouldn't you think, no pun intended," Finnegan surmised.

It had taken Sally several years to trust anyone else with the combination and key to the safe, besides Bill. Magda was the first non-owner to have access, and Sally was glad she took it so seriously, not letting too much cash pile up in the till. Though these days, more and more people paid with a card.

There were a couple of stores in town that only took cash, but Sally thought that was very old-fashioned. She may not be 20 anymore, but she was smart enough to roll with the times.

"Any times? Anyone else?" he asked, pulling her out of her reverie.

"Oh, yes," she replied, getting to the juicy bits. "Rose told me she saw Jack Arnold come out of my office. And get this, Gilbert claims he saw Roy coming out of my office. But none of them could recall when."

Finnegan shook his head. "Was everyone in and out of your office?"

Sally laughed. "No, but there were a couple of sightings. I still can't believe one of them did it, though I have my suspicions about who the top suspects are."

Sally had thought of naming them Roy, Rose, Bethany, and Gilbert, but decided to keep that information to herself until she got closer to picking one of them for certain. A part of her also was having a very hard time admitting to herself that someone she had known for years was a killer, but that's what it looked like at the moment.

"Who would that be?" Finnegan asked.

"I'd like to keep that to myself until I have a clearer picture of what is going on," Sally replied.

Finnegan snorted. "Look, Sally. Why don't we try to work on this together? And you know I can have you come down to the station to make a statement or even arrest you for obstruction of justice," Finnegan said, leaning forward, his face red and a vein bulging from his forehead.

She didn't think he could arrest her for that, but then again, she wasn't a lawyer. But she also didn't want him to have a heart attack. She sighed and revealed her thinking.

"Yeah, I guess that makes sense," he replied.

"I'm surprised a bit that I suddenly got something out of the people, but maybe the heavier police presence meant it was time they told you or me something, even if I think at least one of them is lying."

Finnegan nodded.

"So what did you find out, Detective?" Sally inquired, pulling her notebook out of her backpack as he began speaking.

"Rose also told me she saw Jack Arnold come out of your office, though he denies it," Finnegan began.

"I guess there's no proof unless you find fingerprints," Sally surmised.

"True, even better if you had a camera in the hallway," Finnegan replied.

Sally had to stifle a curse word. Just like no lock on the office door, she didn't believe having a camera in the back hallway made sense. She did now have cameras outside at the front and back doors to hopefully ward off burglars, but she instinctively trusted her customers, even if that was probably pretty stupid or, worse, naïve.

"And you said Gilbert told you he saw Roy?" Finnegan said.

Sally nodded.

"Roy claims he saw Gilbert. Though everyone claims they didn't note a time," Finnegan told her, shaking his head.

"Oh geez. It's all a bunch of nonsense at the moment, isn't it?"

"Someone put the aspirin bottle and note on your desk. Probably the murderer or an accomplice. We're getting closer to the truth, aren't we?" Finnegan replied.

"True, but there are still too many suspects and not a lot of evidence."

"I hope we get something from the sweep of your office."

Exactly what Sally was hoping, though not too certain of it. Now she decided to be bold. "Mark told me tonight that there was other information you had gathered. He told me to come in Tuesday, I mean tomorrow," Sally said, hoping Finnegan wouldn't be too upset. Now that it was after midnight, the next day really was Tuesday. Time was flying, and ugh, it was now the year she turned 60. Why was that at the top of her mind at the moment?

Luckily, Finnegan began speaking, so that got her mind off that difficult subject.

"Not really," Finnegan admitted. "We have a list of people who bought aspirin from the pharmacy over the last two months, but it seems like half the town. We also have analyzed the video showing someone pushing Dr. Wiggams, and the hand is quite hairy, so we guess that a man did it."

"If that's true, I guess we can rule out Bethany Wells," Sally replied, thinking out loud.

"That still leaves a lot of suspects," Finnegan replied.

"Anyone on the list who matches our suspect list?" Sally asked.

"You mean your suspect list?"

True, she had revealed her thinking, but he was keeping his cards close to his chest. She knew she was right, so she didn't push. Well, she hoped she was right.

Finnegan pulled out his phone and scrolled through what was likely the list of aspirin buyers. The painkiller was ubiquitous, so Sally didn't think that was going to help. And someone could have purchased the medicine a year before and then decided to use it. Or the person had been planning this for even longer.

Or waiting for the old people to get older, Sally added cynically.

"I've found Roy, Gilbert, and Bethany on the list," Finnegan told her, looking up.

"No Arnolds?" Sally asked.

"And no Rose," Finnegan added.

"Rose was at my house a while back and had a headache. She told me she couldn't take aspirin for some reason," Sally explained.

"Though that doesn't mean she didn't buy it," Finnegan replied.

"You told me the person who pushed Dr. Wiggams was probably a man," Sally commented. They seemed to be going in circles.

"Yes, but maybe we have more than one killer on our hands," Finnegan said.

"So what's your next step, Detective?" Sally asked, though she was about to say "our next step," but she tried to stay on his good side.

"I'm going to take Jack, Gilbert, and Roy in for questioning. Hopefully, someone spills the beans. You're welcome to join. Be at my office at one in the afternoon," Finnegan said.

He moved to leave the storeroom, and Sally followed. She was definitely ready for bed. All the discussions and information at the bar would hopefully percolate into a solution by morning.

Chapter Twenty-Eight

The first morning of the year didn't turn out quite like Sally had planned.

She had slept in, trying to recover from the insanity of the night before. Surprisingly, she had slept fairly well, in spite of a bit of tossing and turning in the middle of the night.

And the bar was closed January 1, so she would have plenty of time to rest that day before working again on the second.

A flash of light and an aspirin bottle on her desk in the bar kept popping up in her mind, but she managed to get back to sleep. It helped that she never looked at her clock on the nightstand, which she often did if she awakened during the night.

Stretching, she glanced over and saw it was 10 a.m., which meant she had gotten almost seven hours' sleep. The police had questioned everyone in the bar about what Sally had found in her office. There hadn't been that many people left, but the questioning still took time.

She was due at the police station later to listen in on the interrogation of the three people Detective Finnegan had taken into custody: Jack Arnold, Gilbert Rock, and Roy Barnes.

Sally was glad the list of suspects in these terrible killings had been narrowed. She wasn't 100% certain one of the three men was behind the aspirin poisoning, but at least they seemed to be getting somewhere with the investigation.

She got out of bed and put on her fluffy blue robe. As she did, she noticed one of the elbows was worn. She sighed. She had had the robe for years, though not quite as long as Gladys. Unlike the car, she wasn't quite ready to give up on the bathrobe just yet.

Heading downstairs to make coffee, she heard what she thought was a car pulling into her driveway. She frowned. It was New Year's Day, and she was definitely not expecting any visitors at the early hour. Everyone in town knew she worked at the bar and had many late nights. No one would have just stopped by unless it was an emergency.

Now her blood ran cold. She froze on the bottom step, hoping they would just go away. She hoped it wasn't an emergency. Though from the things she had had to go through over the last year or so, this would not really be a surprise.

She heard two car doors slam, several beeps, and footsteps on the walkway to the front door. She was curious what was going on, but somehow her feet were frozen in place.

She waited to move until the doorbell rang or someone knocked. She held her breath, hoping it wasn't bad news. A hard rap at the door sent her into motion.

She stepped down to the floor of the foyer and walked the three steps to the door. Unlocking both bolts, she swung it open, and her eyes went wide.

Her emotions ran from happiness to horror to shock.

"Mom, Dad, what are you doing here?" she cried, pushing the screen door open and letting them in. The three pulled together into a tight hug. Tears flowed as they did. After a long moment, they pulled apart.

Sally was about to open her mouth when her mother put her hand up. "I know you told us not to come because you were worried about us being victim to the killings, but we just had to see you. And we have a surprise," her mother explained while Sally considered how to respond.

"Um, well, it's so great to see you, but I hope you'll head back home soon. I'm really worried about you, though there have been some developments."

Sally related the latest happenings while her parents listened to her, slack-jawed.

"Oh, Sally, we're so worried about you," her father exclaimed, not usually the emotional type. He pulled her in for another hug.

"I'm fine. I'm OK," Sally said, muffled in her father's sweatshirt.

Her mother touched her shoulder. "Let's take your mind off of this for a bit and show you what we brought," her mother said, smiling widely, heading back outside with Sally on her arm.

"Let me at least put some clothes on, Mom," she said, pulling away.

Sally bounded up the stairs to put on her standard jeans and sweatshirt. She took the couple of minutes to steel herself for what was coming and try to calm down her beating heart, her reaction to having her parents here, in Berry Springs, with all the death around the town at the moment.

She walked downstairs more calmly and slowly than she had gone up and pushed open the screen door.

Once she cleared the big bush next to the door that blocked her sight of part of the driveway, she stopped, her mouth dropping.

There were now three cars in the not-so-long driveway. The last car, her parents', was hanging off a bit.

In the middle, between their car and Gladys, was a medium-sized blue SUV she had never seen before.

"You bought another car?" Sally asked. "Didn't you tell me you only needed one car for the both of you? And why drive two cars from Oklahoma if you were both coming here?"

Sally was wondering what was going on.

"No, dear, this is your new car!" her father exclaimed, grinning. He walked over and dropped the keys into her open palm.

"My new car?!"

Her mother came over. "Honey, we know you got the inheritance from Momma Arnold's estate and were thinking about putting it toward replacing Gladys. We just thought you should use that money to spruce up the house and the bar. Or maybe you want to take a nice, long vacation to get away from it all. So we thought we would take care of the car situation," her mother said, now grinning like her father was.

Her parents were just too much.

She was frozen in place, trying to process the gift. This was meshed with her continued worry that her parents were here, where she had told them they shouldn't be.

Love won over, and she ran over to them and gave them another big hug. Though she would be 60 that year, she felt six again. "Thank you so much, Mom, Dad. This is a wonderful surprise."

"Let's have a look inside," her dad said, leading her to the SUV.

She was glad they hadn't splurged on a gigantic SUV like a lot of people in town drove. As she pushed the clicker to unlock the vehicle, she hoped it was a 4×4. First world problems, she told herself.

Sally pulled open the door and hopped up into the driver's seat.

Looking around, she inhaled the new car smell. It was an automatic, which she thought would be a godsend. The hills in Berry Springs were very difficult to navigate with stick-shift Gladys, particularly if she was hanging at an angle at a light.

"It's got four-wheel drive," her father said.

Sally breathed a silent sigh of relief. There was so much room. It would be perfect for transporting stuff for the bar or taking friends for a hike or dinner out in the county.

She got back out. "I love it. Thank you so much."

By now, her parents were beaming. An only child can do that.

"Let's go inside and celebrate," her mother suggested.

Sally checked her phone. It was just coming up on 11 o'clock. That reminded Sally she hadn't had anything yet that morning to eat, or had her coffee. She needed to get caffeine inside her, or she might get one of her terrible caffeine-withdrawal headaches.

"Good idea. I haven't eaten anything yet. And I am desperate for coffee," Sally replied, leading her parents inside and into the kitchen.

"Now you just sit down, and we'll take care of everything," her father told her.

Sally knew there was no point in arguing with them, so she planted herself in one of the chairs surrounding her large kitchen table and let them work.

She quickly texted Magda to tell her about the car.

"That's so cool, Sally," Magda texted back.

In no time, there were plates of pancakes, scrambled eggs, and toast in front of them. Sally gulped her coffee.

"Dig in," her father said, grabbing his fork.

The food was delicious. She didn't cook or bake that often, though she seemed to be doing more of it recently. On the other hand, her mother and father were outstanding cooks.

"This is the best breakfast I've had in a while," Sally said.

"Of course it is, dear," her mother replied.

Sally grinned. Besides being good at cooking, her parents had very healthy egos. There was no point in commenting on her mother's last statement.

"When did you say you have to be in town?" her father asked, putting down his fork.

"One o'clock. So we still have a little time. It won't take me long to shower and get ready."

"You can take your new car to show it off downtown," her mother suggested.

"Mom, this isn't Beverly Hills, where people go downtown to see and be seen," Sally replied, winking.

"Oh, I know, dear, but won't the townspeople be surprised at what you're driving?" her mother declared.

Sally nodded. "OK, yes. Many people will probably be shocked I'm not driving Gladys."

That last thought hit her in the gut. Gladys.

"What will you do with her?" her father asked, reading her mind.

"I want to keep her, somehow, but it's probably better to get rid of her for a clean break."

Her mother nodded sagely, "Yes, that would be better."

They spent another hour talking about everything but the Senior Slayer murders. Her parents filled her in on what was going on with the rest of the family, which wasn't very much. Her parents had two sisters each, and they were strewn about the continent: her mother's sisters lived in Savannah, where the family was from, while one of her father's sisters lived in Missoula, Montana, and the other in Toronto.

"I'm so glad everyone is doing well," Sally said, finishing her last piece of toast.

Sally had enjoyed the full breakfast, but that is what her stomach was feeling at the moment: full. She'd have to get a hike in, she considered.

She checked her phone. "OK, I've got to get ready to go over to the police station." As she said that, she debated whether she should tell her parents to leave, but she knew she couldn't.

"Everything all right, dear?" her mother asked, seeing the doubt in Sally's eyes.

"Yes, I'm fine. So what will you two be doing?" Sally asked neutrally.

"Well, it was a long drive for us, and we hoped we can stay here overnight, if you're not too worried," her father answered. Ah, they knew her too well.

Sally hesitated before responding. "Well, I do love seeing you, so yes, please stay overnight, but I'd feel better if you stay here in the house with all the doors and windows locked," Sally replied, realizing she sounded more than slightly paranoid.

"Now, dear, we will be fine. But we will stay here and lock the house up," her father said, looking over at her mother, who nodded.

Sally smiled and got up. She picked up her plate to bring it over to the sink, taking a jam jar with her.

"Oh, Sally, we'll clean up. Just you go get ready," her mother chided.

"Thanks," Sally called as she headed over to the stairs and up to her bedroom en suite.

She really was glad to see them. She just hoped they would be alive when she got back from the police station.

Chapter Twenty-Nine

Sally bumped into Randall Wentworth as they were both heading into the main town building.

"Joining us this afternoon, Ms. Witherspoon?" Wentworth said, overly formal.

"Yes, as a matter of fact. Detective Finnegan asked me to listen in from the room next door," Sally explained.

"Fine by me. I expected you'd be here," he replied.

Of course, he was representing all three. Sally smiled as they walked together into the police station, part of the building.

Detective Finnegan was already there to greet them. Sally followed the detective and the lawyer into the back silently, her mind more on her parents than what she was about to hear. She tried to push those thoughts aside as she debated if she should offer any questions Detective Finnegan could ask the three suspects.

They approached the small room next to the interrogation room, and Finnegan led Sally and Wentworth inside.

"I'll check with my clients and let you know if they have a problem with you listening in," Wentworth explained, walking out.

Finnegan shut the door. Through the one-way glass, Sally saw Wentworth enter the interrogation room, where Jack Arnold was already sitting. She thought that made a lot of sense to start with him.

Wentworth sat down and conferred with his client. They only exchanged a few words, and she saw Jack nod his head. Wentworth looked at the one-way window and gave a thumbs-up.

Sally didn't expect anything different, but she was still relieved she could stay and listen.

That was Finnegan's cue. "You OK in here?" Finnegan asked.

"Sure," Sally replied as Finnegan turned to leave the room.

He didn't ask her for her thoughts beforehand, and she decided she needed to stay on his good side, so she just offered a "good luck" as he shut the door. Sally shook her head. Good luck? That was a weird thing to say.

She tried to concentrate on the task at hand, but she knew a part of her was still back with her parents at her old Victorian on Maple Street.

* * *

Detective Finnegan entered the interrogation room next door and sat down across from Jack Arnold and Randall Wentworth.

He didn't have a folder with him this time, just a large notepad and pen. He looked down at it and jotted some notes. Maybe it was just gibberish to make Jack Arnold nervous.

It worked. Jack was tapping the table and shifting in his chair. Wentworth's hand on his shoulder made him stop.

"You were seen coming out of Sally's office," Finnegan said, jumping right in.

Jack shook his head. "No way. I was in the hallway, sure, as I had to use the restroom a couple of times during the party. You know, long night, a few beers..." Jack countered.

"Our witness is very reliable."

"Who is it?" Finnegan asked, leaning forward as if that would intimidate the ace detective.

Finnegan shook his head, "That's confidential."

Wentworth scoffed but said nothing and leaned back.

"You must have had a good reason to be in Sally's office, Jack. Did you plant the aspirin? Are you the killer?"

Finnegan was quickly putting the pressure on Jack, though Sally would probably have taken a slightly different tack.

"No," Jack yelled, pounding the table.

Finnegan grinned. He really seemed to be enjoying this. "Well, if you weren't in there and aren't the killer, how do you explain that someone saw you?" Finnegan asked, shifting his bulk in the chair. It creaked, but held.

Wentworth leaned over to whisper something in Jack's ear. Jack sat back and closed his eyes.

Sally was holding her breath for what was to come next. She didn't think Jack had anything to do with the killings, though he and his brother would probably have a good reason to get rid of her, as they were very upset their mother had left Sally so much money.

But why would they kill their beloved mother or the others?

Finnegan said nothing and waited for Jack to respond. His eyes opened, and he first looked at Wentworth, who nodded.

"All right, I was in Sally's office, but I didn't plant any aspirin," Jack explained.

Finnegan nodded. "Did you see a bottle of it on the desk?" Finnegan asked. Jack shook his head.

"No, but I was more interested in the safe, so I wasn't looking at the desk," he said.

"What time was this?" Finnegan probed.

Jack shrugged. "No clue, I wasn't watching the clock."

Finnegan looked down and scribbled something on his pad. Looking up, he asked, "So what about the safe? Need money?"

Sally didn't think that was the case. Even with the reduction in inheritance, the Arnold boys had a house, large property, and the family business. Thinking about it, all that together made it even less likely that they had anything to do with the killings.

"Are you kidding, Detective?" Jack asked, laughing.

Finnegan turned his head toward the window so Sally could see he went red, whether in embarrassment or anger, Sally couldn't tell. "So what was it?" Finnegan asked, his voice raised.

Jack grinned. He seemed to be enjoying this. Wasn't Finnegan supposed to be in charge, Sally asked herself.

"Well, I was trying to get into the safe to see if my momma's check was in there?" he admitted.

"You mean Sally's inheritance?" Finnegan asked.

Jack nodded.

"What would that do for you?" the detective asked, tapping the table with his pen.

"I was going to tear it up," Jack replied.

"But she'll just get another. The will is clear," Wentworth added.

Sally wondered why he had suddenly spoken out. Wasn't he supposed to be supporting his client? Wentworth obviously realized his mistake when he coughed and stared at the floor.

"Well, I'd had a few beers, as I said. I was pissed that Sally got some of our money, and I guess I wasn't really thinking," Jack admitted.

Sally might not think they had anything to do with the deaths, but she hoped she wouldn't have to be looking over her shoulder the rest of her life. Jack Arnold could sometimes be difficult, but Steve Arnold could be outright dangerous.

Finnegan looked like he was going to speak when a klaxon shrieked.

Sally jumped in fright at the loud sound, the stool she was sitting on crashing to the ground.

Sally watched Finnegan race out of the interrogation room. She fled her hideaway and followed him. As she came out of the room, she saw him turn the corner at the end of the hallway. She ran down after him. As she turned the corner, she saw him enter the cell area. He left the door open, so she followed.

At the second cell on the left, they found Mark Soder pointing inside.

Gilbert Rock was lying on the ground, not moving.

A paramedic raced in from the other side of the corridor and began working on him.

Sally saw froth around his mouth, his face blue. One shoe was off and a few inches away from his foot. There was a small bag of white pills hanging out of it.

She pointed to the shoe. Finnegan's eyes went up. He strode into the cell, pulled out gloves, put them on, and took the evidence.

After a few minutes, the paramedic got up and shook his head.

As he did, another paramedic came in with a stretcher. They loaded Gilbert Rock onto it and sped out. Though Sally didn't think there was anything they could do for him.

Another death. And in the town jail?

Chapter Thirty

Once the paramedics had left with Gilbert's body, Finnegan led Soder and Sally back to his office to review what had just happened.

Sally was glad Finnegan hadn't just shooed her out, but maybe he really did believe she could help with his investigations. She was really getting into this side hustle as an amateur detective, though it was complicated juggling it with her bar job.

Getting back to the task at hand, she took a seat on his couch, while Soder took a chair next to the desk, and Finnegan seated himself in his own imposing leather reclining executive chair.

"Tell me what happened, Soder," Finnegan requested, or more demanded. His face was beet red.

"I went in to check on the prisoners and get Gilbert and Roy ready for questioning. I looked in on Roy, and all was fine. Then I walked over to Gilbert's cell and saw him unresponsive, frothing at the mouth. I hit the alarm and called the paramedics. Then you came racing around the corner. Everything was locked up. I don't know how this could have happened," Soder said, shaking his head.

Finnegan didn't say a word but just held up the small bag, still wearing blue gloves. He handed it to Soder. "Get this tested immediately. I'm assuming it's aspirin."

Sally nodded, "I agree."

Soder quickly left the room.

"So we know that Gilbert is a killer," Finnegan concluded.

Sally frowned.

"Isn't that being a bit hasty, Detective? Yes, he had a bag of something. Yes, he seems to have taken it. And yes, he is dead. But it doesn't immediately mean he is the Senior Slayer," she retorted. The moniker slipped out before she had time to really think about what she was saying. Well, at least the use of that name. She hated it because it always made her think of her parents.

Her parents. They would probably be wondering when she was going to get back home. They did know that she would be at the police station for a while as the interrogations were underway.

She'd had to give them a call soon or maybe try to get out of there and just drive home. It would be better if she told them in person about what had just happened.

"Well, it has to be aspirin. But if he isn't the killer, how did that bag get into the cell?" Finnegan said, thinking aloud.

"It looks like he brought it in himself, doesn't it? His shoe was off, and the bag was hanging out of it. Don't you check prisoners before you put them in the cells?" Sally asked a bit indelicately.

"Well, none of them were prisoners per se. We had just brought them in for questioning…" Finnegan said, his voice trailing off.

"So you don't really check them." Sally finished his sentence.

Finnegan went red again. "OK, right. Well, we do look for weapons," he replied, "but not for pills in someone's shoes."

Sally was going to mention that seemed to be a bit lax, but she decided to remain on Finnegan's good side, particularly at this stage of the investigation.

"I guess that makes sense. Why would you think to look in their shoes? And it really does seem like a weird thing to keep there," Sally said.

Finnegan harrumphed.

"Looking on the bright side," Finnegan said, "We are definitely getting closer to catching our killer. Though he may have just died in my jail."

"Even if Gilbert was the killer, which I'm still finding hard to believe, why would he kill those people? He was such a happy, helpful figure in Berry Springs, and he definitely adored Momma Arnold, Belle, and even Dr. Wiggams," Sally said. "He was always cooking meals for them when they were sick, delivering books from the library, and helping them all with online research and support."

"I agree that most of the town loved him and vice versa, but he's dead, the pills were apparently in his shoe, and I'm one step closer to concluding this case."

"What about Roy?" Sally asked, thinking that they should speak to him as well.

"I'm putting that off until we get the test results and autopsy. That way, I have more information to try to draw Roy out, if he knows anything," he mansplained.

She hated mansplaining, but decided to not ask him why he was going to try to draw Roy out if he thought Gilbert was the Senior Slayer.

"I need to call the chief," he said, finally waving her out of his office.

Sally wasn't too upset about that. She had a lot to think about, and she needed to get home quickly to make sure her parents were OK and hadn't left the house. And she had to relate everything that had just happened at the police station.

* * *

Late that afternoon, Sally and her parents were seated around the kitchen table. Her mother had made an early dinner of chili and fresh bread, and they were just about to dig in. Each had a glass of red wine and water.

"I just can't believe it," her mother said, sipping her wine, "Gilbert was such a gentle, kind man."

Sally nodded. "I know," Sally replied, scooping up a bit of chili and enjoying the heat and spiciness. "This is delicious, Mom."

"Thank you, dear," her mother replied, ripping her piece of bread in two and dunking it in her own bowl.

"So Gilbert's the killer?" her father asked directly.

Sally shrugged. "It's not clear. He had pills with him, apparently, though they could have been planted; he was supposedly seen coming out of my office, and he's dead," Sally replied.

She had filled her parents in on everything that had happened over the last 24 hours. She trusted them implicitly, and they certainly weren't going to run to the press or call Finnegan to tell them Sally had spilled the beans. At that last thought, she laughed out loud.

"What is it, dear?" her mother asked, putting down her spoon.

"Oh, nothing, just a funny thought," she replied. "Thank you again for the car and for surprising me with a visit. It really is wonderful to see you two," Sally said, her hand shaking a bit.

"But you're still worried about us," her father replied. "We get it. We really do, but it was more important for us to surprise you and see you than worry about what might happen to us in Berry Springs."

Her mother nodded, smiling broadly. "Of course, we are staying at least one night. You shouldn't have to go through this on your own," her mother said. Her tone told Sally it wasn't worth even trying to talk them out of it.

And she had some extra time on her hands anyway. The bar was still closed pending the final investigation of the premises, and she was waiting for the test results on the pills.

Pulling out her phone, she texted Magda the latest update. News of Gilbert's death had probably gotten all over town.

"Stay safe," Magda's reply said. "We are hunkering down at my place. You let me know if you need anything."

As she read Magda's reply, she saw she had several unread messages. They were mainly from the people at the bar's New Year party, making sure she was safe and also relating their shock at Gilbert's death.

She replied to a few before she heard a cough. "Not at the table, dear," her mother said, tsking. She felt like a little girl again.

Sally blushed and put down her phone, and tried to clear her mind of the happenings in town and concentrate on the conversation and time with her parents.

* * *

Later that evening, after her parents had gone to bed, Sally sat in her living room reviewing the events of the past month or so.

If it was what it looked like, Gilbert was the Senior Slayer. If he had been, they weren't going to get a confession out of him, though maybe he had left some kind of evidence at his house. As she was pondering this, her phone vibrated.

"Aspirin," the one-word message from Finnegan said.

Sally sat back. Well, now it was definite. Though it still didn't prove Gilbert was the killer. They needed to have concrete evidence connecting Gilbert to the deaths. She wasn't sure how they were going to do that, barring finding a confessional note or something else at his house or the library that tied him to the deaths.

On the bright side, she thought, if he was the killer, then there would be no more mysterious deaths in Berry Springs.

Chapter Thirty-One

The next morning, her parents persuaded her it was OK for her to leave them alone locked in the house. She was still nervous, but an early-morning text from Detective Finnegan had asked her to come in at nine o'clock to listen in on his questioning of Roy Barnes. He had written that Jack Arnold had been let go and that he didn't consider him a suspect anymore.

Sally was sure the Detective was just questioning Roy for the sake of thoroughness, and he clearly was ready to conclude the case with Gilbert Rock's death.

Though if it wasn't ruled a suicide, then the case would still not be concluded.

Before heading to the police station, she decided to stop in at The Nutmeg Café to hash through the happenings with the owner and her good friend, Joanna. The café was just past the town square, so she could chat with Joanna, have a quick breakfast, and still be on time for the police.

Though the weather was crisp, it wasn't snowing, so Sally had gotten up early and was walking into town. She pulled her coat tighter and was glad she had remembered her gloves. Her breath was visible in front of her, and all the signs told her she needed to pick up the pace to not freeze to death before she got to The Nutmeg.

Joanna beamed when she saw her. "Oh, Sally, so nice to see you," she called as she finished up a takeout order for a customer.

Sally saw it was Bethany Wells. Ugh, she hoped Bethany was just going to leave and not come over and give her the third degree. Bethany paid for her order and came over to Sally. "Terrible, terrible," she said. "I'm so worried, but I'm sorry I don't have time to chat. I'm having a few friends over." With that, Bethany left the café.

Sally was sure Bethany had organized her own gossip circle, but she was glad that meant that she wouldn't be at the center of it if Bethany had stayed there for a chat.

Sally found an open table in the back, and Joanna came over to take her order, not before giving her a big hug. "Oh, you poor thing," Joanna said, sitting down.

"What a poor town, you mean," Sally replied.

"I hope you figure it all out soon, Sally," Joanna said. "What will you have?"

"Just a coffee and one of your yummy blueberry muffins. I'm due over at the police station soon," she replied, lowering her voice as if that made a difference. Since the events of the year before, the whole town knew about her side hustle.

Joanna winked and got up to get her order.

Sally put her backpack on the floor and considered getting out her trusty notebook, but she didn't have much time, so she decided to just sit and think.

Gilbert was such a kind soul. She wondered how he had gotten mixed up in all this. He may not be the killer, but he was dead.

Joanna returned after a couple of minutes.

Sally got out her wallet, but Joanna put up her hand. "You do enough. This one's on me," she explained. Joanna smiled and went back to the counter to serve other customers.

Sally noticed Joanna's son, Kent, in the back, pulling something out of the oven, chatting with the baker Joanna had hired.

She sipped her coffee and pulled apart the muffin. Dunking a piece of it in her coffee and stuffing it in her mouth, she sighed. Coffee and a muffin were akin to heaven in her book.

It didn't take her long to finish it. The coffee was in a to-go cup, so Sally grabbed her backpack and the coffee and waved goodbye to Joanna.

"Thanks," Sally called as she headed out and to the left. A block away lay the police station and hopefully, finally, some answers.

* * *

"Roy, why don't you tell me what you saw New Year's Eve," Finnegan began.

Sally was back sitting in the small room next to the interrogation room. Her coffee was next to her; her notebook and pen poised for action.

Randall Wentworth was seated next to Roy, no surprise there. He had a neutral expression.

"Well, I told you I saw Gilbert come out of Sally's office, right?" Roy began.

"Yeah," Finnegan replied, "That's nothing new."

"Well, there was someone with him," Roy added.

Sally was stunned. Finnegan didn't say anything at first. He turned back to the one-way mirror and raised his eyebrows. Sally nodded in response, though he obviously couldn't see her.

"Who was it?" Finnegan asked, finally.

Roy looked at Finnegan, then at Wentworth, then at the one-way mirror.

Sally wondered why he didn't just blurt out a name. She knew him to be a gruff, direct person.

Roy sighed.

"Can I speak to you in private, Detective?" Roy asked.

This got a response from the lawyer. "You need me, Roy," Wentworth said.

"It's OK, Randall. I really need to talk to John alone," Roy replied, using Finnegan's first name.

Randall didn't say anything for a bit, but then slapped the table and got up. As he walked out, Sally saw that his expression said he was none too happy about this development.

"OK, Roy," Finnegan said.

Roy shook his head. "Sally's in there, isn't she?" Roy asked, pointing to the one-way mirror.

"Yes, to be honest, but she's helping with the investigation. Anything you say to me, you can say to her," Finnegan replied, taking the soft tone of a grandparent.

Roy sat back and closed his eyes. There seemed to be a lot of that in this room, Sally thought, considering Jack Arnold had done the same.

She tapped her pen on the table.

Finally, Roy opened his eyes. "OK, she can stay," Roy said.

"So who was with him, Roy?" Finnegan asked, his tone now sharp.

"You aren't going to believe this," Roy replied, dragging the agony out even further.

Sally was close to getting up, running into the other room, and yanking it out of him. She had even started to get up from her chair.

"Randall Wentworth," Roy declared.

Chapter Thirty-Two

"Randall Wentworth?" Finnegan repeated, getting louder.

"Yes," Roy announced again, sitting back and crossing his arms. Sally couldn't move. Randall Wentworth, she thought, the town gentleman, everyone's lawyer. What was his part in all of this? There must be a simple explanation, but Sally knew in real life a lot of things were much more complicated than they should be.

She scribbled the lawyer's name in her notebook as if that would help the answer to it all pop out. She thought about heading into the next room, but that might shut Roy up, and she and Finnegan needed answers, not silence.

"Now why would he be coming out of Sally's office with Gilbert?" Finnegan asked, his voice tense.

Sally could feel the emotions through the plate-glass window. It would be very difficult to pin anything on the town's powerful lawyer, who knew everyone's secrets and was tight with all the power figures in Berry Springs and elsewhere.

"I just saw them for a split second as I headed back into the bar. I don't think they saw me, and I have no idea what they were talking about. Their mouths were moving, but the music from the bar made it impossible to make out the words. And I'm not a lip-reader, especially in that short amount of time. You'll just have to ask Mr. Wentworth," Roy said, now quivering.

"Are you cold, Roy?" Finnegan asked, moving to turn up the heat.

Roy shook his head. "No. Scared. I probably shouldn't have told you what I just said. Randall will get me, I'm sure of it."

Sally's gut told her he might just be right, even if she still couldn't believe old Randall Wentworth could be mixed up in all this. Though she had told herself in the past, she wanted to stay on Wentworth's good side. Who knew what his bad side was capable of?

Ugh, maybe Roy really was in danger. She wanted to help him, but she had no idea how.

The blood drained from her face as she realized what this meant. If Wentworth was told what Roy said, then he would certainly know that Sally knew.

This was not turning into the start of the New Year that Sally had hoped. Though with Roy's information, they may be closer to the truth of the Senior Slayer deaths, if Wentworth was behind it all.

Then again, with his influence, she had no idea what would happen. She couldn't imagine the lawyer being convicted or, worse, going to jail or being on death row.

Sally looked through the one-way mirrored glass and saw Finnegan get up. He motioned for the officer at the door to come over.

"Take him back to a jail cell," Finnegan ordered.

Finnegan followed them out and came back in a few seconds later with Randall Wentworth. It was showtime, Sally thought, trying to bring some levity into the situation.

Both men sat down across from each other. Randall looked grim, crossing his hands on the table with a piercing look at Finnegan.

Over his shoulder, Wentworth was looking directly at Sally. She could feel his intense stare, even if he really couldn't see her. Knowing Wentworth, though, he had probably somehow acquired X-ray vision.

"Now what is this all about?" Wentworth whispered.

Sally felt like she could be in the middle of a horror movie. She knew Wentworth was ruthless, but this was just frightening.

Sally felt her mouth go dry waiting for Finnegan to respond. She wondered how he was feeling at the moment. Both men didn't move, time standing still.

All she could hear was her own breath. The chair beneath her creaked, and she jumped.

She clapped her hand in front of her mouth to stop it from making a sound. She stared out at Wentworth, staring back at her. His eyes then went back to Finnegan.

"OK, I have to ask you some questions," Finnegan said finally.

Sally exhaled loudly. She picked her pen up, holding it over her notebook. She looked down, and the pen was shaking. She held it steady with the other hand.

"Oh, do you?" Wentworth replied. "Do I need a lawyer?"

Sally laughed, releasing tension.

"Well, it depends on what you have done," Finnegan said, leaning toward Wentworth.

The lawyer remained frozen in place. "What do you think I've done?" Wentworth asked, his voice tight.

Sally saw his eyes narrow. Finnegan remained silent. She wondered whether this was to get Wentworth worked up or because he was dreading the next few minutes.

She saw Finnegan open the folder in front of him, a typical Finnegan delay tactic. She wanted to go into the other room and tell him to just get on with it. Delaying wasn't really going to help now.

"Shall I call the mayor?" Wentworth asked. He pulled his cell phone out of his breast pocket, his fingers poised above the screen.

"No need for that," Finnegan said, his voice raised. "If you've done something illegal, none of your connections are going to help you. I'll be certain of that" His words sounded more assured than his voice did. "Roy saw you with Gilbert coming out of Sally's office at the New Year's Eve party," Finnegan said, his words shooting out like bullets.

Wentworth just looked at him, then let out a belly laugh. It went on and on. Sally felt chills down her spine.

Finally, he stopped and looked right at the detective. "That is ridiculous. I wasn't even at that party," Wentworth declared.

"Well, there is a back door to the bar, isn't there? You could easily have slipped in," Finnegan said.

Sally nodded in agreement, as if either man could see her.

"I was at the police chief's New Year's Eve party, which even Mayor Pulasky attended. Ask any of them," Wentworth replied, looking self-satisfied.

Ugh, she hated when people name-dropped.

"Oh, I will, I will," Finnegan said. "But first, I'd like you to tell me what you were doing at Sally's bar with Roy."

Wentworth started to get up.

"Sit down," Finnegan said sharply, "You are being questioned by a police detective."

Wentworth hesitated before returning to his seat. "I have nothing to say to you, Detective. I was at Chief Sanford's party with at least 20 other guests, including the mayor, I say again."

"Stop with the power plays, Wentworth. If you did something illegal, I will get you I told you. So spill it," Finnegan barked.

Sally jumped in her seat, and even Wentworth twitched, though he held his ground.

"I wasn't there, Detective," Wentworth repeated.

Sally wondered how the detective was going to prove the lawyer was there. They probably wouldn't find his fingerprints. He was too smart for that, and Sally couldn't remember a time over the last 17 years when Randall Wentworth had been in her office. He always made appointments at his own office in town, mainly to show off his power and wealth, Sally knew.

Finnegan didn't say anything. The men sat still at a standoff for what felt like several minutes.

Sally couldn't move.

Finally, Wentworth leaned forward and spoke. "Look, Detective Finnegan. I don't know what you're playing at. Roy is lying. I was never in the bar New Year's Eve. I have no idea what you're talking about, and if you need to speak to me again, you go through my attorney," Wentworth said in an even, powerful tone.

Finnegan didn't move.

Wentworth got up. "Oh, did I mention my attorney is friends with the Attorney General and the Governor in Little Rock?" he added as he walked out.

Sally heard him walk down the hallway, and she waited until the footsteps were gone before she left the small anteroom and went into the main interrogation room. She sat down across from Finnegan.

"Well, that was fun," he declared. Both laughed.

"But do you think he had anything to do with the deaths?"

"Definitely. Roy may be gruff, but he's no liar," Finnegan answered.

"True. Belle thought he was one of the most honest people she knew," Sally added.

"Exactly. I just have no idea how I'm going to prove anything, though. There probably aren't going to be any of his fingerprints in your office," Finnegan said.

Sally nodded. Exactly what she had been thinking.

"I just wish Roy had heard more, and now Gilbert's dead, so I can't ask him," Finnegan said, tapping the table with his pen.

"You could have Randall's house searched," Sally offered.

Finnegan shook his head. "That would be a very difficult search warrant to get. And I don't have any proof. Yet."

"What about searching Gilbert's house for any clues?" Sally suggested.

Finnegan smiled. "Good thought, Ms. Witherspoon. I'll go talk to a judge right now," Finnegan replied, getting up. This was Sally's cue that it was time to leave. "Thanks for coming in, Sally," Finnegan said as they walked out to the front of the police station together.

She hadn't done much, she felt, but they had certainly learned a lot from the questioning.

"Will you talk to Roy again?" Sally asked as they reached the door.

Finnegan nodded. " But first, I'm going to search Gilbert's house, so I have more to go on. I'll talk to Roy, and hopefully I can put together a stronger case against Wentworth. I don't care who his lawyer is or who he knows. If he's behind the Senior Slayer, I'll get him," Finnegan declared. He pushed the door open for Sally, and she headed back to her house and her parents.

She was glad she had walked. She could digest everything she'd heard that morning.

As she walked down the block toward home, she passed Randall Wentworth's office. Sally looked up, and he was staring down at her. She shuddered and picked up her pace.

On the whole way home, she kept looking over her shoulder to see if Wentworth was following her.

Chapter Thirty-Three

Her parents were in the midst of preparing a nice light lunch, replete with fresh, crusty bread and a salad with chicken.

She didn't want to panic her parents, but she decided to come clean about all that had transpired at the police station over lunch. There were a lot of gasps from them as she relayed the goings on.

"Oh, Sally, this is really turning into a dangerous game," her mother cried, putting down her fork.

She hadn't realized how hungry she had been until she sat down to eat. "Thanks for the food. Always delicious, Mom. It's been quite an eventful morning."

"We're just glad you are here, safe and sound."

At the last words, her father jumped up and ran around double-checking all the doors and windows downstairs. He even ran upstairs. She could hear him running around. She and her mother exchanged glances.

"Men," her mother said, shrugging her shoulders.

Sally grinned and dug right back into the salad. She took a sip of iced tea to wash it down.

While her father seemed a bit on the anxious side, Sally felt like the calm in the storm. She'd been through so much over the last year or so. Another possible threat to her life wasn't going to keep her locked up inside, even if that is what her parents, well, her father, seemed to be planning.

She had texted Magda on the walk home. She was just as shocked as Sally and even suggested closing the bar until everything calmed down. Sally would never do that. She loved running the bar, meeting people, and her mischievous side knew that the goings on would bring in more customers.

Besides, why should they all be scared to leave their homes? Life was meant to be lived, regardless of the dangers or risks. And there were always risks when one left one's house, she texted Magda.

Sally laughed at the reply, "OK, Grandma."

Her father came back downstairs.

"All secure," he said, as he sat back down and dug into his salad.

"OK, corporal," her mother replied.

That got a laugh out of all three, relieving the tension of the current situation.

"Thanks, Dad, but nothing's going to happen," Sally told him. She didn't really believe that everything would be perfect, but her father seemed more concerned than he usually was. Maybe it was time to send them both back to Oklahoma.

"Mom, Dad, thanks so much for visiting me and for the car—" Sally began.

"We are not leaving you now, if that is what you are suggesting," her mother scolded, tapping her fork on the table.

Sally took a deep breath. "I am worried more about you two than me, to be honest," Sally finally replied. The deep breath hadn't really helped.

"We know," her father said, taking her hand, "But we want to be there for you. I just hope you can solve the crimes quickly." His voice was tight, which gave Sally another sign he was more nervous than he was letting on. Her mother was usually the worrywart, but perhaps her father was concerned something would happen to her or Sally, or both.

Sally admitted that made sense and made them all human.

Though if Gilbert had been the killer, they would all be safe now, Sally thought.

If Wentworth was behind it, maybe not.

Sally was in turmoil, but putting on a brave face for her parents, even if they could read each other like a book.

Her mother glanced over at Sally, lost in thought, and frowned. "Time for coffee," her mother said, getting up.

Sally knew this was code for "find me something to do with my thoughts."

"Mom, I think it's time for something stronger. Why don't we go into the living room for a bourbon?" Sally suggested.

Her father glanced at the clock on the wall. "Isn't it a bit early in the day for bourbon?"

As Sally was debating the question, the doorbell rang, followed by a sharp knock at the door. Sally froze and then realized her parents had as well. She relaxed.

"If someone was going to kill me, do you think they would announce their presence?" Sally asked.

Her father grinned, "Guess you're right."

Sally got up to see who it was. As she walked through the foyer, she picked up her large walking stick, just in case.

Through the window next to the door, she saw it was Mark Soder. She leaned the walking stick against the wall and then unlocked and opened the door.

"Hi, Mark. What's up?" she asked as if she couldn't figure out why he was here. "It's Mark Soder from the police," she yelled toward the kitchen.

"Your parents still here?" he asked in a whisper.

Sally nodded. Whether she told people something or not, most of the town knew what everyone else was up to. Someone would have seen the cars in Sally's driveway and announced the news to whomever they saw.

Sometimes that was a good thing because it meant neighbors watched out for each other. Other times, she felt constantly spied on.

"Can I come in?" Mark asked.

"Of course you can," her mother said behind her.

Sally blushed for some reason, and Mark grinned. This was not going to be easy.

"Hello, Mark. George and I are so glad to see you again," she said, pointing to Sally's father, who had joined them in the hallway.

"Won't you join us for lunch?" her father offered as Mark came in.

"Thanks, but I just had something to eat," Mark replied.

"Coffee, bourbon, iced tea?" her mother recited.

"Why don't we all go into the kitchen?" Sally suggested.

Her parents led the way with Mark, then Sally in procession. As they all sat down, Sally caught her mother winking at her as she nodded at Mark. Sally blushed again.

"Would you like something to drink?" her father asked.

"Coffee would be great, thanks," Mark replied, grinning at Sally.

"How's Candy?" Sally asked, reminding her parents that Mark was a married man.

"Oh, she's off with some girlfriends, so I had time to pop over and see you," Mark replied, telling it like he and Sally were having an affair.

She noticed her parents were hanging on his every word. Her father had even stopped mid-coffee-pour. Sally sighed and shook her head. Mark laughed. Her father put the coffee in front of Mark and sat back down.

Sally was thinking about jumping up to get that bourbon they had been talking about. It might calm her nerves. Instead, she just decided to change the subject. "Any news?" Sally asked, finally getting down to business.

"As a matter of fact, yes," Mark replied. "But uh…." He looked at her parents.

"We'll just go into the living room and have that bourbon," her father said, nodding to her mother.

Sally didn't mind what they did, so long as they didn't get the wrong impression, though what Mark had just said could be misconstrued. She would have a talk with them after he left.

They both watched her parents leave the kitchen and cross the hall to the living room. The door shut. Sally got up and closed the kitchen door. That was one of the moments where Sally was glad she had an old Victorian with many rooms and not a modern house with a great room and open-plan kitchen.

"So what's up?" Sally asked.

Mark grinned. "You love this stuff, don't you?" he asked, already knowing the answer to the question Sally assumed.

Sally took a moment to think. "Well, yes, but it is sad that people have died. I feel like I can somehow avenge their deaths by trying to find out who killed them."

"Yes, these deaths have been particularly hard. I still can't believe Momma Arnold, Belle, and Dr. Wiggams are gone," Mark replied.

"Momma Arnold was a saint in the town and will be sorely missed. I wonder if her sons will be able to continue her legacy."

At this, Mark laughed. "Oh, right. They will be lucky to live out the year the way they play with guns and their tempers flare at the drop of a hat."

Sally thought back to the struggle the year before when Momma Arnold had revealed a long-buried secret to her in the Arnold kitchen, and Steve had burst in with a shotgun. Luckily, no one had been hurt before the police could arrest Steve.

"You're probably right, though I hope you aren't," Sally finally replied.

Both sat silent for a few seconds.

Sally broke the silence, "And Gilbert."

Mark nodded, "Poor man."

"You don't think he had anything to do with this and just happened to die in your jail?" Sally retorted.

Mark frowned.

"Sorry, I didn't mean for that to come out that way," she replied, putting her hand on his.

Now it was Mark's turn to blush.

He pulled his hand away.

"OK, getting back to the subject at hand. We searched Gilbert's house. Luckily, my boss was able to get a judge to sign off on a search warrant quickly."

Now they were finally getting somewhere, Sally felt. She leaned forward in anticipation.

"What did you find?"

"Not that much. Well, maybe something. On the surface, he seems to be exactly as we expected his house to be. Well decorated, clean, neat, and books everywhere.

Sally laughed, "Not surprising, considering he was a librarian."

Mark hesitated.

"What is it?" Sally asked.

"Well, he does seem to have very expensive furniture and clothes," Mark replied.

Sally shrugged.

"So?"

"Well, as you said, he was a librarian. How much do you think he made?"

Sally considered that for a moment.

"Well, maybe he comes from money or is economical otherwise?"

At that, Mark laughed.

"Have you ever known Gilbert to be economical?"

Sally grinned.

"OK, you're right. But what does this all mean?"

"Well, we're looking to get access to his bank account to see about what kind of money he had. That might tell us more."

"Oh, Gilbert was such a kind soul. It's sad that he somehow seems to have got himself caught up in all this."

"We don't know that at this point, but it does look like we are a lot closer to finding out what's been going on here."

"How is Randall Wentworth mixed up in all this?" she asked.

"That's what we also need to find out as soon as possible. Randall denies everything, as I guess he would."

"But he did threaten your boss with a hotshot lawyer from Little Rock, who apparently knows the Governor and Attorney General of Arkansas," Sally replied, the whole time wondering how they would finally get to the bottom of the whole mess.

"Well, John Finnegan hates being threatened, and I know he has a couple of powerful contacts in Washington, so this should make things interesting," Mark said.

Sally had not thought Detective Finnegan was one to have contacts, as it were, but if they were legit, they could certainly help.

"Finnegan's bringing in Wentworth again for questioning. We still have Roy in protective custody. I just hope we can break Wentworth, get him to confess, and we can finally wrap this all up," Mark said.

"Mind if I join you?" Sally asked, getting up, assuming it was time to head out.

"Sure. That's why I stopped by to see you and give you the update," Mark replied.

Sally wondered why he hadn't just called, and she was going to ask him that, but then her parents came back into the kitchen.

"Sorry to interrupt," her mother said, looking back and forth at Sally and Mark and smiling, "We felt like coffee."

More like they felt like eavesdropping, Sally thought, but did not verbalize. "No problem. We're just leaving," Sally replied.

"Back to the police station?" her father asked.

She was glad her mother didn't say something like, "Oh, going somewhere for coffee together?"

"I just need to get my coat and backpack, Mark," she said as they walked out into the hallway together. She ran upstairs and used a few seconds in her bathroom to freshen up and recover from the embarrassment. She knew, though, that her mother would be giving her the third degree when she returned.

She plodded back downstairs with her backpack. Putting it down, she put on her coat while her parents watched. "I'll see you later," Sally said, giving both of them a kiss.

Mark held the door open for her, and they headed out to his car.

"Should I take mine?" Sally asked, seeing her parents waving from the front window.

"I can run you back here later." Mark saw her parents, too, and waved back. Sally almost melted on the ground. "They are such a cute couple," Mark said.

Sally laughed. "That's what they are probably saying about us just about now."

Mark turned red. "Um, well, um…"

Sally shook it off. "Forget about it. Let's take your car. At this point, I don't care what they think," though she didn't really believe those words as they exited her mouth.

Chapter Thirty-Four

Back at the police station, Sally and Mark stopped in to Finnegan's office.

He was on the phone when they walked in, but he motioned them to sit down across from him.

"Yes, great. Thanks for the fast help on this," Finnegan said, putting down the phone.

It may be the 21st Century, but Finnegan still had an old-fashioned corded phone on his desk. Sally thought it looked like it had been there since the building was built. She probably wasn't wrong, she thought.

Finnegan scribbled some notes and then looked up.

"That was the bank manager in town," he explained.

Sally leaned forward.

"You got his bank records already?" she asked.

Finnegan frowned, looking over at Mark.

Mark went red.

"Sorry, boss. You did say we wanted Sally's help…" he began.

"But not give her all the information," Finnegan replied, his voice tight.

Mark shrugged.

Sally thought Finnegan might say something else or admonish his employee in front of her, but luckily, he turned back to her.

"Yes, they are emailing them over now. I can't wait to see what they reveal," he said, grinning.

A ping from his computer made him turn to the keyboard.

He typed in what must be his password and double-clicked.

He began scanning, while Sally and Mark leaned forward.

Sally wished she had X-ray vision at that moment to read what Finnegan was seeing.

"Aha," he said.

"Wow," he added.

"What? What?" Sally cried, almost waiting to jump across the desk.

Finnegan stopped reading and turned his monitor around for Sally and Mark to see.

Sally quickly scanned the screen.

Gilbert's bank balance was larger than any she'd ever seen, well, private bank accounts at least. She was in finance in Atlanta, and those corporate balances were insane.

"But he was just a librarian," Mark said, stating the obvious.

"So where did this money come from?" Finnegan asked.

He scrolled through.

"There are large payments coming in regularly."

"From where?" Sally asked.

"Looks like from a foreign bank account, but I'm not sure. I'll have to check with the bank manager."

Sally sat back.

"But what does this all mean?" she asked, thinking aloud.

"Someone paid him to kill," Finnegan said.

Sally shrugged. "Well, it does look like someone was paying him for something. His librarian salary was not that much."

"No, I would guess it wouldn't be. The infusion of cash seems to explain a lot. I know he's always been a smart dresser, but turned even more luxurious over the last, let me see, well yeah it does seem like the last year or so. I just thought he got great bargains," Sally replied, not too convinced about her own conclusions.

"Aren't we all jumping to conclusions?" Mark asked, "Maybe he got an inheritance."

"Well, the money was coming from somewhere," Finnegan replied, not too helpfully.

"But how does this tie into Finnegan?" Sally asked.

"He's involved in this somehow. Roy wouldn't lie about him seeing Randall and Gilbert together in your back hallway."

Sally had a light go off in her head. Her thought for a second about how this was all connected, but she hoped her conclusion wasn't true.

"Sally, what do you think?" Mark asked, pulling her out of her woolgathering.

"Why don't you interview Wentworth and see what he has to say about the money going into Gilbert's account?" she suggested.

"You think he was the one paying Gilbert?" Mark asked.

"Well, that's what it looks like."

"But why did Gilbert die?" Sally asked, thinking she knew the answer to her own question.

Finnegan tapped the desk, "He somehow knew it was all going to come out and couldn't take it. If Gilbert was poisoning people with aspirin, he was paid to do it, so there is a mastermind behind it all. At the moment, this looks like Randall Wentworth."

* * *

Sally was back in the anteroom, pen and paper poised, as she saw the door of the interrogation room open. Detective Finnegan was already sitting there looking like he was ready to pounce.

Mark Soder led Randall Wentworth in. They were followed by a short, thin man in a three-piece double-breasted suit. Sally noted the pinstripes on the charcoal fabric.

Almost an attorney cliché, she thought. She assumed this was the all-powerful lawyer from Little Rock. She hated him already. Though that made her think of her mother again, and her saying that 'hate was a very strong word.'

Randall Wentworth had agreed to allow her to listen in. He had apparently said he had nothing to hide, and if Sally wanted entertainment, she could get it.

Sally thought he had a lot to hide, and she was wondering how much of that would come out in this session. Hopefully, it would be the one and only, but Sally wasn't really that optimistic that would be the case.

Mark Soder started the recording device, with Finnegan noting who was present. From that, Sally learned the Little Rock lawyer was named David O'Malley. That immediately reminded her of poor Jim O'Sullivan, from her fated river cruise.

"Detective," O'Malley began, "I am outraged by this questioning and am currently in contact with the Attorney General's office in Little Rock to stop it immediately."

"Oh, give it up. I am a police officer in this county and have legal reason enough to question your client. If you'd like this information splashed all over the local rag, be my guest," Finnegan barked in reply.

Wow, the testosterone was strong in that room, Sally noted to herself, still surprised by Finnegan's words and tone. He definitely wasn't playing games here. O'Malley leaned over and whispered into his client's ear. Wentworth shrugged.

"Fine, but keep it short," O'Malley said, pulling out his notebook and placing his cell phone face up on it as if the governor might call any minute.

What an ass, Sally quickly concluded.

"So, as I told Randall already…" Finnegan began.

O'Malley put up his hand. "Please refer to my client as Mr. Wentworth or Attorney Wentworth."

Sally felt ill. This was getting ridiculous with the silly power plays, as if Finnegan would be swayed by them.

"Fine. As I told Mr. Wentworth already, we have a witness who places him at Sally's Smasher bar on New Year's Eve. He was seen together with the deceased Gilbert Rock coming out of the owner's office. Later that evening, Ms. Witherspoon found a large bottle of aspirin on her desk, along with this note."

He held up the paper with the cut-out letters. "As your client has no doubt informed you, we are currently investigating several deaths in town due to aspirin poisoning. This puts him in the middle of it all."

Randall Wentworth remained silent while his attorney was sending daggers to Detective Finnegan with his eyes. "As I learned from my client, there are no cameras in that hallway, so there is no proof of this. It seems, Detective, it is my client's word against the witness's. And I know who will win that contest," O'Malley declared smugly.

Sally felt like she needed to shower after listening to this guy. She was glad she was not in the room with them.

Finnegan didn't immediately respond. Instead, he pulled out a stack of paper from the folder in front of him and slid it across the table.

Neither attorney looked down at them. "What's this?" O'Malley asked. Apparently, Wentworth wasn't planning to utter a peep.

"These are bank statements belonging to Gilbert Rock indicating large monthly payments into his account over the past year," Finnegan explained.

That got a reaction from Wentworth. He shrugged, and his mouth opened. "So?" Wentworth replied, looking at his attorney.

O'Malley looked across at Finnegan and sneered.

"This is proof you were paying Gilbert to kill those people," Finnegan accused.

Now both attorneys laughed. "Oh, come on, Detective. Is that all you have?" O'Malley stated when they had finished laughing.

"I will connect them to your client. At the moment, I have the FBI in Washington investigating the source of these payments, which came from offshore bank accounts," Finnegan replied smugly.

Sally was enjoying the entertainment, but she wasn't sure where Finnegan was going. Did he really have FBI contacts in Washington? And could they really trace the payments?

And when had Finnegan contacted the FBI? She had just been in his office. There was only a few minutes when he had shooed Sally and Mark out to print out the bank statements, he had told them.

She guessed he was keeping his additional investigation close to his chest. Maybe he had used the time to call someone in Washington.

She considered he might know someone there, but she had never heard him talk about it before. The deaths a year ago in town hadn't needed anything of that sort, and anyway, she and Finnegan weren't the best of friends, and it's probably not something he would just drop into conversation.

"FBI?" Wentworth squeaked, his mouth apparently dry.

Gotcha, Sally thought. O'Malley tapped Wentworth's shoulder, who said no more.

"Do you really want us to believe you have contacts in Washington, Detective? That is ridiculous. If anyone has contacts, it's me. This questioning is over," O'Malley declared, getting up.

Wentworth went to stand when Finnegan said, "Sit back down, or everything I know will be in every newspaper I can get it in."

Sally didn't think that was really possible, but she was seeing a new side of the detective. Who knew what he was capable of at the moment? She could feel the tension in the room through the one-way glass. There was a standoff for a couple of minutes. Wentworth didn't sit back down, but O'Malley also did nothing, just standing, staring at Detective Finnegan.

Finally, he went over to the table and sat back down, motioning for Wentworth to do the same.

"I will be keeping your client here in the jail until I get the information from Washington. If it turns out the money came through him, I will be putting him away for a long time, and I don't think any of your contacts will be able to help, Attorney O'Malley," Finnegan declared, his voice rigid.

O'Malley looked like he was going to burst a gasket. His face went red. He took a couple of deep breaths when his phone rang.

Looking down, he smiled. "Ah, just the call I was waiting for," he said, "May I?"

Finnegan nodded.

Sally wished she could see his face at the moment.

"Good afternoon, Governor," O'Malley began, a smile on his face.

Sally's stomach dropped. This was it. Finnegan tapped his pen on the table. Sally couldn't take her eyes off the Little Rock attorney. As O'Malley listened, his smile left his face, and it turned into a frown.

"But, I don't..." he said, apparently cut off.

Sally felt like he was trying his utmost not to yell into the phone. That wouldn't help his political situation at all, she thought.

"Yes, sir. I understand," he said finally, taking the phone off his ear and disconnecting the call.

Wentworth looked at him, and O'Malley shook his head. "Well, fuck," Wentworth roared. Finally, some emotion out of the man.

"What was it the governor wanted, Mr. O'Malley?" Finnegan asked quite self-satisfyingly.

"It seems he got a call from the FBI in Washington. He told me that they said they were assisting you in this matter and they asked him not to interfere," O'Malley said.

Sally felt his reluctance to speak about any of this. Of course, he and Wentworth had expected the governor to call and force Finnegan to release Wentworth immediately. Sally felt glee as she realized this was definitely not to be the case.

"Oh darn," Finnegan said.

Sally burst out laughing. Apparently, it was so loud that all four men turned toward the window. She stifled it.

Mark Soder hadn't said a word the entire time. Sally couldn't wait to get alone with him to find out what he thought of the whole situation.

"Now what?" O'Malley said.

"Detective Soder will be bringing Mr. Wentworth to one of our cozy jail cells to wait until I get the information I need. You are welcome to stay in town, and I will notify you about any further developments."

Sally could tell he was loving this.

O'Malley slapped the table. "Fine," he said, getting up and swiftly walking out.

Wentworth looked frozen in place as he watched his attorney desert him.

Mark Soder got up and led Wentworth out.

Sally waited a few seconds for the footsteps to quiet down before she slid out of her chair and over to the interrogation room to pick over the carcass of the conversation.

Chapter Thirty-Five

"What's the reason? I want to know," Finnegan asked, shaking his head.

Sally had been thinking about this for a while. What was the reason for all these killings?

She had come to a conclusion, though that conclusion didn't really make sense.

Sally sighed. "I think there is no reason, beyond simple cruelty," she declared.

Mark Soder frowned. "Cruelty is never simple, Sally," he replied.

Finnegan leaned forward. "If it is cruelty, that just doesn't work for me. There has to be a reason behind the cruelty. I can't let this case go if I don't understand the why."

Sally nodded. "I know, Detective. But maybe it's just a mean streak, a troubled past that turned Randall cruel."

"And Gilbert. I still can't imagine him poisoning the people."

Sally had been thinking about this as well, ever since Gilbert was found dead in his cell. "To be honest, I always wondered how he got the seemingly nice clothes and colognes. It seems someone was paying him for something, and that's how he could afford it."

"But why Gilbert…" Mark added.

"Maybe Gilbert was made to steal, or who knows what. Or he was being blackmailed." Sally thought back to the events of a year ago and what Jeff Bartholomew was made to do because of blackmail.

"Randall will talk," Finnegan concluded.

Sally wasn't so sure, so she folded her hands and just smiled. "You'll figure it out, Detective."

"Definitely," Finnegan replied.

"What's next?"

"Well, I should have the bank information soon from the FBI. Then I'll have him."

"But you said you wanted to know the why. Do you think he'll tell you?" she asked.

"I'll get it out of him. I will," he said, pounding his fist on the table, making Sally and Soder jump.

Sally got up. "I have to get back to my parents. Let me know what you find out."

"You too, Ms. Witherspoon," Finnegan retorted. He knew her too well. She wasn't going to just go home and talk to her parents.

She knew exactly who to talk to next.

But first, she did want to check on her parents. Their presence in town worried her, and she wanted to make sure they stayed alive, even if Gilbert was dead and Randall was behind bars. She wasn't taking any chances.

* * *

"Please," Sally said, her eyes filling with tears.

Both her parents shook their heads vigorously. "We are not going anywhere, young lady," her mother declared, making Sally feel like a six-year-old.

Sally took a deep breath to not say something she would regret, or worse, yell at her parents. "I am so thankful for the new car and your visit. But I just worry so much about you. It would be so great if you went back to Oklahoma until this is all sorted out," she pleaded.

Her father chuckled. "You mean, so you have more time to sort this all out?"

"Well, I…" she began.

Her mother put her hand on Sally's and rubbed it. "We love you so much and want to spend time with you. We'll be fine here, but…" At this point, her mother looked over at her father, who nodded. "… we'll go home tomorrow. It's a bit late to start the journey now, and we can have one final dinner together before we head out around lunchtime."

"OK, but you promise me you will stay in the house the whole time until you leave?"

Both parents nodded.

"I've got to see someone to try to get to the bottom of all this. It won't take me long," Sally explained.

"That's my ace detective," her father said, getting up and coming over to give her a big hug.

This was not going to be easy.

Chapter Thirty-Six

Sally knew exactly who to talk to next to get the most information in the shortest amount of time. If Bethany Wells, the town gossip, didn't know what was going on with Randall and Gilbert, then nobody did.

Bethany lived outside town in a secluded wooded area south of Berry Springs. As Sally jumped in her new SUV and sped down Route 10 toward Bethany's log cabin, she began to sweat.

As she passed several streets, she realized that was where she and Magda had been held the year before. They both had been lucky to get out alive. Sally never wanted to relive the feeling of being tied up with seemingly no way to get out.

She tried to brush those thoughts aside as she turned right onto Bethany's street and headed to the end. Pulling up, she enjoyed her view of Bethany's home. It was a log cabin, but a fancy one.

Like the Arnolds, Bethany was from one of the oldest and wealthiest families in town.

Her home was across Silver Lake from where Jeff Bartholomew, the high school teacher and coach, lived. Bethany was the assistant at the same school. With her wealth, Sally always wondered why Bethany worked. Actually, she didn't really wonder.

Bethany's side hustle was gossip. Being at the center of the high school definitely provided her with a lot of gossip about what was going on in town. Sometimes, Bethany was just incorrigible. But that was exactly the reason Sally decided to visit her.

Bethany probably already knew about Gilbert's death, knew that Randall was arrested, and probably had as much information as if she had been in the anteroom with Sally.

Usually, Sally tried to avoid chatting with Bethany too much. Anything you say can and will be used against you in the court of gossip. And that was the last thing Sally needed. Although she had to admit to herself that she also loved a bit of gossip, she tried to keep most of it to herself. Being a bartender meant you heard and saw a lot, but it would scare her guests away if she blurted it all out around town to whoever would listen.

Sally jumped out of her car and went over to the door. She had called ahead to make sure Bethany was home. Bethany had been as excited to hear from Sally as Sally had expected.

"Oh yes, come right over. I'll put a fresh pot of coffee on," Bethany had said breathlessly into the phone.

Sally didn't even have to knock on the door. Bethany had obviously been watching through the curtain as Sally made her way up the granite path to the door.

"New car?" Bethany asked.

Sally nodded. "You notice everything," Sally said. "It was a gift from my parents."

"What will you do with Gladys?" Bethany asked as she led Sally into the living room with a glorious view of the lake. The question that Sally really didn't want to think about now.

"I don't know. I was thinking of keeping her as a memento. You know, park it next to the house," Sally replied, knowing full well that really wasn't an option.

"It's such a classic. It must be worth something," Bethany offered.

"I doubt it," Sally replied, planting herself on Bethany's couch.

"That's not really why you're here, is it?" Bethany asked, smiling.

Sally grinned. "No."

"Would you like something to drink?" Bethany asked, standing next to the couch. She hadn't yet taken her seat.

"You mentioned coffee on the phone. That would be great," Sally replied.

Bethany nodded and headed into the kitchen.

Sally had only been to Bethany's house a couple of times. Bethany may be the town gossip, but she kept to herself, obviously not wanting people to find out too much about her.

Sally thought this was odd, but then again, she knew that people who expect or worse demand certain things from others rarely follow their own rules. One of the many dichotomies of life.

That reminded her of her boss in Atlanta, who she only thought of on a rare occasion. The toxic boss was always extremely upset if someone was late for a meeting by even a minute, yet let people often wait or, worse, sweat it out, 30 minutes or more before joining.

But she wasn't there to think about her Atlanta life, either.

Bethany returned with two steaming mugs of coffee and a plate of sugar cookies on a decorative silver tray.

"How lovely," Sally noted, rubbing her hand over the tray.

"Yes, one of the souvenirs from my travels. This one is from India, and it cost a pretty penny," Bethany beamed.

Well, la-di-da, Sally almost blurted out, reminding her of mostly unpleasant Amy Wong from her boat tour. Sally had to admit to herself that Amy grew on her throughout the trip, even if she talked down to most people like she owned the world.

Bethany placed the tray on the lovely wood coffee table carved from a thick slice of oak tree. She sat herself down across from Sally and leaned back. Taking a sugar cookie, Sally dunked it in her coffee, giving her a few seconds to think about her first question. She chewed the cookie and swallowed. "So I guess you've heard the latest," Sally began, assuming it all.

Bethany nodded. " I know everything that's going on in town. All its secrets," Bethany replied, grinning widely.

Hopefully not every secret, Sally considered. "The biggest question is why Randall and Gilbert would do all this to their supposed friends."

Sally wasn't holding back. Bethany probably knew all the details anyway, and it had already been several weeks since Belle's death after the Thanksgiving dinner. She needed to get to the bottom of it all. Though wasn't that what she had been telling herself since then? Sally was not a patient person.

"Randall has a cruel streak, doesn't he?" Bethany replied, more as a statement than a question.

"What do you mean?" Sally asked, wishing she had taken her notebook with her. She had had it out just before she left to see Bethany, but had forgotten to put it back into her backpack.

Was it the beginning of forgetfulness? She would be 60 that year, something a large part of her was dreading. Then again, her parents were in their 80s, and both fit as a fiddle.

"Well, he is everyone's lawyer, and he acts like he is doing you a favor by providing you services, rather than the fact you are paying him a hefty fee for whatever you need. I find that man dreadful," Bethany explained, admitting a truth she really let slip.

"But if he has all that money, why would he spend it paying Gilbert?" Sally replied, taking another sip of coffee.

"You think that man would do his own dirty work?" Bethany retorted.

"Good point. He wouldn't want to be caught doing something directly. But if he was paying Gilbert, why would he want Belle or Momma Arnold, or Dr. Wiggams, for that matter, dead?" Sally asked.

Bethany got up. "I need something stronger to help me think," she explained, heading over to a large wall unit with glass doors. Sally saw a few crystal carafes filled with dark liquids.

Sally watched as Bethany opened one of the glass doors, took out a small crystal goblet, and poured herself what Sally guessed was bourbon. Bethany took a small sip before returning to the couch.

"Ah, that's better," Bethany declared.

Sally checked her phone. It was just after 4 p.m., not too early for a drink. Well, for her, maybe, but she was at Bethany's house trying to get something out of her, so she wasn't going to comment on the drink or the pre-cocktail hour it was imbibed.

"He once told me, or rather admitted to me, that he hated getting older and he hated seeing old people suffer in rest homes and the like," Bethany began.

"But what does that have to do with the deaths?"

"Well, I did say he seems cruel, but maybe it's his way of absolving people of their suffering before it happens."

"That seems like a weird thing to do," Sally admitted.

"Randall thinks he is all-powerful and tries to pretend he runs the town. Oh, who are we kidding? He knows so much about people and has so much money, he is controlling the town. If something upsets him, he just picks up the phone to call the mayor or the chief."

Sally made a mental note to talk to Tim Sanford and get his real take on Randall. Tim may be police chief now, but he and Sally were good friends ever since she had moved to town. His now deceased father had been Sally's next-door neighbor, and she always tried to look out for him as he became frailer every year.

As she was contemplating this, her phone rang. She looked down and saw it was her mother.

Her heart skipped a beat.

Chapter Thirty-Seven

"Oh, hi, Sally, how are you?" Ugh, the "something happened" voice. "Mom, what's going on?" Sally said matter-of-factly, even if her voice was trembling.

Bethany was frozen, staring at her.

"Well, I, well, your father went out for a walk and said he would be back a half hour ago."

She told them to stay in the house and lock all the doors and windows. But she wasn't going to yell at her mother now about that.

She checked her phone. It was coming up on 5 p.m., and looking outside, she could see it was getting dark. It had started snowing while she had been chatting with Bethany.

"You know, Dad. He loves his walks," Sally said, trying to sound more cheerful than she felt.

"It's snowing, Sally. I'm starting to worry," her mother admitted, something she rarely did.

"I'll be home as soon as I can, Mom."

"What's wrong, Sally?" Bethany asked as Sally put the phone away.

"My father went for a walk, as he loves to do, but he still isn't back. It's cold and snowy outside. My mother is worried…" Sally began.

"And of course, you are too," Bethany replied.

Sally nodded, a tear forming in her left eye.

"What can I do to help?" Bethany asked.

"I'm going to head home now and see if Magda can help. The bar will open soon, but Annette should be there. You stay here nice and safe. Thanks for the coffee and delicious cookies," Sally rattled off the words as if she was on autopilot.

They hugged, and Sally ran outside and ripped open the door to the SUV.

On the way home, she frantically called Magda, who would be at the bar ready to open.

"Hey, boss. Where are you?" Magda asked, adding, "Are you driving and talking?"

"The new car has hands-free," Sally said. "But that's not why I'm calling." She quickly filled in Magda on the events of the day and that she needed her help to try and find her father.

"Oh, Sally. I'll be right there. Jeff's with me, so he can help. Annette and Zeke can handle the bar tonight."

Sally could hear Magda talking in the background. "Of course, we're there for you," she heard Annette yell.

Her friends. Every time something like this happened, she felt blessed to have them.

Magda came back on the line. "I'll be at your house in 15 minutes."

"Thanks so much, Magda," Sally said, tapping the touch screen on the dashboard to end the call.

She flew up Route 10 and only slowed when she passed the Berry Springs sign at the edge of town. The snow wasn't too heavy, and her 4×4 was the perfect vehicle to be driving in these somewhat slippery conditions.

She was home in no time, and she peeled into the driveway, slamming on the brakes in a car chase maneuver. Her new SUV stopped just in time behind her parents' car. Gladys would have gone careening into the back of it. Adrenaline was pumping through her body as she jumped out of the truck and headed toward the house. Her mother was waiting on the porch, and she threw her arms around Sally.

"I'm so worried," her mother whispered.

Sally was thinking it too, but didn't verbalize it. And if her mother admitted being worried, then this was a very serious situation.

Hopefully, her father wasn't the next Senior Slayer victim. Though if he were, Wentworth and Gilbert had nothing to do with it. Gilbert was dead, and Wentworth was still in jail.

Sally took off her winter coat and accessories, led her mother into the kitchen, and sat her down at the table. "I'll make us some tea," Sally offered.

Her mother nodded.

Sally put on the kettle and sat down with her mom to wait for it to boil. "So when did he leave for his walk?" Sally asked.

Her mother looked at her, her mouth open as if she were paralyzed.

"Mom?" Sally asked, taking her hand, which felt cold.

"Oh, I'm sorry. I'm just terrified." Stiffening, she raised herself in the seat and took a deep breath. "Well, he left just after you did. I told him not to go, that you would be worried, but you know how your father is," her mother explained.

Sally nodded as her heart sank. That was a long walk to be outside in the cold, and now with the snow.

"Was he properly bundled up?" Sally asked, now sounding like her mother.

"Yes. He was wearing a heavy sweater, winter coat, his thick boots, gloves, hat, and scarf. You know the dark blue one I knitted for him when you were young," her mother choked up at the end and put her head in her hands.

The kettle screamed, making both women jump. Sally took a deep breath and got up quickly to make them both a cup of tea, placing the mugs on the table.

The doorbell rang, and Sally was glad to find Magda and Jeff at the door. She led them into the kitchen. When Sally's mother saw the visitors, she wiped her face and put on her "everything's fine" look.

"We're here to help, Mrs. Witherspoon," Magda said.

"Please, call me Dorothy," Sally's mother replied.

"I don't ever think I'll get used to that, but I'll try," Magda replied. That got a light laugh out of all of them.

"What can we do?" Jeff asked.

Sally looked down at her mother. "Where was Dad headed for his walk?"

Her mother took a sip of tea, and this seemed to lift her spirits. Or maybe it was the fact that there were helpers there.

Sally hoped he hadn't wanted to hike in the woods. That could be extremely dangerous in these conditions, even if he did have the proper footwear on.

"Just into town, he said. You know, to the other end of town and back," her mother explained.

"That's a relief. It shouldn't be too hard to find him," Sally replied, trying to sound more confident than she felt.

"Maybe he's fallen. Oh, I hope he's OK," her mother said, sniffling, but holding it together for appearance's sake.

"We'll head out now, and I know we'll find him Mrs, um, Dorothy," Magda said.

"Yes, let's go," Sally added, leaning down to give her mother a kiss.

"Now you call me the minute you find him, dear," her mother ordered.

"Of course," Sally replied as she walked to the hall to get ready again for the winter weather.

She put on every cold-weather thing she had and, this time, even her winter boots. She hadn't needed them to drive to Bethany's.

The three headed out and decided to walk into town so they could scour every inch of the streets as they went along. If her father had fallen, it was now dark, and the slow pace would make it easier to spot him.

Unfortunately, Sally knew her father preferred dark colors, so there would be no bright orange jacket or the like to alert them.

They headed down Sally's street, Maple, and turned right on Oak, the main street through town.

They walked slowly, stopping at every house and bush to check for her father.

"Dad?" Sally yelled every few feet, while Magda and Jeff called, "Mr. Witherspoon?"

"I almost yelled 'Dad' too," Magda admitted, lightening everyone's mood.

The walk wasn't easy as the snow had started to accumulate on the roads and sidewalks. The small town of Berry Springs didn't do a very good job of clearing snow and ice, so it could be treacherous. Sally was glad she was wearing her boots and noted that her companions were properly dressed as well. You had to be ready for all kinds of weather in the Ozarks.

They headed further down Oak and reached the town square. It was really dark with only a few streetlights to help light their way.

Sally looked over at the main town building and thought of Randall Wentworth inside. She even considered heading back in to file a missing person's report on her father, but she decided to first try to find him with her friend's help. If that didn't work in the next hour or so, she would break down and inform the police. Her mother wouldn't want the "scandal," but in the end, that might be the best and fastest way to find her father, alive.

That last thought gave her a punch in the gut.

"Sally, are you OK?" Jeff asked.

"Sorry, just really worried," Sally admitted, something that was as difficult for her to do as her parents.

Magda touched her arm in solidarity.

They reached the end of Oak and hadn't seen a soul, let alone her father. They kept calling and calling his name, but no response. And the weather and temperature was keeping everyone indoors.

They turned right on Fern Street, thinking he probably headed that way rather than left and back around on South Street, past St. Luke's Methodist.

If they didn't find him by the time they got back to Sally's, they decided to head to South Street and look there.

Sally pulled out her phone and tried to read the time. 6:15 p.m. They had been walking for a long time, and still no George Witherspoon.

Then Sally had a thought. Maybe he had stopped in at Betty Jo's Diner for something hot. Sally knew they didn't close until nine, and while they had walked past the diner, they had only glanced in, thinking her father had been walking and fell.

Sally related what she was thinking to her friends.

"Good idea," Magda agreed.

They headed back to Oak St. and picked up the pace as they walked back to the town center. As they passed The Nutmeg Café, the door opened, and George Witherspoon came out.

Sally screamed, tears running down her face.

She ran to him and gave him a big hug. "Oh, Daddy, I'm so happy to see you!"

Magda and Jeff came over, and they all hugged.

George pulled away, a bit confused. "What's going on, dear?"

"Mom was worried because you didn't return when you said you would," Sally explained, adding, "'We've been scouring town for you. And I told you both to stay inside, but you didn't listen, which isn't surprising."

Her father chuckled. "Oh, I'm sorry. I know I should have stayed at home, but I was getting antsy and decided to go for a walk. I lost track of time and left my phone at your house. I thought you'd just assume I stopped somewhere for a coffee or a snack," he said.

"You know, Mom. She expects everyone to do exactly as they've said," Sally said, her brow furrowed.

Her father frowned. "You're right," he concluded.

Sally called her mother with the good news as they walked back to Sally's house. "Oh, thank you, Sally. I'm so relieved. That man should be more careful. He knows how I worry, sometimes," her mother said.

Sally knew her mother worried more than sometimes, but would rarely, if ever, show it, even in front of her daughter. Her mother would never admit to weakness.

The group headed back to Sally's Victorian for a quiet meal indoors.

As they ate, Sally wondered if they would get to the bottom of the mystery. What would the FBI find out, and would Randall Wentworth go to jail?

Chapter Thirty-Eight

The next day was a whirlwind of activity. It was only the third day of the year, but Sally felt like it had been at least a month or more with all that was going on. She hoped the crimes would be solved that week and not later. She was glad her parents were away from Berry Springs, but the whole town was tense as the deaths hung over them. And the revelations surrounding Gilbert Rock and Randall Wentworth were slowly making their way through the small-town grapevine, edged on by Bethany Wells and her gossiping.

After having seen her parents safely off back to Oklahoma, Sally had gotten a call from Detective Finnegan. He filled her in on what the FBI had discovered. As they both expected, the accounts that had paid Gilbert Rock the huge sums of money belonged to Randall Wentworth through numerous subsidiaries and shell companies. It had taken a lot of digging, but the FBI had come through.

Finnegan told her he would be questioning Randall that afternoon about the money allegations. That gave Sally time to check in on the one person that might be able to bring the terrible days to a close: Wentworth's son, James.

A year before, Randall had told Sally a touching story about James getting back on his feet after his mother had died. Looking back, Sally hadn't quite bought it that Randall really cared. She had said nothing at the time because every conversation she had had brought her closer to finding Bill Arnold's killer.

She knew from her own experience and from conversations with others that Randall and James were not that close, though Randall pretended differently.

James was in his last year of the local community college and planned to attend the University of Arkansas. Randall claimed he was doing pre-law, looking to follow in his father's footsteps, but James had told her he was more interested in history and becoming a teacher.

The fact that James was gay irked Randall, Sally knew. Though he pretended that wasn't the case. Randall Wentworth was all about appearances, and having a gay son did not fit with his idea of the 'proper' life. Thinking about that made Sally sick to her stomach. Her gut really did seem to know what was going on.

James worked part-time at the local car dealer, and that is where Sally was headed after she finished her coffee. She made herself several cups each morning, and she was not about to leave the house until she finished every drop.

Looking around the kitchen, there was a lot to clean up. Her mother had made a hearty breakfast, and Sally had persuaded her parents to leave before her mother could spend time cleaning up. They couldn't get out of town fast enough for her. If they were not in Berry Springs, they were safe, she told herself, though she was still a bit tense waiting for them to call or text that they had gotten home safely.

It wasn't that far, but at their age, they often stopped for at least one break along the way.

Sally downed the last of her coffee and headed upstairs to shower and change.

Once that was done, came the hard part. She slowly walked outside and was hit by a wall of Arctic air. She smelled what she felt was snow in the air, though it was only cloudy and dreary at the moment. The perfect atmosphere for Gladys's going away.

She pulled her heavy coat tighter around her and headed down the steps and over to the carport. She stopped and sighed.

It was time for Gladys to leave her. Though she was still considering keeping her as a memento, Sally knew she would just rust away. And the last thing Sally needed was to slide off the road in winter because of her ancient car.

Gladys was her pretense for having a chat with James at the dealership. She had called ahead and knew he would be there. While her parents had bought her a new car, which was the original reason she was going to see James, she still had Gladys. Maybe he would give her a good deal on the old Datsun, or maybe he knew someone that was looking for a collector's item, her way of saying old clunker.

She opened the door and peered inside. She had cleared out most of the stuff in the car with her father's help and put it in her new SUV. That car was parked partly on the lawn so she could get Gladys out. She went to the back of the car and checked the trunk, nothing there.

Then she went through the glove compartment and checked under the seats for any last bits.

As she shone her phone's flashlight into the dark recesses underneath the seats, her eye caught a bit of paper. She slowly pulled it out from under one of the set rails.

As she read it, it brought tears to her eyes.

It was a rock concert ticket from 1983, her freshman year of college, when she had met Bill Arnold for the first time. They had quickly become best friends, and it was Bill who had helped her start the bar. It had been almost a year-and-a-half, yet so much still reminded her of him.

She tucked it in a small pocket in her backpack and planted herself in the driver's seat for the last time. She sniffled as she backed out, but tried to quickly clear her mind for the talk with James ahead. She wanted to sell Gladys for a good price, but she also wanted to enlist James' help in getting his father to confess to paying Gilbert and planning all the murders. Gilbert, it looked like, was the Senior Slayer as the press called him, but Randall Wentworth was the planner and payer.

The dealership was just south of town, not far from Sally's bar. That was where she would be heading after listening in on the Wentworth questioning. Magda had texted her that morning to see if she was OK to work, but Sally was desperate to get back to the bar and its atmosphere to take her mind off the happenings and hopefully give her that creative boost to tie everything together. The biggest question on her mind was why Randall Wentworth would plan all these deaths of the elderly. That just didn't make any sense. As long as she had known him, he had had a purpose and reason for doing everything she felt. Yet the deaths of Momma Arnold, Belle, and Dr. Wiggams seemed almost random. Dr. Wiggams had been pushed, not poisoned with aspirin, so that added another twist. The only thing the three had in common was that they were getting on in years.

At that, Sally laughed. Only Belle and Dr. Wiggams would have admitted to that; Momma Arnold had always claimed she was still a spring chicken if asked.

As Sally pulled into the lot, James waved to her. She saw him taping price sheets to a couple of windows.

She parked Gladys as close to the door as she could. Checking her phone, she saw it was just above freezing, and snow was predicted that afternoon. Good thing she now had the SUV from her parents to navigate the winter weather.

Getting out of her car was slow going. Gladys, oh Gladys, she thought. Come on, Sally, pull yourself together.

"Hi, Sally," James called in greeting. She put on a big smile and followed him inside. She couldn't look back. "Want some coffee?" James led her to his desk in the back of the showroom.

Since Berry Springs was so small, the dealer sold multiple makes and models. Sally saw the same model SUV she had gotten from her parents parked near James' desk.

Sally sat down and shook her head. "I think I've had enough coffee this morning, thanks," she replied, placing her backpack on her lap. She gingerly put the car keys on the desk.

"So you're looking to sell the old clunker," James said as undiplomatically as he could muster, it seemed.

"Yes," Sally replied, stiffly. "I was going to buy a new car, but as I mentioned on the phone, my parents took care of that as a late Christmas gift."

Or maybe it was an early 60th birthday gift. She hadn't thought of that up to that point. She would have to ask them about that.

"Well, let's see what we can do for you. The car isn't really worth too much, to be honest, but on the other hand, some consider it a classic. I'm sure we'll get a good deal for you," James explained, smiling. He was such a nice lad, the opposite of his father.

"I've done a bit of research online and asked around since you first called me about seeing the car. There are a couple people in the county that are interested. If you want, we can handle all that for you, and we'll just take a 10% commission."

Sally considered for a moment. The car wasn't going to get her much anyway, and James assisting would help her put Gladys behind her. If she had to handle all the showings and paperwork herself, she couldn't be sure of her emotional state. This was something she didn't want others to see. It was just a car, Sally kept reminding herself, but it had been with her for a long, long time.

"Yes, that would be great, James. Where do I sign?"

James pulled out a stack of paperwork from a folder on his desk. Looking through each page, he marked where Sally needed to initial or sign. At the last page, he added his own John Hancock before passing the stack across the desk to Sally.

She took it in her hands and sighed. As she went through the paperwork and signed, she did feel a bit of relief. This was a tough decision she had made, but it needed to be done. Getting rid of the old allowed space for the new.

She pushed the paperwork back to James and topped it with the car keys.

"Anything else I can do for you, Sally?"

Sally's reputation preceded her, and she knew he didn't mean something to do with cars. She chuckled. "Is it that obvious?"

James laughed. "Well, to be honest, I'm glad you came in with the car. I'm worried about my father, even if we don't have much contact these days," James confessed. "He won't tell me what's going on, and now I find out he's in jail and being questioned."

Sally thought he would have noticed his father not at home, then Sally remembered James lived with his boyfriend, Michael, in Jefferson, where James attended community college. Sally knew the fact that James was gay was just one of the reasons Randall rarely mentioned him.

Sally filled him in on all the information she had, including the arrogant lawyer from Little Rock with his so-called connections. She didn't hold back, including the latest from the FBI. James' mouth dropped, and there was a lot of "What? No!" as Sally related everything she knew up to that point.

"But why?" James asked when Sally had finished.

"That's the biggest question, isn't it?"

James shook his head. "From what I could tell, Dad loves the Arnolds and is pretty close to a lot of people in town."

Sally didn't want to add salt to the wound, but she felt Randall Wentworth was more interested in people's money and the power he had over them than anything else.

Which, in the end probably was somehow connected to why he had them killed. If that's what it was. Nothing was 100% at that point.

Randall also may have pushed Dr. Wiggams himself. His law office was on the town square right next to the main town building that housed the police and coroner, among other town offices and services.

"What will happen to Dad?" James asked.

"Well, he needs to confess. All evidence points to him, and as hard as this may be to hear, he is guilty," Sally concluded, perhaps a bit prematurely. She believed people were innocent until proven guilty in a court of law, but it wasn't looking too good for Randall. A part of her was gleeful with schadenfreude, she had to admit to herself.

"Oh, he'll never do that. He's got that hotshot lawyer from Little Rock representing him," James said.

"Well, our Detective Finnegan has one up on that hotshot lawyer with his own FBI connections. But in the end, shouldn't it be about proof and facts rather than who knows whom?" Sally asked, thinking aloud.

"Maybe someone else is behind it. I just can't believe Dad hated people enough to kill them, or rather to pay someone to kill them."

"It really looks like he did it, for reasons we have yet to discover," Sally said.

"So how can I help?"

"Maybe you can get him to confess or at least tell the police what he knows. I know you two are estranged, but he does seem to have a soft spot for you," Sally explained.

"Yes, somewhere inside that tough nut," James replied, shaking his head.

Sally didn't want to push him, but James' help may be the key to solving the whole mystery.

And Sally was not going to stop until she did.

Chapter Thirty-Nine

"What the heck are you doing here?" Randall barked as he walked into the interrogation room.

James was seated at the cold metal table, but didn't turn as his father arrived. "I want some answers," he replied just as loudly.

"OK, everyone, just calm down," Finnegan pleaded.

Sally laughed from her vantage point in the anteroom. Telling people to calm down usually got the exact opposite.

Randall took a seat across from his son, his lawyer taking the chair beside him. Finnegan sat down next to James. From the other room, Sally had a great view of Randall Wentworth, the main person in this investigation.

It had taken some pleading to get James to agree to come to the station, but he was as sickened as the rest of the town about the deaths, and even if his father was involved, he wanted to bring closure.

Sally had left Gladys at the car dealer and hoped James would sell it soon to a kind soul.

He drove them into town to the police station.

Sally had called ahead to alert Finnegan to what she had planned.

He hadn't been too happy that she didn't share her plan with him beforehand, but he also admitted that he hoped this would be the final straw in getting the facts out of Randall Wentworth.

The four men sat at the table, no one speaking.

Sally had her notebook and pen out, but they were lying ignored on the table next to her. She was perched on the edge of the stool, leaning as far toward the one-way mirror as she could without tipping over.

"Dad, why have you done all this?" James began, breaking the silence.

Randall leered at him across the table. "I've done nothing, son. I don't know what these gentlemen are talking about," Randall replied quietly.

Sally couldn't believe his gall. The proof was there that he had paid Gilbert Rock for the killings. He had somehow gotten Gilbert killed, probably to hide the crimes and keep him silent permanently. Now Randall was caught, and Sally couldn't see how he was going to get out of the situation. He may have his fancy lawyer who knew the governor, but Finnegan was like a bulldog who would get him eventually. And he had the FBI in Washington helping him.

"Yes, you are a perfect gentleman," James continued, "You know exactly what to do at all times. You control everyone. You make their wills. You have the power. Yeah, I've heard it all for years."

Randall slammed his fist on the table. Oh, good start, James got him to lose a bit of his perfect control.

"Don't you talk to me that way, boy," Randall yelled, starting to get up.

O'Malley put a hand on Randall's arm. That got him to sit back down. At least there was at least one adult in the room, Sally thought.

James wiggled in his chair. She wished she were in the room to help him work through the anger he must be feeling. She hoped he would be able to finally get through to Randall and get him to confess.

"Dad…" James began quietly.

Sally could feel the emotion through his voice, even if she was only listening through a speaker and could only see into the room and not feel the room in person, as it were.

Wentworth looked like he was about to speak, or yell, but O'Malley's hand on his shoulder kept him quiet.

"The evidence against you is pretty dramatic, so why hold out? I know you are upset that this has all come out, but isn't it time to give yourself up? Your name, our name, has always been so important to you. Don't you want to keep the reputation of being honest, speaking the truth, even if it means going to jail?" James continued with words that took Sally's breath away.

Wentworth's eyes went wide.

Sally could see that he was shocked that his son would stand up to him for once. He looked like he was either going to sock James or run out of the room. Neither would have helped his cause, which he seemed to realize himself.

There was silence in the room.

Sally was frozen in place, waiting for the next move, whoever would make it.

Finally, Wentworth spoke. It was a whisper, but it was powerful.

"My power in Berry Springs is everything, don't you see, boy? I need to maintain power."

"And that's the way to do it, by killing people?" James replied, his voice raised.

"Whatever it takes," Wentworth replied.

This got raised eyebrows from his attorney.

Sally could only imagine what Finnegan was thinking.

James really seemed to be getting through to his father.

"So you did kill all these people, Dad?" James asked, point-blank.

Randall cackled, which sent a shiver up Sally's spine.

She really thought he was about to confess, but maybe he was just playing games with them all.

Randall Wentworth must know his career was over, Sally thought. Finnegan had so much evidence against him. Why else would Randall pay Gilbert Rock if not for the deaths in town?

"You are too dumb to know why I did what I did, not that it had anything to do with the deaths," Wentworth stated matter-of-factly.

"Such a disgrace…" Randall added, glaring at his offspring. He really was playing games with them.

James stood up at that. "This is ridiculous. I don't know why I came. He hates me. He hates me for who I am. He hates that I don't want to become a lawyer…" James was raging.

Randall turned red in the face. He looked like he might implode, but he kept quiet.

"Burn in hell," James screamed, tearing open the door and running out.

Sally rushed after him. She caught up to him as he threw open the main door and gulped some fresh air. "James, James," she cried, taking him into her arms.

He burst into tears.

"I'm so sorry I made you go through this," Sally said, tearing up herself.

James pulled away and shook his head. "It's not your fault. I agreed to come, remember?" he replied, wiping his eyes with his shirtsleeve. He sniffled. "I really thought I could get him to confess, but he just makes me so angry. I wish Mom were here to control him. She'd get it all out of him."

Sally wasn't sure how much more he could do, but it wouldn't hurt to ask. "Do you want to go back in?" Sally asked as Finnegan joined them.

"All right, son?" Finnegan asked.

James frowned at him. "I'm sorry. I thought I could help."

"Don't worry. He's a tough nut to crack, but we'll get him."

"So you don't want to try again?" Sally asked, repeating her question.

James shook his head. "No, I won't be able to control my emotions, and I know Dad will just try to continue to manipulate me. I'm heading back to work."

He headed over to his car, jumped in, and squealed down the road out of town.

Oh, Sally, so much for your brilliant idea.

"What now?" Finnegan asked, sounding genuine.

"You know, James gave me an idea. Can I try with Randall?"

Finnegan's eyebrows raised. "You want to chance it?"

Sally nodded vigorously, her ponytail swinging.

"Well, it certainly can't hurt," Finnegan replied.

Sally didn't quite know what she was going to say, but she had a minute or so to collect herself before heading into the interrogation room with Finnegan.

They walked back inside, and Finnegan led her into the back.

"Can I get a coffee first, Detective?" she asked.

Finnegan nodded and stopped in the small breakroom to pour a cup of cop sludge. He added a good amount of milk, so when he handed the paper cup to Sally, it looked a bit more presentable.

She took a sip. It wasn't as bad as she had anticipated, and the caffeine certainly helped to raise her energy level for the fight ahead.

And it would be a fight to get anything out of Randall, but she had a feeling she knew his weak spot.

Chapter Forty

Finnegan opened the door and watched Randall Wentworth as Sally came in behind him.

"Where's my son?" Randall demanded.

"He's gone. He's sick of you," Finnegan replied a bit harshly.

"That boy is a sissy," Randall spat.

Finnegan ignored that bigoted comment.

Sally wasn't sure why they were throwing barbs at each other. She thought Finnegan was a bit dull by trying to provoke the town attorney. She didn't think that would get him to confess more quickly.

She needed everyone to be calm, well as calm as possible, and maybe she would be the one to finally get the truth out of the haughty small-town lawyer.

She seated herself across from O'Malley, as Finnegan took his proper place across from the accused. She had thought to bring her notebook and pen with her, so she could scribble notes, or at least pretend to, to perhaps make Randall wonder what was going on.

"You know, Randall, I always wondered something," she began, trying to make sure her voice sounded strong even though she was shaking inside.

She was already starting to regret her suggestion to try and get the truth out of Randall Wentworth.

He leaned forward.

"What's that, my dear?" he said, leering.

"Your experience, your stature seem to be bigger than small-town life," she continued.

Randall frowned, but quickly seemed to pull himself together after that barb.

She may be wary of him, but she definitely seemed to know his weak spot.

"Well, my family used to live in the area, and I really enjoy small-town life," he replied.

"But wouldn't you rather be in the big city, in a bigger job, getting a bigger salary," she continued, jabbing the proverbial knife in further.

Randall didn't reply, but rather sat back and smiled. He tapped the table.

"To be honest, you are partially right, but I discovered long ago, soon after I arrived in this town, that I'd rather be a big fish in a small pond rather than the other way around. Yes, I'd probably make more in, say, Little Rock, but it would take a lot of clawing and scratching to climb the ladder. Faster and more lucrative here."

Sally wasn't sure she believed him completely, but she could see him being happy about the reputation and power he had here, even if Berry Springs was a small town tucked in the Arkansas Ozarks.

Now was Sally's chance to pounce.

"So why would you ruin your big-fish-in-a-small-pond reputation with killing?" she threw at him.

Randall just laughed. "Oh please, Ms. Witherspoon. Why don't you give it up? I've done nothing and, even if I did, I certainly wouldn't tell you." He looked like he might jump up and lunge across the table, but O'Malley's look put him in place.

"Why did you hate Belle, Momma Arnold, and Dr. Wiggams to do them harm?" she continued, staring right at him.

Randall crossed his arms and harrumphed.

"What do you think your wife would think of all that you had done?" she said, throwing her one dagger in his direction.

That got a reaction. Randall leaned forward and stabbed the table with his finger. "You leave my dead wife out of this!" he cried, actually sounding human for once.

His wife had passed away ten years earlier. Sally had liked her, liked her much more than she did her husband. She had always wondered why a kind soul like Missy had married a rough man like Randall. Maybe Missy had thought she could reform him, or maybe she loved the money and position that came with being married to him.

"Is that why you wanted the elderly dead? Some kind of revenge?" Sally continued.

Randall looked at the floor and didn't respond.

She felt that everyone in the room, including Wentworth himself, felt like the reason for everything would be coming out here and now. She just had to keep pushing to get it out of him. And she wasn't going to stop until she did.

"Why the elderly? Why now?" she continued.

"Well…I…" Randall said, slipping. He clapped his hand over his mouth when he realized what he had started to say.

O'Malley was throwing daggers with his eyes at Randall.

Finnegan was scribbling away, but gave Sally a side glance with a faint smile. Finally, they were getting somewhere. Sally kept silent for a few moments, considering what to ask or say next.

Randall seemed to be starting to break, but she knew he was too smart to just spill everything now. He regretted what he had said, so he was going to be very careful for the rest of the questioning. Of that, Sally was sure.

"Was it revenge? Did you want more money, more power?" she asked.

Randall sneered. "Gilbert did it. We know that. So I don't know why you are wasting my time here."

"Um, we have financial records tying you to the payments to Gilbert," Finnegan reminded him.

"Faked. The FBI has it in for me for some reason," Wentworth replied, not too convincingly.

Sally shook her head. She was here to get to the bottom of the killings, nothing else.

She scribbled in her notebook to help calm herself. She finally looked up and smiled.

"Well, you tell us all the time how smart you are. Do you think Gilbert was smart enough to do this on his own?" Sally asked, tapping the table with her pen. She had to admit this was a similar tactic they had used to get Diane to confess a year ago, but if it had worked with her, it might work with Wentworth.

"Oh, I am smart. Smarter than all of you," he said, pointing his finger at the other three seated at the table.

Sally looked at O'Malley, who did not look like he wanted to be there at the moment, but he was probably getting a lot of money to sit there, so he stayed quiet.

Even if O'Malley spoke, she didn't think he was going to be able to control his client anyway.

"Why would you want them dead?" Sally asked again, "What did they do to you?"

Randall looked like he was going to reply, but kept his mouth shut.

"Was it money? Was it power? What was it?" Sally repeated, relentless in her pursuit of the truth.

She believed she had more patience than he did. She reminded herself she wasn't going to leave the room until Randall confessed.

"Belle, the lovely waitress at Betty Jo's. Momma Arnold, who must have paid you quite a bit of money over the years. And Dr. Wiggams, who must have given you a lot of details from autopsies. And Gilbert Rock, unassuming librarian, living a quiet life." Sally decided to throw out the names to see if Randall would flinch. He didn't.

"Listen, Detective. You may want to keep my client here, but you can't keep him here indefinitely," O'Malley intervened.

At that, Finnegan laughed. "Listen, Mr. O'Malley. I have a dead Gilbert Rock, payments to him from an account belonging to your client, and enough to hold him here until I get a confession or an indictment. You know that. I know that. And he knows that," Finnegan said, the final phrase pointed directly at Wentworth.

Sally felt the adrenaline rushing through her. This was definitely her favorite part of an investigation, now her third, and hopefully not her last, she admitted to herself.

"What I want to know, Randall, excuse me, Mr. Wentworth," Sally continued, giving him a verbal finger, "Why now? What happened this year, right at the holiday season, to bring things to a head?"

She leaned forward, as if this would intimidate Wentworth.

She was therefore surprised when he leaned back slightly.

Maybe she was getting to him.

Randall finally spoke.

"It's been a difficult year," he admitted, though Sally didn't know what kind of difficulty he was referring to.

"Difficult," she quickly replied.

Randall shrugged.

"Difficult to control my clients," he admitted.

Now it was Finnegan's turn to lean forward, though his bulk meant he only moved a couple of inches toward Wentworth.

"What do you mean, 'control my clients'?" Finnegan asked, breaking into the questioning.

Randall replied slowly, each word enunciated, "My power was not what it used to be."

To Sally, he seemed like he was deflated. Maybe the stress of maintaining a mask and a method was finally getting to him. She did think they were getting very close to the truth.

"Power?" Sally asked.

O'Malley tapped his client's hand, obviously to get him to stay silent, but Randall quickly pulled his hand away.

All four were silent, with Sally praying Randall would finally open up.

He didn't look like he was going to say anything more, but Sally knew they were right about to get a confession.

Finnegan suddenly got up. "It's time to call the district attorney and a judge," he said, walking out.

"I own them. You have nothing!" Wentworth screamed after him.

Sally grabbed her notebook and pen, jumped up, and followed the detective out. She did not want to be alone in the room with Wentworth and his slimy attorney.

Finnegan headed to his office, so she followed him. Finnegan shut the door after Sally entered. He sat behind his desk, while she took the couch in the corner.

Chapter Forty-One

"Are you really going to call the district attorney and a judge?" Sally asked.

"I will, but first I need to fill in the chief," he admitted.

Sally had thought of calling Chief Sanford herself that morning. She was friends with him, but she knew from the last time that Finnegan would have hated that, so she had decided to wait and see what happened at the station.

Looking back, she was glad she did.

Finnegan picked up the old-fashioned phone and dialed some numbers. That reminded her that this was a small town and things changed slowly. This was something Sally loved and hated at the same time.

"Yeah, it's me. I've been questioning Wentworth based on the new evidence from the FBI, but I don't seem to be getting anywhere. Want to stop by?"

Sally thought it was presumptuous that he would ask his boss to come to his office, but she knew Tim Sanford was not your typical police chief.

Finnegan put down the phone. "He'll be here in a couple of minutes," Finnegan explained, leaning back in his chair. It creaked under his weight, but also looked like it had been there since 1970, so Sally assumed it wasn't about to collapse.

The door opened, and Tim Sanford walked in. He was in full uniform, as he always wore it at the station.

"Hey, Sally," he said. Sanford sat in the chair across from Finnegan. "So what have you got?"

Sally and Finnegan filled him in on everything, including the attempt by Wentworth's son to get a confession out of him.

Sally admitted she thought they were getting somewhere, but wasn't sure when they would really get to the heart of the matter.

"Well, we have enough on him to hold him. Let me talk to the district attorney and a judge to see what we should charge him with. In the meantime, I suggest you two head back and keep at him. Maybe he will crack," Sanford suggested.

"Yes, sir," Finnegan replied. Sally wasn't sure if he was mocking the chief, but she wasn't about to comment on that.

Sanford got up and walked out. "Say hi to Andy for me," Sally called after him. Sanford waved and headed down the hall.

"Shall we?" Finnegan asked, pushing his bulk up.

Sally nodded and picked up her pen and notebook from the spot next to her on the couch. They walked back to the interrogation room. Sally followed the detective inside.

"Are we done, Detective?" O'Malley asked.

Finnegan laughed. "No, we're just getting started," he replied, planting his ample behind in the chair.

"Well, fuck," Wentworth barked.

Sally knew he was getting upset, which meant he would probably make another mistake. And then she would have him right where she wanted him. Sally sat down in the chair she had used before.

"So where were we?" Finnegan began.

"I was telling you I had nothing to do with anything, and it was Gilbert," Wentworth replied almost immediately.

"Well, actually, you just told us that your power was not what it used to be. What does that mean?" she said, not letting him forget about what he had just told them, even if he probably regretted admitting to it.

"I, well, I…" Wentworth began, going limp again.

"You know, I'm sick of your obfuscating," Finnegan replied.

Sally was surprised he knew the word, but there seemed to be a lot she didn't know about the detective.

"How do you explain how money from offshore accounts that belong to you got into Gilbert's account?" Finnegan demanded.

Wentworth didn't reply, but just stared at him. This really was the crux of the matter. How would Wentworth explain that away, she wondered.

Wentworth coughed before speaking. "You ever wonder where he got the money for his rich clothes, fancy colognes, and luxury trips?"

Sally also loved somehow the dichotomy of her small town. It was fairly liberal, with an openly gay police chief, for example, but there were still a lot of cliché small-town conservative views about.

"So you were paying him for services rendered?" Finnegan asked, knowing full well that would get a rise out of Randall.

"I'm not a pansy like my son," he yelled.

"Never said you were," Finnegan replied calmly. "But maybe you were paying him for something?"

Like killing, Sally thought, but kept her mouth shut.

"Well, he is a librarian, isn't he?" Wentworth said. "I love perfect first editions, and he did research for me and bought the books. A bit of a side hustle to supplement his meager librarian income," Finnegan explained.

Sally thought this was a pretty weak excuse for the payments, especially because they were in the tens of thousands. She assumed say a first edition Shakespeare would be a lot, but she couldn't imagine Wentworth buying that, or being able to afford it for that matter.

"Where did you get all this money?" Sally asked, having another thought.

"I'm an attorney. I earn it," he retorted.

"You're a small-town attorney in a remote part of Arkansas, not a lawyer on Wall Street," Finnegan replied. That must have stung, because Wentworth went red again. He kept quiet. Sally wondered what he would say next.

"True," he replied, "But I have a lot of clients across the county. Many of them quite rich."

"Like the Arnolds?" Sally asked.

Wentworth nodded. "Oh yes, they are very rich."

"But then why would you kill the matriarch who was your client all these years? Might that not cut off the money supply?" Finnegan asked.

Wentworth kept quiet for several minutes as he apparently contemplated what to say next. He kept looking over at his attorney, who returned the glare with a straight face. He stared at Sally until she had to look away.

Finally, he looked at Finnegan and slapped the table. "She was getting a bit stingy," Wentworth replied, and it seemed the floodgates had opened. He put his head on the table.

"So that was the power you were losing?" Sally asked, relentless in her pursuit of the truth.

Randall shrugged.

"She must have paid you a king's ransom over the years, what with wills, the company legal affairs, and who knows what else? Finnegan added.

Randall didn't immediately reply.

"Wasn't that enough?" Finnegan continued.

At that, Randall laughed.

"There is never enough money or power for me in this world," he boasted.

"But why now? Why Gilbert? Why ruin the holidays?" Sally asked, as if that last question was the worst part of the whole affair.

"She was getting stingy," Wentworth repeated, not responding to her question.

"Stingy?" Sally offered.

Wentworth nodded.

"Yes," he replied.

"But what does that mean?" Finnegan asked.

"Well, I have certain fees I require for my services, which never seemed to be a problem for Carol Arnold in the past."

"Up until now?" Sally asked.

Sally wanted to rip the truth out of him at that point, but she knew it would be better to keep at it little by little. The truth was on the tip of Wentworth's tongue, and it wouldn't take much more to get it out of him.

"You know," Sally began, trying a different tack, "James told me he wished you had been a better father. Don't you owe it to him to tell us what happened?"

"I don't care what he thinks!" Randall screamed.

"But what about your family reputation in the future? It will be forever tarnished by what you did now, but maybe if you confess, James will feel like you are a better man than he thought you were. He is your son," Sally rattled off, though she spoke the last sentence slowly and quietly.

Randall frowned and couldn't look at her.

"Let's get back to the subject of your fees and Carol Arnold," Finnegan interrupted, obviously uncomfortable with the family topic.

Randall Wentworth went pale.

"I'm sorry," he whispered, his head in his hands all of a sudden.

Sally and Finnegan weren't sure where that had come from, but Sally thought maybe there was a real father in there somewhere. A year earlier, he had told her a warming story about his son.

O'Malley looked like he was going to hit his client, as if that would help things at the moment.

Wentworth looked up, and Sally's eyebrows went up as she noticed a tear streaming down his cheek.

He coughed and started talking.

"Just before Thanksgiving, Carol Arnold came to adjust her will," he began.

Sally's first thought was that must have been when Momma Arnold bumped up Sally's legacy.

"OK," Finnegan replied.

"Well, I told her my fee and my extra service fee," Finnegan continued.

"Extra service fee?" Sally asked, beginning to understand where Finnegan got all his money to spend on such things as the ultraluxury office.

"Yes, I always tacked on an extra fee for wills and estate planning. She didn't want to pay it anymore."

"What do you mean, fee?" Finnegan asked.

Wentworth coughed and coughed. O'Malley slapped him on the back and asked if he was OK. Wentworth nodded. He stopped coughing and continued. "Well, it was more a special little thing I made people do so that I would handle their estates," Wentworth confessed.

Sally and Finnegan looked at each other. "What was that, Randall?" Finnegan asked, using his first name for effect.

"Well, if I did someone's will, I always made them make me the executor. This gave me part of the estate as an additional amount of money, next to the attorney's fees I charged."

"That is smart," O'Malley blurted out.

Randall laughed. "Oh yes, yes it is."

"But Momma Arnold wasn't playing anymore?" Finnegan asked.

Wentworth shook his head. "No, she wasn't. And she threatened to tell everyone in town that it wasn't usually the way an estate should be handled. She was going to tell people I was strong-arming them, which I wasn't. It was just a suggestion," Wentworth explained.

Yes, a suggestion made by someone a lot of people in town feared. She wasn't surprised many or most went along with it.

"So you decided to kill her. Is that an answer?" Sally asked, jumping into the fray.

"Oh no, that would have been too easy. I got Gilbert to kill," he replied, now spilling everything.

"Why aspirin?" Finnegan asked. The question on the tip of Sally's tongue.

"I did some research, and it can look like symptoms of food poisoning, and, well, old people often take it. I thought it was quite clever, cleverer than using a poison. And conveniently, it was the holiday season, so I knew there would be a lot of people about. If one or two old people died, there would be a lot of suspects."

Sally was not too surprised at his audacity. "And why Gilbert?"

"He needed money to fuel his luxurious habits. Apparently, he was running out of credit cards to max out and was desperate to keep up the facade of luxury clothes and trips enough to do my bidding," he replied.

Sally felt bad for Gilbert. He must have been in a very bad way to help Wentworth. But maybe somehow he did enjoy the killing and subterfuge. Though with him dead, he wouldn't be explaining that to her any time soon.

"Well, you were certainly successful," Finnegan admitted, getting up.

"I think I have enough," he added.

"Wait, Detective, I have one more important question," Sally said.

Finnegan sat back down. "Be my guest."

"Yes, dear, what do you want to know?" Wentworth sneered.

"Why older people? And what about Dr. Wiggams?"

CHAPTER FORTY-ONE

"Isn't that two questions?"

"Just answer the lady," Finnegan said.

"Well, let's start with Dr. Wiggams. He was getting too close to the truth. The old, doddering man had seen me meeting with Gilbert at my office and was close to putting two and two together for some reason. He needed to be done away with."

"So you pushed him," Sally added.

Wentworth nodded. "Yes. He never was too sure on his feet, and with all the ice that day, I just needed to tap him before he went down," Wentworth replied proudly.

"But what about any cameras?" Sally asked.

"I know where those are and made sure I wasn't seen," he replied.

"It worked," she admitted.

"And the old people? Wouldn't they be your most lucrative clients?"

"Bingo," Wentworth replied. "And old people are just a burden on society. I got some money from them, though admittedly more from Momma Arnold's estate than Belle's. That was my little thing, as it were." As he said this, he smirked.

Sally gasped. She couldn't believe what she was hearing. He wanted to rid society of old people. Though somehow, she felt he might just be adding insult to injury and throwing that in at the last minute to make himself seem even more evil. Though evil, he was most certainly.

"What do you mean?"

"A part of my will service, in addition to making me executor, was that the person had to leave me some money in their will. You know, that gave me one more fee."

"You really are evil."

Randall Wentworth sat back and sneered.

Chapter Forty-Two

"To Gladys," the three women toasted, clinking glasses. Sally had invited Joanna and Rose over that evening. She needed some company after the terrible events that had transpired since Thanksgiving. And some emotional support, as Gladys was now gone.

James Wentworth had gotten her a good deal. A collector in the next county had bought the car for $2,000. He was going to restore it completely, he told James. And Sally was welcome to come and see it when it was ready.

She wasn't sure she wanted to do that. It would remind her of the years with the car and, worse, seeing Gladys like brand new would remind her of her lost youth.

She usually looked forward, not back, but turning 60 was such a big milestone she wasn't sure she was ready to face. Though she told herself the alternative was much worse.

"Oh, Sally, thanks so much for the invite," Rose said.

"How are you holding up?" Joanna asked.

Sally had called Magda after leaving the police station to fill her in and ask her to run the bar that night with Annette. She needed a night off, something she rarely did.

"Oh my god, what an awful man," Magda had declared. " We'll definitely help out. You relax and rest."

"Thanks so much! I'll definitely be in tomorrow. It will help to get my mind off of it all," Sally replied, wishing she could give Magda a hug. But that wasn't possible through a phone call.

Sally looked at Joanna and smiled. "What a month it has been for everyone, but at least we have some answers," Sally replied.

Joanna laughed. "I meant about Gladys," she declared.

"Oh well, it was time," Sally replied, choking up but quickly calming herself.

"Honey, you don't need to be strong in front of us," Rose offered, taking her hand.

"OK, it's been difficult, but she was really on her last legs, so…" Sally replied, sniffling.

"… you are putting the past behind you and just looking forward," Joanna said, finishing her sentence.

"Something like that," Sally replied, taking a big gulp of wine.

"Dig in, you two," Joanna said, waving a hand over the spread on the kitchen table.

Joanna had brought an assortment of tapas from her café, and it was probably enough to feed 20.

"Thanks so much for the food," Sally said, leaning in for a hug. "It all looks delicious."

Rose nodded in agreement.

They quickly and quietly filled their plates with olives, spreads, breads, stuffed grape leaves, cheeses, and the like. "It's like a Thanksgiving feast at New Year's," Sally said, looking at their plates heaped with food.

"Bon appétit," Rose called, and they all dug in.

There were several minutes of quiet while they devoured the food. There was a lot of mmming and "Oh, this is so good." Sally made sure their wine and water glasses were kept full as they enjoyed the meal and each other's company.

Putting her fork down, Rose looked at the two other women at the table.

Sally was wondering when they were going to get to the topic of Randall Wentworth, which she definitely needed to process with them, though she wasn't sure when she would actually be ready for it.

"I have an idea," Rose said.

Sally was silently relieved; she didn't have a question about Wentworth.

"Oh yes, what is it?" Joanna asked.

"Well, the three of us get along so well, don't we?" Rose asked.

Sally and Joanna nodded.

"Well, I was thinking, why don't we go into business together? I've been thinking about finally retiring from the hotel and doing something else. I've been there forever, and it's time for a change," Rose explained as if she were talking about the weather.

"Retire? But you are the Grand Hotel," Joanna declared.

"I know, I know. But I've been there for a long time, maybe too long. I want to do something different before I keel over," Rose explained.

Sally nodded. "I get it. If I think back to my finance job in Atlanta and that if I were still doing it, I would scream. I divorced my husband, left my job, and moved here and opened the bar. I don't regret a minute of it," Sally agreed.

"Exactly," Rose cried.

"So what do you mean 'go into business together'?" Joanna asked.

"Well, you make wonderful food, Sally is an amazing bartender, and I am a great organizer… why don't we three set up our own catering company? I can run it while you two provide the food and drink, keeping your regular jobs, of course. It gives me something to do, you know, I love organizing events, and I'm sure there are plenty of people, churches, and the like that would love our service," Rose said in rapid fire.

Sally and Joanna sat back and were quiet for a moment.

Then at the same time, they yelled, "Let's do it!"

Rose was beaming.

"Oh, I'm so glad you think it is a great idea," Rose replied.

"It is a great idea and sounds like a lot of fun," Sally said.

"Do you have any ideas of what the business will be called?" Joanna asked.

Sally's first thought, as usual, was to run to the hall to grab her notebook and pen out of her backpack to start scribbling ideas.

"Well, yes, I have. How about The Catering Coven?" Rose asked, looking anxiously at the other two women.

Joanna laughed. "Oh, people will love that," she said.

"We aren't witches, but the name is catchy, isn't it?" Rose asked.

Sally nodded. "I think it's a great name. And what a great idea to start the

New Year," she said.

"I agree," Joanna added.

Sally poured some more wine for all of them and then raised her glass. "To The Catering Coven!" she toasted.

"Oh, this is going to be so much fun," Rose said, smiling.

Sally smiled back. She was thinking of bringing up Randall Wentworth when her phone beeped.

"Hey, Sally," Magda wrote, "We miss you here tonight. All's going well. I can't wait to hear what went on with Randall Wentworth. Care to pick over the carcass tomorrow morning?"

Sally laughed. That phrase had been used a lot recently.

"What's going on?" Joanna asked.

"Oh, just a text from Magda."

"Everything OK at the bar?" Rose asked

"Yes, no problems. She wanted to come over for breakfast tomorrow," Sally explained.

"She's such a great girl," Rose replied, making Magda sound like a six-year-old, or maybe it was just the era of Rose's youth speaking.

Sally debated mentioning why Magda wanted to come over, but she didn't want to spoil the atmosphere or the evening. She knew she needed to decompress with someone over the events since Thanksgiving, but she decided Magda was probably the best person for it. Over the years, working together at the bar, they had become close friends.

And this evening with Rose and Joanna had turned into a simpler and more elegant celebration than a discussion about evil warranted.

Chapter Forty-Three

"I still can't believe Randall was behind it all. Ugh," Magda said, stuffing a piece of croissant in her mouth.

Sally had made plenty of coffee, and Magda had thankfully brought the breakfast with her. There were rolls, jams, butter, croissants, and cheeses laid out.

Sally decided she would need to go for a hike later that day. After the big dinner the night before with Rose and Joanna and this breakfast, she would need to work it off.

"I know, though, don't you agree that we all thought he was a bit strange with his high-and-mighty attitude? Sally replied, buttering a roll.

"Well, yes, but aren't all lawyers like that?" Magda asked.

Sally considered that question for a moment as she ate the roll, which she had topped with raspberry jam. She laughed, finally. "Maybe you're right."

"And how did Gilbert get involved in all this?"

"Randall really knew everything that was going on in town. He was snooping on people and overheard a conversation Gilbert had with the bank manager about getting another credit card. Apparently, they denied him one, and Randall put two and two together. I have to say, looking back, I did always wonder about his trips, clothes, and colognes," Sally related.

Magda laughed and shook her head.

"Hindsight is 20-20, boss."

"OK, true."

"But the killings just started recently. He's been going on trips and wearing wonderful clothes for years," Magda replied.

"It seems two things came together. Randall Wentworth was milking his clients when making their wills, forcing them to add him as a partial beneficiary. And Momma Arnold was wanting to cut him off from his extra fees right before the Thanksgiving dinner. Coupled with the information about Gilbert he gathered at the bank, he concocted the scheme and blackmailed Gilbert to go along," Sally said, thinking aloud.

"Poor Gilbert," Magda declared, shaking her head.

"I know. He was so nice, the opposite of Randall."

"What will happen to Randall now?" Magda asked, taking a sip of coffee.

"Finnegan has enough on him, definitely. The payments to Gilbert came from an offshore account the FBI traced to Randall, and he confessed quite a bit yesterday. He'll go to trial, and I hate to say it, but the death penalty might be on the table. These were cruel killings, even if he didn't do them himself."

"What an awful way to die. I can't stand the thought of someone being put to death by the state, even if other people died. Can't he just go to jail for life?" Magda asked.

"I agree, but I'm thinking the county prosecutor will want the death penalty for the cruel way the people died," Sally replied, hoping one of them would change the subject.

"I wonder what will happen to the Arnold sons," Magda said, as if she had read Sally's thoughts.

"Yeah, I'm wondering the same thing. They can probably manage with the business, but keeping up the Arnold compound will be a chore. I can't see them selling it, but who knows?"

"What about your inheritance? Now that your parents got you that snazzy SUV, you can use the money for something else," Magda said.

That got Sally thinking of her parents. She had called them the night before to fill them in. They were both relieved the Senior Slayer had been caught, and Sally and the town could put that behind them once and for all.

"I still can't decide whether to do something with the bar or the house."

"With that amount, you could do something with both," Magda suggested.

"True. But maybe I'll invest in a van for the bar or something like that, too," Sally said.

She explained Rose's idea for the catering service to Magda.

"Oh, what a great idea. And what a great name for the company. I am glad to help out," Magda offered.

"We'll definitely need it," Sally replied.

"But you won't close the bar, will you?" Magda asked, now turning serious.

Sally shook her head. "No, I love my bar. The catering service will be a side job. Sally's Smasher will definitely stay open."

"That is a relief," Magda replied.

Sally was just about to ask Magda if she wanted something more to drink when the doorbell rang. "Who could that be?"

"It's a small town, Sally. People just stop by," Magda replied.

Sally still couldn't get used to that after so many years in Berry Springs.

She went to the door and saw through the small window slit that it was Mark Soder. He was always a sight for sore eyes. She opened the door and gave him a hug.

"Mark, what brings you by?"

"Just stopping in to see how you are doing. Glad it's all over?" Mark asked as Sally ushered him into the kitchen.

"Hey Magda," Mark said, planting himself on one of the kitchen chairs.

"Oh, hi Mark," Magda replied, giving Sally a sly wink.

Sally turned red and spun around quickly, hoping neither of them saw that. "Would you like some coffee?" she called, pulling a mug out of the cabinet and taking a couple of deep breaths.

"Sure. Thanks, Sally," he replied.

She turned around and poured him a mug. Sitting back down herself, she busied herself with her own cup of coffee.

"I was just asking Sally what she thought would happen to Randall Wentworth," Magda said, skipping over the bits about Sally's inheritance or Rose's catering plan.

"Death penalty," he stated seriously. "Even if I hate that idea," he quickly added.

Sally and Magda nodded in agreement.

"Though what he did was definitely cruel," Sally replied, even if she hated the death penalty too.

"It seems this was all just below the surface for years, but no one caught on. And poor Gilbert," Mark said, shaking his head. He sipped his coffee. "After all that's been going on, this could perhaps use a kick, but I'm on duty," he said, laughing.

Sally looked at the clock on the wall. "And it's only 11 in the morning," she teased.

Magda pushed back her chair. "I'm going to get going, Sally. I'm meeting Jeff at his cabin for a nice walk. It's freezing outside, but at least it's not snowing. And we both need to get some fresh air."

Sally kind of guessed why Magda was suddenly leaving, but she didn't say anything. She got up and gave Magda a hug, then led her out to the hallway. Opening the door for Magda, she said, "Thanks for the breakfast. I'll see you later at the bar."

"Have fun," Magda whispered.

"Stop it!" Sally replied just as quietly.

Sally was just about to close the door when two cars pulled up. "Grand Central Station here this morning," she muttered, using one of her mother's favorite phrases.

She recognized the three people getting out as she waved to Magda, who pulled away and honked her horn. Roy Barnes, Jack and Steve Arnold came up the walk. That was definitely a surprise.

"Good morning, Sally," Roy called as they approached the porch.

"What brings y'all here?" she asked, dropping into her seldom Southern drawl.

Jack coughed. "Thanks," he said.

Sally still wasn't sure what was going on.

"What Jack means is that the three of us want to thank you for your help in bringing the killers to justice. Momma Arnold and Belle didn't deserve it," Roy explained, pulling Sally into a hug.

Jack and Steve then gave her a manly mini- hug and pat on the back. A lot of hugging going on this morning.

"What's going on, Sally?" Mark called from behind her.

"Oh, I see you have a visitor," Roy said, winking at Sally. Did the entire town know what she thought of Mark Soder? Ugh, small towns rarely have secrets.

"Magda was just here for breakfast, and Mark just stopped by to say hello," Sally replied, hoping no one would make another comment on the subject.

"Well, yes, so we're here to present you with this," Roy said as Steve and Jack looked on, nodding.

Roy reached into his pocket and pulled out a small piece of paper. He unfolded it and handed it to Sally.

She was stunned and didn't know what to say. It was a check made out to her in the amount of $20,000!

"I... I... can't accept this," she said quickly, trying to hand it back to Roy.

Roy brushed her off. Jack and Steve did the same and wouldn't take the paper.

"You have done so much for us and for the community. It's a small token of our appreciation," Jack said, surprising Sally at his words.

Sally was really surprised at the Arnold men, because not too long ago, they had been upset that Momma Arnold had left her $50,000 in her will. But perhaps helping solve the crime and being the one person to finally get the truth out of Wentworth was worth something.

Her other side job.

"I don't know what to say," Sally said, choking up. "Thank you," she added, quickly brushing away the tears.

"You are very welcome," Roy replied, leading the Arnold men back to the cars.

"Would you like to stay for coffee?" she called after them.

Roy waved her away. "No, we have to get going. You have a great day," he said as he opened his car door.

In no time, both vehicles were heading down the block toward town, leaving Sally alone with Mark.

A Note from the Author

I've been overwhelmed by the feedback I've received for the first two Sally Witherspoon mysteries, *Death in the Ozarks* and *Murder on the Mississippi.*

I hope you have enjoyed this third book in the series, *Death for Sale*!

If you are interested in learning more about me and my writing, please check out my website (https://www.erikmey.com)

Be well!

Acknowledgments

Thank you to Cindy Bullard, my literary agent, and to Shawn Reilly Simmons and everyone at Level Best Books for helping to bring Sally Witherspoon into the wider world. I am eternally grateful!

About the Author

Currently in Austria, Erik S. Meyers is an American abroad for years and years who has lived or worked in six countries on three continents, the longest in Germany. He is an award-winning author and communications professional with over 25 years of expertise in a variety of corporate roles. Reading and writing are his passions, when he is not hiking one of the amazing trails in Austria or elsewhere.

AUTHOR WEBSITE:
   https://www.erikmey.com

SOCIAL MEDIA HANDLES:
   Facebook: https://www.facebook.com/ErikSMeyersAuthor/
   Instagram: https://www.instagram.com/erikmeyauthor/

Also by Erik S. Meyers

Sally Witherspoon Book 1: *Death in the Ozarks* (https://www.amazon.com/dp/B0CKWT4FY2/)

Sally Witherspoon Book 2: *Murder on the Mississippi* (https://www.amazon.com/dp/B0F1HVT9PY)

Connections: A Short Story Anthology (https://www.amazon.com/dp/B0DJ7N98R5)

The Accidental Change Agent (https://www.amazon.com/-/en/dp/B08BSR9CDS/)

Caged Time (https://www.amazon.com/Caged-Time-Tarniss-desire-faith-ebook/dp/B08VRCR5FS/)